THE ONLY ONE

BOOK TWO

MELISSA ELLEN

This book is a work of fiction. Names, characters, places and incidents are the product of the author's imagination or are used fictitiously. Any resemblance to actual events, locales, or persons, living or dead, is coincidental.

Fifth Edition: April 2018
Printed in the United States of America

PROLOGUE

We were three days into our road trip to California before I finally answered his call. He'd called me every day, sometimes multiple times a day, since the day I last saw him in my apartment—the day I left my life in Wellesley behind to move to California and start a new one. I always ignored it, turning my phone to silent. Every night he'd send me the same text message:

R: I'm sorry. Goodnight, beautiful. x

And every night I'd silently cry myself to sleep in the hotel bed, hoping Stephen couldn't hear me from across the room.

We were at a gas station somewhere in Nebraska. Stephen was inside getting us some drinks and snacks for the road. I stared at the phone in my hand as the screen silently lit up with Rhett's name and number. Again. Before I knew what I was doing, I pressed the green button to answer the call.

I didn't say hello. I didn't say anything. I just held it to my ear, wanting to hear his voice no matter how painful it'd be.

"Ava?" His deep, beautiful voice filled with disbelief sounded in my ear. "Ava, are you there?"

I could hear the stress and exhaustion in his words. I didn't respond, only squeezed the phone tighter, fighting back tears as his voice washed over me. He quieted, waiting for me to give him a response, before releasing a heavy sigh.

"Ava, you don't have to say anything. I just need you to listen. I'll give you space, if that's what you need right now. I'll wait patiently, but I *will* come for you. This isn't over. You are the only one for me."

Silent tears fell down my cheeks, the phone suddenly ripped from my hand. Stephen had taken it, hung it up, and was navigating through the screens.

"What are you doing?" I choked out through the tears rolling down my face.

"What I should've done three days ago. I'm blocking his number and deleting it from your phone."

I wanted to scream at him to stop and fight him to get my phone back, but I was still too weak to fight. Resting my head against the seat, I stared out the window, letting the tears continue to dampen my cheeks as he started the car and drove back onto the road.

The warm summer sun radiated through the window as we drove down a country road lined on both sides by emerald green rows of corn. Rhett's words replayed in my head as I watched the fields go by in a blur, numb. My heart and mind were at odds with each other. But my heart had been weakened. Shattered.

The more distance I put between Rhett and me, the more frequently my mind would win out. I felt the wall being rebuilt around my heart the closer we got to California. But this time, it wasn't just a wall; it was a fortress.

CHAPTER 1

"Come on! Move already!" I yelled at nobody in particular as I beat on my car horn.

It was pointless, the yelling and honking. We were in a typical Los Angeles gridlock on the interstate. Nobody could move. I'd lived in California for over two years now and still wasn't used to the traffic.

I was running late for work, once again. Thankfully my boss was lenient about our work schedules. He never seemed bothered that I arrived an hour late every day. He knew I stayed late most nights and often worked the weekends. I put in my time, and I got the job done. All my clients were happy with my work, so he let me get away with my regular tardiness and occasional long lunches.

The traffic slowly rolled forward a few feet as my phone began to ring. Lizzie's name popped up on the center display of my car dash.

"Hey!" I answered, excited to hear from my best friend.

With our busy lives, we rarely got to talk, but made it a point to talk at least once every couple of weeks, even if only for a few minutes. It was hard being on opposite sides of the country over the last few years, especially after we'd lived together through college and been inseparable growing up.

She was living in New York City with her husband, Mike, who'd become a successful chef. They'd moved there right after we graduated from Wellesley. He had worked as an executive head chef at a restaurant owned by our former boss, Christopher. Recently though, he'd received backing from an investor to start his own restaurant. I was more than excited for the both of them.

I had a suspicion about who the investor might be. But I never asked, and they never volunteered the information. We avoided the topic of Rhett altogether after the fight Lizzie and I had, when Rhett and I first broke up. It was the only time we'd ever fought in all our years of friendship. She'd begged me to hear him out. I was hurt she'd take his side and didn't understand why I needed to move on. He'd made his choice—Serena—and hadn't been there for me like he'd promised when my father passed away.

In the end, she stopped pushing, and we made up. I knew she still kept in touch with him, though. He was living in New York now. He'd recently taken over his father's business after his father announced his retirement.

It was all over the news, tabloids, and business journals. I couldn't avoid hearing about it, even all the way across the country. Shortly after taking the helm of Blackwood Industries, he'd also been named 'New York's most eligible bachelor.' I'm sure the women were throwing themselves at him, even more than they already did.

Lizzie wasn't the only one who still spoke to him. I knew he was keeping in touch with my family, too. He'd been to see my mom and Nana a few times, and I knew he often spoke to Jackson from the times my sister would let it slip in conversation.

At first, it infuriated me that everyone didn't turn their backs on him, shutting him out. I slowly realized it wasn't fair to ask of them. After all, I was doing the same thing keeping in touch with his sister, Valerie. She was in town this weekend, looking at the USC campus. We had plans to meet for lunch today.

"Hey! Did I catch you at a bad time?" Lizzie's voice came through the car speakers.

"No, I'm just sitting in traffic on my way to work. What's going on?"

"Well, I was hoping I could invite myself out to California. I have some free time coming up in a couple weeks. Are you willing to put me up for a weekend?"

"Put you up *or* put up with you?" I teased her.

"Both," she laughed.

"Of course! I can't wait. Will Mike be coming with you?"

"No. He'll be stuck here, taking care of business. You get me all to yourself, you lucky bitch."

"Perfect," I laughed. "We can have a girls' weekend."

"I'll send you my flight details as soon as I have it booked. Sorry to cut this short, but I have to run. I'll call you later?"

"Sounds good. Miss you and tell Mike hi for me."

"Will do and miss you, too," she said before hanging up the call.

~

I walked into Willis & Associates, the small architecture firm where I'd been working for the last few years. I started working as an intern while finishing my graduate studies. Tom, my boss, had offered me a full-time position as soon as I graduated earlier this year.

At the time I started, he was a one-man operation. He hired Jocelyn and me a few months apart after landing a couple larger residential projects he wouldn't be able to do on his own. We both worked as interns, becoming fast friends, so when he offered us both a permanent position, I was relieved. I didn't know if he offered me the job because he truly thought I had talent, or because he needed the "Associates" his firm name suggested he already had. Either way, I happily accepted.

I loved my job, and our little firm seemed to be growing quickly, which was exciting to be a part of. There were now four of us working in our tiny, quaint office. Tom recently added a new intern to our little group, Drew, to help us with drafting.

"Morning!" I beamed, passing Drew on the way to my desk.

"Morning, Ava," Drew greeted, standing near the door. "I was about to make a Starbucks run. Do you want anything?"

Drew was your average good-hearted guy. He had boyish good looks but was not someone I'd call strikingly attractive. He was cute in his own way, with his curly, brownish-blond hair, and cheeks that always seemed to be flushed. He had an average build and wore thick-rimmed glasses befitting of his quirky personality and sense of humor. He was often laughing at his own jokes, which somehow had a way of making us laugh with him.

"No, thanks. Brought some from home, today," I said, lifting my travel cup into his view.

"All right, be back in a few." He waved, leaving through the front door of the office.

Our office wasn't the most impressive, as far as size or layout, but I loved it nonetheless. It had a long, narrow, open floor plan, with only three rooms toward the back of the space housing Tom's office, a restroom, and a small room used as both a break room and a makeshift meeting area.

The walls were all painted white, but the warm wood floors, desks, and exposed wood beams above all helped keep it from feeling stark and bland. Tom had commissioned photographs over the years of some of his most impressive projects. They were stretched across large canvases that hung on the walls all the way down the space, giving it a gallery feel.

We each had our own desk facing the front of the space, allowing us to intercept clients and visitors as they came in. Not having a receptionist, we all did our part answering phones and greeting people.

I sat down at my desk. Joce's desk across from me still sat empty. I wasn't the only one running late today. After putting my purse away, I began checking my messages. A few minutes into reading my emails, Joce came blowing through the door looking a little rough, but still gorgeous, with her unfairly beautiful long, red hair, pale green eyes, and tall, slender figure. She had fair skin covered with a smattering of the faintest freckles. Her lips and cheeks were a natural pale pink, requiring her to wear little makeup. She reminded me of a beautiful, antique porcelain doll.

She moved quickly to her desk, dropping her stuff on it with a huff as she sat.

"Another bad date?" My eyebrow arched with my question.

"How did you guess?" she responded with a sarcastic roll of her eyes.

We both knew it was an easy guess. Joce was boy crazed and seemed to have a knack for picking the wrong guy. She met most of the men she dated through social apps like Tinder and Bumble. She always scheduled her dates for Thursday nights, which meant most Friday mornings she arrived in the same fashion and mood.

"I'm thinking I should swear off men, like you have, Ava."

I didn't respond. I just gave her my best sympathetic smile. I hadn't exactly sworn off men. I had at first, but eventually I decided the best way for me to move on was to date. The problem was, most men didn't compare to Rhett, and the few I'd gone on more than one date with ended up losing interest in me after the second or third date. It was like I was cursed to be alone forever.

"What do you say we get some drinks tonight? I could use a little girl time and who knows, maybe I can meet a good man the old-fashioned way," she said, looking at me hopefully.

I wanted to tell her meeting a guy in a bar wasn't exactly her best option for finding husband material, but who was I to judge?

"Sure," I reluctantly agreed.

"Ladies," Tom interrupted our little chat, "I have some exciting news! I just got off the phone with a new potential client who wants us to work on a home in Malibu!"

Tom was a little more ecstatic than usual, his smile stretching wide across his face. Malibu meant money, so I didn't blame him for being overly enthused.

Tom was a family man in his mid-to-late forties, with a receding hairline of brown hair speckled with grays. He'd spent the first part of his architecture career working for large corporations, and eventually got burned out from the high stress of commercial architecture. He left his cushy salary job to start his own firm, doing residential architecture.

He started out with mostly remodels and smaller new-construction homes. But he was quickly becoming a recognized architect in the area and had built up his portfolio of residential work. He had more recently gained exposure to larger projects and clients with more money to spend.

"That's great news!" Joce radiated.

"That is! When do you meet with them?" I asked, equally happy for him.

"We," he corrected me. "Ava, you'll be coming with me. You're going to help me run point on this one. And the meeting is today. This'll be a vacation home for the client and they're in town for the weekend."

Crap.

My excitement deflated a tad, afraid I was going to have to cancel on Valerie. We were supposed to meet up after she finished touring the campus this morning.

"What time is the meeting? Will it be here in the office?" I asked, hoping I could figure out a way to both meet with Valerie and make the meeting in time.

"The meeting is at two downtown. I'll send you the address. We'll need to drive separately. I have to head straight home after the meeting. My son has a baseball game tonight."

Tom's wife, Marie, was pregnant with twins and had been recently put on bed rest for the remainder of her last trimester after having some complications. He often took off early from work to help with their son and do things around the house. He'd been assigning projects to Joce and me to run point on, so the clients always had someone available to them if he couldn't be. Neither of us minded. It was good experience for us.

"Sounds good," I responded, starting to feel a little stressed.

A two o'clock meeting didn't give me much time to meet Valerie at The Ivy for lunch. It'd been awhile since we'd caught up, and now it looked like I'd have to cut our lunch date short.

I spent the rest of the morning responding to emails and getting as much work done as possible. My day had just been derailed by this unexpected meeting. It appeared I'd be working some this weekend to catch up on the time I was losing this afternoon.

I was wrapping up some final touches to a rendering when my phone vibrated on my desk.

V: Just finished the campus tour. Still on for lunch?

I looked at the clock, seeing it was nearly noon. I'd been so focused I lost track of time. I saved my work and rushed to pack up my things, responding to Valerie as I headed for the door.

"Don't forget, drinks tonight!" Joce hollered from behind me.

"I won't! Text me the time and place," I said, waving as I ran out the door.

～

Valerie was already at a table on the patio when I arrived. She was looking as stunning as ever in a little emerald-green sundress, with her long brown and golden hair down in wavy locks. She looked casual enough, but I was sure her dress probably cost more than my rent. She'd been watching for me, and when she saw me approach, she stood, waving with excitement.

"Ava!"

"Hey, Val!" I hugged her as I reached the table. "You look cute. I love your dress."

"Thank you! I'm so glad you could make it."

"Me too, but I'm afraid I had an unexpected meeting come up, so I won't be able to stay as long as I'd hoped," I apologized.

"Oh, it's fine. I know you're a busy professional woman now," she said, grinning with a wink.

The server approached us and took my drink order. We went ahead and ordered our lunch, so I wouldn't be rushed to make my meeting. We visited and laughed about random things like clothes and the boys she'd been dating. I was enjoying my time with her, and hadn't realized how much I'd missed her.

"So how was the campus tour?" I asked as we ate our lunch.

"Good, just a typical campus, I guess," she shrugged, impartially.

"I'm kind of surprised your family is on board with you coming all the way to California instead of following in the family footsteps at Harvard."

"Well, I wouldn't say they were exactly on board. Dad obviously would prefer me to go to Harvard and get a law degree or something boring like that. But *I* want to be an actress. Mom finally got him to agree I could come out here as long as I attended college and got a degree."

"An actress, huh?"

"Yep!" She grinned from ear to ear.

I didn't know if Valerie had any acting talent, but she definitely had the face for it. I could see her gracing the red carpets as one of the glamorous Hollywood starlets someday.

"Well, it'd be great to have you living here. I still can't believe they let you come all this way alone."

Valerie's family was extremely protective of her. I was a bit surprised when she told me she was flying out here and her mother wasn't joining her for the trip.

"I am *eighteen* now, Ava."

I gave her a raised eyebrow as I tilted my head, knowing her age didn't make much difference.

"Ok, they may have sent a chaperone with me," she conceded, changing the subject to me and my job.

"Speaking of work," I looked at my clock, "it looks like I better head out or I'll be late. How long are you in town?"

"Only the weekend."

"Well, let's meet up again before you go. I hate that I couldn't take a longer lunch."

"Sounds good to me!" she said, smiling. "I'll text you later."

We hugged our goodbyes before I rushed to my car, leaving for my meeting.

~

I cursed the highway gods when I got stuck in Friday-afternoon traffic on the way to the meeting. I looked at my GPS, and I was sixteen minutes out for my meeting that started in thirteen minutes. As soon as I made it downtown and parked, I sent Tom a text apologizing and letting him know I was on my way up.

As I made it through the revolving door of the massive glass-and-steel building I was entering, my phone chimed with a new text. I pulled it out, rushing to the elevator bank, expecting it to be Tom responding. Instead, it was Joce letting me know the time and place for drinks. I started to text her a response when I collided with a hard figure, sending my phone to the ground.

"Oh my gosh, I'm so sorry!" I apologized, lowering my eyes to the gentleman who'd already bent down to kindly retrieve my phone.

I halted, unable to continue my apology, stunned silent when I saw the head and broad, muscular shoulders crouched below me. My heart dropped to my stomach. My lungs tightened in my chest. He stood back up with his smile that dripped with sex appeal.

"Ava," Rhett replied smoothly, handing my phone to me, smiling, with his beautiful blue eyes reminding me of the Pacific Ocean. I stood there paralyzed, unable to move or speak, his voice rendering me incapable of anything.

"We really have to stop meeting this way," he teased.

I had no words as emotions bombarded me. I broke our eye contact, looking at my phone. I took it from him carefully, ensuring our hands didn't touch. I knew if I touched him, this would be a losing battle for me. And I intended to win. I heard the elevator ding to open, and I thanked God for the escape.

"Excuse me," I said flatly, side-stepping around him, keeping my distance.

I rushed into the elevator, repeatedly pushing the button for the top floor, pleading the doors to close faster. Just as they started to close, a masculine hand stopped them, pushing them back open as he stepped into the elevator with me.

Damn it.

Just like the highway gods, the elevator gods were against me. And apparently, Rhett was determined to follow me.

I scooted to the other side of the elevator, trying to put as much space between us as you could in a claustrophobic six-foot-by-six-foot box. He moved to stand next to me, where I could smell his sinfully good fragrance. I stepped backwards toward the rear of the elevator to regain some much-needed space. He followed me like we were doing a square dance.

I moved forward trying once again to get away from him. Before he could follow me, I turned around, glaring at him. "Stop it," I scorned pointedly before facing forward, careful not to look at him for too long.

"Stop what?" I could hear the smirk in his voice from behind me.

"You know damn well what." I didn't bother explaining. He'd always known the effect he had on me, especially when we touched.

I watched the numbers light up as we ascended into the sky, praying for the dreadful elevator to go faster. I could feel his eyes on me, and I suddenly wished I hadn't chosen to wear my sheer cream blouse and form-fitting, pale pink pencil skirt that hugged all my curves.

As if things couldn't get any worse, we stopped halfway up to my destination. The elevator doors opened and a crowd of people got on, cramping the space, leaving just inches between everyone. I attempted moving to the side, hoping the others would help be a barrier between us. Unfortunately, Rhett used the opportunity to move right behind me, so his front was to my back.

I stood rigid with my hands to my sides, praying he wouldn't touch me. The elevator doors closed, and I felt the familiar intense magnetic energy pulling between us. He lightly brushed the tips of his fingers with mine. That was all it took for the electric shock to course through my body, bringing every nerve alive.

I held my breath and closed my eyes hoping, somehow, it'd be enough to fight him away. As if knowing what I was doing, he leaned forward, putting his lips near my ear, where I could feel his warm breath tickle the delicate skin at my neck.

"Breathe, Ava," he whispered.

My knees weakened. I didn't know if it was from him or the fact that I was holding my breath. I let out the air I was holding in, trying to regain my strength. The elevator doors opened and closed a few more times as the others made their way off the elevator, leaving us by ourselves, once again.

Before I could step away from him, he turned us, pinning me against the elevator wall, his arms on each side of me, caging me in. He didn't touch me. He didn't have to. I felt the heat radiating from his body. He looked down into my eyes as we breathed each other's air.

"You know what you're doing to me right now," he gritted through his teeth. "I'm having a hard time controlling myself. It's been too long, Ava... Too long since I've been inside you."

I felt the throbbing between my legs from his words. My body responded to him like it always did. My lips parted, wanting to feel his lips on mine. The elevator door dinged open, breaking my trance. I quickly ducked under his arms, running out of the elevator, not looking back. I hoped he wouldn't follow. I was panicked and breathing fast as I quickened my steps, walking up to the receptionist.

"Ava Conner, with Willis & Associates." The words rushed out in a pant as I spoke.

The nice lady behind the desk smiled sweetly. "Yes, the other man is waiting for you in the conference room, through the frosted-glass doors on the left. No need to stress. The meeting hasn't started," she said, pointing me in the right direction.

My rapid breathing had clearly clued her in to my skyrocketing stress level—little did she know, it had nothing to do with being late for the meeting. I quickly made my way into the conference room, finding Tom alone at a big, long, wooden table.

"I'm so sorry, Tom," I said, trying to catch my breath as I spoke.

"Don't worry, Ava. It's fine. He hasn't made it back from lunch yet. They expect him any minute. Have a seat, dear. Catch your breath. You look like you just ran a marathon." He patted my back.

I sat next to Tom, trying to level my breathing and gain some composure. I needed to focus. We had a very important meeting, and I didn't want to mess this up for Tom. We sat there for about five more minutes, waiting for our client to arrive. I had finally started to feel calm when the frosted-glass doors opened. Looking up, I plastered a smile on my face to greet our new client. My smile dropped and was replaced by a wide-open mouth as Rhett walked through the door.

CHAPTER 2

R hett smirked as he strode confidently across the room to greet us. He looked sexy and poised, and I hated him for it.

Tom stood, making his way around the table. "Mr. Black-wood," he greeted him in a lower voice than normal, shaking Rhett's hand. It was obvious he was trying to impress Rhett. "I'm Tom Willis, and this is Ava Conner." Tom stepped to the side to introduce me.

I sat there, once again stunned silent as my boss stared at me expectantly. *Crap.* He expected me to shake his hand.

Rhett took a step forward to where I was sitting, looking like the devil himself with his impish grin. "Ms. Conner." He offered his hand for me to grasp as his smooth voice floated over me like silk.

I had no idea how he could stand there, greeting me impassively as if he'd never met me and didn't just proposition me in the elevator a few minutes ago. I eyed his hand as

I cautiously stood, knowing I needed to put the whole elevator incident out of my mind. It was a moment of weakness earlier, but that was only because of the initial shock of seeing him. *Right?* I could do this. I had to do this. If not for me, for my boss.

"Mr. Blackwood, nice to meet you." I took his hand in mine, pretending like his presence had no impact on me as his eyes swept down my body.

As soon as I felt the charge between us travel through me, I abruptly tried pulling it away. But Rhett held my hand tight, grinning at me. I yanked my hand forcefully from his, hoping Tom didn't notice. Rhett chuckled under his breath. My temper flared. The man was insane. *Does he think this is a joke?*

We took our seats, and thankfully Rhett sat across the table from Tom and me. Or maybe that wasn't a good thing. I had a direct view of his delectable face and hypnotic eyes. I tried fixing my gaze on anything but him.

"So, Mr. Willis, tell me about your firm," Rhett commanded with a confident smile, not taking his probing eyes off me.

Tom started blabbing his usual spiel he gave to new clients. I could hear him talking, but I couldn't focus on what he was saying. He was more animated than usual. I knew he was really trying to sell his credentials to Rhett. I wasn't even sure if Rhett was listening. I felt badly for my boss, knowing he really wanted the project.

My phone vibrated, pulling my attention. I looked at it below the table.

V: Lunch was fun! Hope you made it to your meeting on time. ;) x

My jaw fell a little as it dawned on me Rhett was her chaperone, and she knew who I was meeting with. *The sly little she-devil!* I quickly typed a reply as Tom carried on, boring us with his credentials.

A: *I can't believe you didn't tell me Rhett came with you.*

V: *Just following your rules. You told me to never mention him to you.*

Damn it.

She was right. I couldn't very well be mad at her. I had that rule with all my family and friends. I put it in place to protect my heart, and now it looked like it was coming back to bite me in the ass. I'd told her that after she'd tried multiple times to get us back together. She was like a kid between two divorced parents. I wondered if this was her attempt at pulling a "parent trap," except for the fact that Rhett was obviously in on it.

"I've brought you a portfolio of some of my recent work. Ava here has been instrumental in many of these projects." Tom passed his marketing portfolio across the table to Rhett, snapping my attention back to the meeting.

Rhett took the portfolio from Tom, breaking his gaze on me momentarily. "I'd *love* to see it."

He spent all of thirty seconds looking through the portfolio before closing it. He looked up, ruthlessly smiling at me before turning his eyes on my boss.

"Well Tom, it looks like this will be a great fit. Send me your numbers and contract. I'll review and sign it."

He'd barely looked at the portfolio. He couldn't possibly know it was a good fit. I knew he had ulterior motives for hiring Tom, making me feel guilty. I didn't know what to do.

I wanted to tell Rhett he needed to find another architect,

but it would be completely unfair to Tom. This was going to be a huge opportunity for him. I'd just have to ask Tom to reassign it to Joce. There was no way I could work on this project with Rhett.

"That's great news! I'll have the proposal and the contract sent over to you first thing Monday morning," Tom said, beaming.

"I'd like to get started immediately, but unfortunately I have another meeting to be at. How about we discuss this further over dinner tonight? You and Ms. Conner will join me," Rhett demanded assertively.

"I have plans!"

The words flew abruptly from my mouth like verbal vomit before I could stop them. I flushed, immediately embarrassed by my outburst. Rhett raised a quizzical eyebrow at me. I didn't even bother looking at Tom, who I'm sure sat with a disapproving look. He was probably wondering what had gotten into me.

Tom took control of the situation, thankfully. "I apologize, Mr. Blackwood, it seems neither one of us can make it to dinner. I hope this doesn't complicate things."

"Not at all. I'm only in town for the weekend, though. Would it be possible for us to do lunch then, tomorrow? We could drive out to the site in Malibu afterwards. I know it's a lot to ask for you to give up your Saturday."

I already knew what was coming. Tom didn't work weekends anymore, with Marie's situation at home. "Do you mind giving us a moment, Mr. Blackwood?" Tom asked.

"Not at all. I'll just be over there, making a quick call." Rhett stood, moving across the large conference room, pulling out his cell phone. He talked in a low, hushed voice as he stared out the large windows, viewing downtown L.A.

"Ava, I hate to ask you to work tomorrow, but is there any way you can meet with him?" Tom pleaded, keeping his voice low.

I watched Rhett with his back to me, wondering how he could be so self-possessed while all the emotions were flooding my mind, unnerving me. He looked good. Better than good. He was sexier and more confident than before. The way he carried himself had me almost wanting to throw my resolve out the window. *Almost.* I wanted to tell Tom no way in hell. He looked so hopeful, though.

"Tom, you know I don't mind working the weekend, but I think maybe Joce would be better suited for this project than me."

He looked at me, confused, and a little distraught by my suggestion. "Ava, I'm a bit surprised you'd give up the chance to work on this. I can give it to Joce if that's what you really want. But I chose you, because I felt you had earned it. You have been doing excellent work for me over the last few years, and this is as great of an opportunity for you as it is me. Plus, I'd hate to switch points of contact after he's just met you."

He was right. If it were anyone other than Rhett, there was no way I'd pass up this opportunity. I smiled weakly at my boss. I couldn't turn this down without telling him the whole sordid story. And there was no way in hell I was doing that. I'd have to figure out a way to keep Rhett at arm's length and our time together strictly professional.

"No. I'll do it. And thank you for the opportunity." I smiled sincerely.

"Are we on for lunch and a site visit tomorrow?" Rhett rejoined us, returning from his phone call.

"Yes, but it'll only be Ava. I apologize. I have other engagements, but I'm leaving you in good hands with Ava. She'll be able to take photos of the site and take down all your specifications. She's more than capable," Tom said, speaking like a proud father.

"I'm sure she is." Rhett grinned knowingly at me.

I wanted to roll my eyes at him and childishly give him the finger, but seeing as how Tom was still present, I smiled sarcastically, instead.

"Well, we won't take up any more of your time. It was a pleasure meeting you, Mr. Blackwood. I look forward to working with you." Tom offered his hand to Rhett.

Rhett shook it. "Let me walk you out," he said, extending his arm for Tom and me to go first.

Tom moved ahead of me. I followed behind him, passing Rhett. Rhett put his hand on the small of my back as he guided me out behind Tom. My breath caught with his gentle touch, my body immediately responding. I quickened my steps to leave Rhett's torturous hand behind.

He stayed close by, walking us to the elevator. We didn't have to wait but a second before the elevator doors opened. Tom walked inside. I started to follow but was stopped by Rhett's hand on my elbow. Tom turned, waiting for me to join him in the elevator.

"I'm going to keep Ms. Conner for a moment to go over the time and location for tomorrow."

Tom nodded his understanding. "I'll see you Monday morning then, Ava. Have a good weekend." He waved as the doors closed.

They were shut before I could respond or move to jump between them. Watching them close was like watching the last life raft leave without me while I stood on a sinking ship.

I jerked my elbow from Rhett, furious he'd trapped me here until I could call another elevator. As I reached to push the call button, he snatched my hand, clasping it with his and pulling me along in the opposite direction. I tried planting my feet, ignoring the thrill coursing through my body. But he was too strong, and my heels didn't have any traction on the shiny wood floors.

"Rhett, let me go," I whispered angrily as he marched us past the nice receptionist, who was watching us closely. His strides were long and determined. I had to walk quickly to keep up as he dragged me along with him.

"No," he firmly stated as he continued to pull me down the long corridor.

He tugged me into an office, closing the door behind us. It was a large, modern executive office of steel, leather, and glass, with floor-to-ceiling windows giving you a beautiful view of downtown Los Angeles. He strode forward, guiding me near a seating area next to a small bar located off to the side of the large, masculine desk sitting in the room.

"Sit," he demanded, pointing to the brown leather couch, finally releasing his hold on my hand. "We need to talk."

He walked across the room, pacing as he ran his hand through his hair and back down his face, deep in thought.

"No." I defiantly crossed my arms over my chest. "There's nothing to talk about. You can email me the time and location in Malibu, and I'll meet you tomorrow. Lunch won't be necessary."

"*That* is not what I wanted to talk about." He stopped pacing, watching me carefully.

"I don't care. That's all we *will* be talking about. Besides, I thought you had a meeting to get to."

"This is the meeting."

"You have some nerve, you arrogant ass! I see nothing has changed." I rolled my eyes, turning for the door.

"Watch what your language, Ava," he gritted through his teeth. "And you're right, nothing has changed. You're still stubborn and defiant as hell. And you're also *still mine.*"

His? Oh hell, no.

I spun at his words, pinning him with narrowed eyes. He wasn't ruffled in the slightest. His eyes penetrated my shielded heart as he slowly moved forward to close the gap between us.

I stepped back, my anger boiling to all-new levels. "Let me be perfectly clear." I paused for effect. "Whatever you *think* you're going to accomplish here, you won't. You may have tied my hands forcing me to work on this project with you, but that's all *this*," I pointed between us, "will be. Strictly professional."

His body stiffened at my words. He stopped his approach, studying me instead. We stood silently, examining each other, both trying to predict what the other was thinking. It was minutes before he finally let out a resigned sigh, "Okay."

I looked at his eyes, trying to figure out if he was really going to accept defeat, or if he was only allowing me to win for the moment. I was afraid it was the latter.

"Okay?" I questioned his intentions.

"Yes, beautiful. *Okay.* We'll do this your way. For now," he added. "I'll pick you up at eleven tomorrow morning."

The "for now" confirmed I'd only temporarily won this battle. But it didn't matter, because I'd keep on fighting until the war was over.

"No. This is not a date. I'll drive separately."

"We'll see about that," he smirked his threat while starting to approach me again.

With each deliberate step he took toward me, I took one back, making my way to the door.

"I need to go. You *will* email me the address." The inflection in my voice was weaker than I intended.

He was getting dangerously close to me, and I was running out of space to retreat. He didn't respond. He smiled his roguish smile as my back landed against the closed door.

"I've missed you, Ava," he whispered huskily as his intense, beautiful blues stared into mine. I reached behind me, grabbing the door handle for stability as I tried to maintain my self-control. I could feel the chemistry between us ricocheting through my body, causing heat to pool between my legs as I watched his masculine body prowl toward me.

"Mr. Blackwood," I cleared my throat, trying to sound professional, "it was good to see you." My words came out squeaky and shaky, exposing my vulnerability.

He grinned, pleased with himself, stopping mere inches from me as he stared down into my eyes all the way to my soul. "Ms. Conner," he crooned as he leaned in closer, bringing one arm above me, resting it on the adjacent wall as his other hand skimmed my cheek lightly. "It's always a pleasure bumping into you." His voice was gravelly as he started to dip his head to kiss me.

I bit my bottom lip, fighting the urge to press my lips to his.

I turned the door knob, flinging the door open, forcing my body to retreat quickly, stumbling out, leaving him alone in his office. I could hear him chuckling to himself as I ran away.

Bastard.

He was not going to make these next few months easy on me.

∼

I sifted through the closet of my one-bedroom Santa Monica apartment, looking for something to wear. I was feeling rebellious and determined. I was intent on putting Rhett's wicked smile out of my mind. I was going to have my first one-night stand tonight, even if it killed me. And I was going to look sexy as hell doing it.

I chalked up my moments of weakness to one thing, the one thing Rhett had been right about in the elevator: it had been *too* long. I hadn't had sex with anyone, since Rhett, and I concluded that was the only reason my body responded to him the way it did.

I pushed the dresses I wore for work aside on the clothes rod, revealing a dress I'd hidden in my closet and never worn. I bought it on a whim after Lizzie had come to visit for a weekend. We'd gone on a shopping spree, and after much internal debate, she'd convinced me to buy it.

It was a stunning, soft, gray dress with spaghetti straps connected to two pieces of material that loosely folded at the top, forming a V-neck cut. The skirt of the dress was form fitting, stopping at my knees, with a revealing slit over the left thigh. The pale gray color complimented my Californian sun-kissed skin. It made me feel elegant and womanly putting it on.

I decided to wear my long, thick, brown hair down in big, loose curls. I wore my makeup natural, using bronzers and light shades of pink on my lips and eyes to help my blue eyes pop. I put on my black, sandaled stilettos, then stood to give myself the once-over in my full-length mirror. I looked hot and felt a sense of payback, even if Rhett wouldn't see me dressed like this. I grabbed my black clutch and headed out the door to the car, where my Uber driver was waiting.

~

We were meeting at The Grand. The bar wasn't our usual scene, with its masculine décor and extensive list of whiskeys, but I guess if the mission was to meet a man, then this was the place to do it. The bar was lively and crowded with younger clientele. It was obviously a hot spot for the young professionals to come and drink their week's stresses away.

I squeezed through the multitude of people in search of Joce, taking in the scene as I went. Besides the deer heads hanging on the walls, I liked the vintage sophistication of the place. It was like stepping back in time to when "the boys" would drink whiskey and smoke cigars. The dark woods and dim lights were inviting and comforting and put me at ease right away. I was ready to relax and enjoy the night.

I spotted Joce at the end of the bar, already being hit on by a suit. She seemed like she was politely trying to ward off his advances, so I did what girlfriends do best and blocked him, pulling her attention away. She thanked me before complimenting me on my sexy ensemble as he walked away. A cute bartender approached us, smiling and flirting while making our drinks. We paid for them, then moved away from the bar, looking for a place to sit.

I wasn't much of a whiskey drinker, but the old-fashioned cocktails were going down easily. I was enjoying myself as Joce and I chatted and scanned the room of good-looking men. I looked at my nearly empty glass, deciding to get another drink.

"You need one?" I asked Joce, glancing at her glass.

"No, I'm good for the moment. You go. I'll hold our table."

"Okay. Be right back," I said, standing.

I navigated my way to the crowded bar, squeezing between two men to get the cute bartender's attention. He immediately saw me. He finished making the drink he was working on before sauntering his way over to me.

"Same thing?" he asked with a flirtatious smile.

"Yep," I innocently flirted back.

"Coming right up," he said with a wink, walking away to make my drink.

"Wow. Impressive." I heard a deep voice next to me.

I looked over at the suit standing beside me, who was giving me his cute smile, revealing a lick-able dimple. He had dirty blond hair, green eyes, and a handsome face.

"I swear I've been standing here at least twenty minutes, trying to get his attention to order a drink. I don't blame the guy. It's hard not to notice a beautiful woman like you, even in a crowd of people," he continued.

I smiled at him, embarrassed. "I'm sorry. I didn't mean to cut in front of you."

"No apologies necessary," he said with a grin, making me flush more.

"Let me make it up to you. What are you drinking? I'll order it for you when he returns with my drink."

"I'd be forever in your debt if you did," he said, pretending to think it over. "I'll agree, as long as you let me pay for your drink." His smirk made my stomach do a tiny flip.

"Deal," I said, smiling back at him. "My name's Ava," I offered, wanting to continue our conversation.

"Ava, it's a pleasure to meet you. I'm Owen." He put out his hand to shake mine.

When the cute bartender approached, I ordered Owen's drink as we continued to talk for a few minutes. I didn't want our exchange to end, thinking he may be exactly what I needed for my one-night stand. He was kind and easy on the eyes, but I realized it was still early in the night. I didn't want to abandon Joce. I also had a little case of cold feet.

Instead, we exchanged numbers. I made my way back to Joce while he went back to the group of co-workers he'd come with. The night went on, and Joce continued scoping the bar for "Mr. Right" while Owen and I kept making eyes at each other from across the room. I wasn't as instantly affected by him as I was Rhett, but his attention didn't make me feel uncomfortable. It made me feel sensual and sexy, and that was good enough for me.

Joce and I were cracking up about something Drew had done and said the other day when she suddenly stopped laughing, grabbing my arm with a tight grip. She looked like she had seen a ghost. Then her face softened, her cheeks turning a bright red that rivaled her hair.

"Ava, I think I just saw Mr. Right," she whispered conspiratorially, looking past me.

I started to turn to see who'd caught her eye.

"Don't look!" she squealed, yelling at me in a panic, stopping me from continuing to rotate my head. "He's looking this way. I don't want it to be obvious."

I rolled my eyes at her childishness.

"Okay, now look," she said, giving me the go-ahead. I slightly twisted, casually glancing over my shoulder, panic instantly shooting through me.

Riley was standing less than twenty feet from us, beaming recognition right at me.

Shit.

He started to make his way to our table as Joce fluffed her hair beside me.

"He's coming over," she squealed.

I turned to her, wanting to explain to her who he was. But before I could, he was at our table.

"Ladies. May I join you?" he asked, with his pantydropper smile.

"Sure," Joce purred in return before I could respond.

He smiled, winking at me, taking a seat next to Joce. She turned up her flirtations. I glared at him. *What the hell is he doing here?* I knew if Riley was here, Rhett couldn't be far behind.

"I'm Riley," he introduced himself to Joce, putting out his hand.

"Jocelyn." She took his hand and batted her eyelashes, oblivious to the fact that I was still sitting here.

I turned from the two of them as they continued to flirt, watching out for Rhett. I found his back turned to me at the bar, ordering drinks with an overly-confident blonde draped on him. I instantly felt jealous and possessive of him. I had no idea where it came from. *Okay...I have some idea...but I shouldn't have these feelings anymore. He's not mine.* I tried to control it.

Her hand was on his shoulder, and she was inching it up his neck as she leaned in closer. My fists clenched under the table as my heart aggressively pounded against my chest.

He gently removed her hand from touching him as he politely dismissed her advances. I hated the relief I felt from that small gesture. He turned from the bar, holding two drinks, catching my eyes as he walked toward us. He strode through the mob of people effortlessly, dominating the room.

I felt the need to flee, but I was chained to my seat, held captive as I watched his muscular body move forward. He was a force of nature. It was like watching a tornado come at me: I knew I needed to take cover to protect myself from harm, but I couldn't help but watch it spin in all its destructiveness.

When he arrived at our table, Riley turned to Rhett, taking the glass of whiskey from him, breaking his conversation with Joce.

"Ava," Rhett said, smiling at me as he placed a glass of water in front of me, silently commanding me to drink it.

Tough shit.

I glared at him, silently refusing it. His glare matched mine as he took in my dress, perusing my body. I felt a small triumph as I watched his brow pinch in frustration.

Joce, catching onto our exchange, looked between us. "Do you guys know each other?" she asked, confused.

"Yes," I intercepted her question, before Rhett could respond. "This is Mr. Blackwood, the new client Tom and I met with today," I said, as professionally as possible.

I knew at some point Joce may meet him for work, and I didn't want it getting back to Tom that Rhett and I already knew each other.

"Oh!" she exclaimed. "It's nice to meet you, Mr. Blackwood. I'm Jocelyn. I work with Ava."

"Call me Rhett, please, and it's a pleasure to meet you, Jocelyn." He turned on his charm, smiling his sexy smile at her. She melted as all women did.

"I assume you know Riley, then? Since you brought him his drink," she concluded.

"Yes. Riley is a good friend of mine. We just stopped in for some drinks after work."

"What a coincidence!" she said, smiling.

But I knew damn well, it was no coincidence. I just wasn't quite sure how he knew I was here. Then the answer hit me like a sledge hammer. He must have looked at my phone in the building lobby.

Ugh. The sneaky bastard!

They continued to talk for a moment until Rhett pulled his phone out of his pocket, feeling its vibration. He excused himself as he took the call, and Joce excused herself to run to the ladies' room. I was about to go with her when Riley caught my arm, silently pleading for me to stay behind. My curiosity kept me seated as Joce left us at the table. When she was out of earshot, I turned my anger on him.

"What the hell are you guys doing here?" I was beyond annoyed they'd shown up to ruin my night.

"Why do you think, Ava?" he snorted.

35

"Well, you two need to leave or I will."

"Why won't you hear him out?"

I turned my head away, not wanting to see the pleading desperation in his eyes. I'd always liked Riley, and I hated that their unwanted presence here was making me feel differently.

"Ava, he's a fucking mess without you. He has been for years, since you left. I'm surprised he waited this long to come and get you."

"Well, it's a little too late for that, Riley." My voice started to shake.

The memories of the night we parted spun uncontrollably in my mind, making me an emotional hurricane. I felt the tears brimming in my eyes.

"He wasn't there when I needed him. He chose *her* over me."

I didn't need to clarify who "her" was. We both knew I was referring to Serena.

He looked at me, confused, then shocked. "You have no fucking idea, do you?" He narrowed his eyes, his own anger spiking. "I guess your little prick friend, Stephen, never told you."

Now it was my turn to be confused. "What are you talking about?"

A sudden wave of fear came over me that I didn't understand. But before he could answer, Joce came bouncing back up to us, taking her seat next to Riley, silencing both of us. He gave me a meaningful look before turning back to Joce, continuing their flirting.

I suddenly couldn't breathe. I needed air. I needed to get out of there. As Rhett started to walk back toward our table,

I grabbed my clutch, quickly telling Joce goodbye and I'd call her later. She seemed unfazed by my sudden departure, happy to be alone with Riley.

I started squeezing my way through the horde of bodies, aiming to bypass Rhett. He cut me off before I reached the door, pulling me into his warm, familiar body. Mine instinctively melded with his. I looked away from him, keeping my eyes on the exit.

"Ava, calm down," he soothed, feeling my heavy breathing.

How the hell does he expect me to calm down, when he's holding me this close?

"Look at me, beautiful. Where are you going?"

"Home," I managed to say, still not looking at him.

"I'll take you."

"No!" I yelled, gaining some fight back in me.

Owen glanced over at me as he shook his friends' hands goodbye. With a sudden surge of adrenaline, I pushed my hands against Rhett's chest, breaking free of his grasp. I took off, shoving my way through the crowd as fast as I could before Rhett caught up to me, aiming to intercept Owen at the door. He smiled brightly upon my approach.

"Can you take me home?" I asked franticly, the panic still swarming me as I looked at Rhett, who was closing in on us. There was no way I had time to call an Uber.

"Sure," he responded cautiously with a concerned face as he looked between Rhett and me.

"Great." I grabbed his arm, leading him out the door. I rushed us both down the narrow staircase to leave, before Rhett could stop me. When we made it outside, I gasped for air, letting it fill my lungs.

"Are you okay?" he asked, guiding me to his car with a hand at my back.

"Yes. I'm sorry. I just...thank you..." I trailed off, not knowing what else to say.

"No worries," he said, giving me a sympathetic smile.

He unlocked the car and opened the passenger door, allowing me to get in. As we drove off, I didn't bother looking back to see if Rhett was coming after me.

When we made it to my apartment complex, I suddenly worried Owen may have gotten the wrong idea. I'd intended to have a one-night stand before, but after the night's events, I couldn't go through with it. Owen walked me to my door and I turned to him after unlocking it.

"Owen, I'm sorry...I don't think..."

"Ava, don't apologize. I don't expect anything," he said sweetly, his smile consoling. "I only wanted to make sure you got inside safely."

I nodded my appreciation, giving him a weak smile in return.

"Would you mind if I called you?" he asked. "I'd like to take you out sometime."

"I'd like that, too."

"Well then"—he leaned in, giving me a kiss on the cheek — "have a good night, Ava," he said, before smiling and turning to leave.

CHAPTER 3

I have no idea what time I finally fell asleep. I tossed and turned all night, reeling from Rhett's unexpected return to my life. I woke at seven in the morning, the anxiety churning in my stomach from the thought of our impending meeting today. I didn't know how I was going to get through it. I was having a hard time maintaining control of my emotions when he was around. I hated how weak he made me feel.

I went for a morning run along the beach, stopping at the Santa Monica Pier to rest and process everything going on in my head. I'd taken up running regularly when I moved to California. It helped clear my mind, release the emotional stress, and relieve the panic attacks I often felt.

Sitting on the pier, I watched a father with his daughter. He was so caring and gentle with her, reminding me of my dad. I missed him more than anything in the world and wished he was here to give me some words of wisdom. I could really use them right now. I sat there for an hour, lost in my thoughts, before finding my way back to my apartment.

It was already nine, and I realized I had no idea where I was supposed to meet Rhett in a couple of hours. I sat down at the table, pulling up my work email on my laptop, hoping he'd sent me the address. I had no emails from him. I wondered if maybe seeing me leave with another man last night had convinced him to back off. I felt a momentary wave of remorse, but quickly pushed it down and went to take a shower.

After my run and a shower, I was feeling better. I needed to put my feelings for Rhett out of my mind. Drying my hair with a towel, I went out onto the balcony of my apartment to stare at the ocean.

I'd rented this apartment for its view and proximity to the beach. I fell in love with it instantly and spent many nights on the balcony, letting the sound of the ocean waves soothe me. After a few moments of reflection, I walked back inside to get dressed.

I pulled on a pair of faded, worn jeans, rolling them at the bottom, and a loose, white shirt. I tossed my hair up in a messy bun, then put on my brown sandals. Grabbing my purse, I headed for the door, deciding to go into the office to catch up on some work.

I exited my apartment, locking it behind me. Turning, I came to a halt, seeing Rhett walking up the hallway. He slowed his stride, stopping a few feet away from me, putting his hands in his pockets as he gauged my reaction.

He looked casual, with his denim jeans and black T-shirt, both hugging his body in all the right places. His face was worn and tired, but otherwise impassive. Neither one of us spoke. We both just took in the other.

"I thought maybe you changed your mind, since you never emailed me," I said, finally breaking our strained silence.

He shook his head no. "I told you I'd pick you up at eleven."

"I'll drive separate."

"No," he said firmly. "I'm not going to argue this with you, Ava. You'll get in my car, or I'll carry you to it and put you in myself," he commanded. We both knew he'd follow through with his threat, so I relented.

"Fine. Let's go. I'll need to stop by the office to grab a few things first." I stomped past him. He turned to follow me, keeping his distance.

~

The drive to my office was quiet and tense. As we headed to Malibu, I wanted to scream, if only to break the silence and release all the pent-up emotions in me. I glanced over at him. He was seething with his own anger as he gripped the steering wheel tightly, staring straight ahead. I turned back to look at the road as we drove along the winding Pacific Coast Highway.

"Are you going to give me the silent treatment all afternoon?" I grumbled, frustrated.

I wasn't sure I truly wanted to talk, but anything was better than the intense silence we were suffering through. He slid his gaze to me momentarily and then back to the road.

"It's not very professional of you to ignore your client's calls," he scorned.

"I didn't realize you called. Your number must still be blocked in my phone."

"Don't you think you should remedy that if we're going to be working together?"

He had a point. I looked over at him apologetically.

"I'll take care of it. Was there something you needed when you called?"

He didn't respond for a minute. I could see he was struggling to maintain control of his emotions.

"Did you sleep with him?" His words came out in a tight, gruff voice.

Maybe I should've suffered through the silence.

"*That* is none of your business. I don't inquire about all of your conquests." My lips tightened, trying to keep my temper in check. "Besides, it's not an appropriate conversation for me to have with a client."

"Damn it, Ava!" His voice boomed through the car. "You have every right to ask me. And so there is no misunderstanding, I haven't touched a woman since you." He breathed heavily.

I knew he was likely telling me the truth. In moments of weakness through the years, I tortured myself by Googling him. The blondes who usually graced his arm had been suspiciously absent from recent photos. I hadn't even seen him with Serena. Lately, he'd been photographed at social events either alone, or escorting Valerie.

"There's only you, Ava. There will only ever be you," he said, his voice softening, the pain and anguish evident.

The same pain and anguish I was feeling. I couldn't look

at him. I focused my eyes downward, seeing for the first time the keys dangling in the ignition. The keys I gave him years ago hung on the key ring. I looked out the passenger window to hide the tears surfacing.

"No...I didn't sleep with him."

My words came out in a whisper, but they were loud enough for him to hear. He let out a sigh of relief, relaxing his body. The thought of me sleeping with someone else was driving him close to a nervous breakdown. I didn't know how to feel about that. I felt relief and fear at the same time.

A few minutes later, we pulled up to a vacant piece of property off the Pacific Coast Highway. It was three acres of untouched land, with a gorgeous view of the Pacific Ocean. The property came with deeded rights to a private, secluded beach cove below.

I got out of the car, breathing in the salty sea air. I closed my eyes, soaking in the sun rays, then opened them, walking deeper into the property to take in the view. It was breathtaking. I knew it had to cost millions just for the land. Rhett came up behind me as I stared out at the ocean, placing his hand gently at the small of my back. I felt my body instinctively relaxing into his touch, until his voice broke me out of my reverie.

"Beautiful, isn't it?" he asked, whispering across my ear.

I moved away, breaking our connection. I gave him a frail smile, not wanting to start another argument but needing to get control of the situation.

"It's a gorgeous view. Give me a few minutes to take some pictures of the property, and then we can go over your thoughts for the home." I tried reminding him this was a business meeting.

I walked back to the car, picking up my camera. I worked my way around the site, taking pictures from different angles. All the while, Rhett had his eyes on me, watching me work. When I was about done with the photos, he moved to the trunk of his car, pulling out a picnic basket. I gave him a curious look.

"You have to eat, Ava. Might as well do it on the beach while we go over our thoughts for the home."

I wanted to argue a picnic on the beach was not appropriate, but I *was* hungry. It also worried me how he said his words, almost as if to imply this was *our* home. We hiked our way down to the beach cove. Rhett set up a blanket and pulled out the picnic lunch he packed with some bottles of water.

As we started to discuss his visions for the home, my worry became warranted. He kept insisting I tell him what I'd want for the home, *if* it were mine. I kept reminding him it didn't really matter what I wanted. This was his home and his money.

A few times, I gave in, as he's a hard man to deny. The few times I shared my thoughts, he immediately agreed and suggested we move forward with those ideas. I'd sigh with frustration, and he'd just give me his sexy smirk in return.

When we finished going over his specs for the house, we started talking like old friends as we ate our lunch. He asked me about my job, keeping the conversation light, and I asked him how it was to be the head honcho at Blackwood Industries. I actually found myself enjoying the conversation and even laughing as we exchanged stories. I was relaxing more than I thought possible as we sat next to each other, watching the ocean tide come in.

The breeze blowing across the sea cooled the air around us as the sun started to set. Feeling a sudden chill, I pulled my knees to my body, hugging them with my arms. Rhett instinctively moved closer, tucking me into his side as his arms enclosed me to protect me from the cool air.

His touch sent heat coursing through my body, contrasting with the shiver running through it. I looked up at his strong, chiseled jawline, losing myself in the moment as I locked my eyes with his. His eyes hooded over as he leaned in, brushing his lips with mine. The instant they touched, I panicked. Moving quickly, I scampered to my feet, looking down at him in shock as he looked up at me, confused.

"Ava." He spoke my name cautiously, as if trying not to scare a timid animal.

"We should go." I looked away from him. "I need to get home. I have work to do."

"Ava," he said again, my name a plea on his lips. "Why are you fighting this? I know you feel it. I know you want this as much as I do. I know you still love me."

I felt the tears prick at the back of my eyes. I wasn't going to be able to hold them in. I spun around, running away.

"Damn it! Ava. Wait!" he yelled from behind me.

He caught up to me with only a few long strides, grabbing my arm, turning me into him as he smashed me into his strong chest. He hugged me to him, comforting me as I cried uncontrollably into his shirt.

"I'm sorry, babe. I'm sorry," he kept repeating, whispering softly as he held me.

I cried in his arms for what felt like forever before he finally picked me up, carrying me to the car. I let him. I was too emotionally confused and exhausted to fight or argue with him. He put me in the car, leaving me momentarily, retrieving the items we left on the beach. I stared out the passenger window, lost in my thoughts.

When he returned to the car, I felt his eyes on me, but he didn't say anything. Turning over the ignition, he steered the car onto the highway, driving us back toward Santa Monica. I closed my eyes, letting the exhaustion from crying overwhelm me as I fell asleep.

~

I woke to his voice and hand floating across my forehead, skimming down my cheek. "Wake up, beautiful. We're here."

My eyes fluttered open as I sat up sleepily, looking around. We were outside my apartment building. I looked over at Rhett as he stared at me fondly, taking in every inch of me.

"I'll walk you to your door."

He opened his car door to get out before I could object, walking around the car to open my door. We walked silently through my apartment complex. He stood there, waiting as I unlocked the door to my apartment. I cracked the door, halting from opening it any farther. I didn't know what he was expecting, but I wasn't ready to let him in, not into my apartment and not back into my heart.

I turned, trying to figure out how to explain. Before I could say anything, he spoke, "Will you join us for dinner tonight?"

I assumed his "us" included Valerie and Riley. I would've

loved to see Valerie again before she left, but I couldn't handle any more turmoil for the day.

"Rhett," I paused, trying to find the strength to tell him goodbye. "I think it's best, if I don't."

I didn't know if it was what I really wanted, but I needed some space. I couldn't think with him near me. His words on the beach were still wreaking havoc on my perseverance.

I could see him struggling to accept my answer as his brow furrowed. His eyes became more intense, as if trying to read me. "I don't like leaving you like this."

"I'll be fine. It's what I need right now." I silently begged for him to understand.

After a few more seconds, he nodded his head, relinquishing the control I know he needed. "We leave in the morning to fly back to New York." He paused, his face hardening slightly. "Fix your phone," he commanded.

"I will," I promised.

He stepped closer to me, brushing the pad of his thumb across my lips. "Get some rest, beautiful."

He leaned forward. I held my breath and closed my eyes as he kissed me on the forehead, and then he was gone.

I walked into my apartment, closing the door, sliding my back down it until my bottom hit the ground. I stared ahead, wondering if I'd just made the biggest mistake of my life.

Finally pulling myself up off the floor, I changed into some more comfortable clothes. I opened a bottle of wine and poured myself a glass. Picking up my phone, I scrolled through it, unblocking Rhett's number and adding it back into my contacts.

With my wine, phone, and a blanket in hand, I went out to my balcony to sit. I called my mom, needing to hear her voice. It'd been a few days since I'd checked up on her. I tried to call her and Nana at least once a week, if not more.

She answered in a jovial mood that was almost contagious. "Hi, honey!"

"Hi, Mom." I smiled through the tears running down my cheeks.

I missed my family daily. It was hard being so far away from them, but it was a necessary evil. My mom, always in tune with me, asked, "Ava, honey. Is everything okay?"

"Yes," I lied. "I just miss you, and it's really good to hear your voice."

"I miss you too, honey," she responded in her sweet, motherly voice, which made me want to cry more. "Maybe I can try to make a trip out there soon? Or you could always come home for a weekend? I know everyone would love to see you."

"That sounds good. I'll try to figure something out," I promised.

We continued to talk about nothing in particular, mostly catching up with each other. After about thirty minutes of random conversation, we said our goodbyes.

"I love you Mom. Tell Emily, Jackson, and Nana I love and miss them."

"I will, dear. Take care of yourself. And, Ava...if there's something you need to talk about, I'm always here for you."

"I know, Mom. Love you. Have a good night."

"Love you, too. Goodnight, honey," she said before hanging up.

Not wanting to be left alone with my thoughts just yet, I tried calling Lizzie, but she didn't answer. I stared at my phone after I hung up. I had the sudden urge to call Rhett. I fought the impulse and put my phone down, looking away from it.

I drank my wine and pulled my blanket tighter while looking out at the stars in the black sky, listening to the ocean. I kept thinking about what Rhett had said on the beach. His words in my head were like knives in my heart, tormenting me. They hurt deeply. There was so much truth to them—truth I didn't want to admit to. I would always love Rhett, no matter how much he'd hurt me.

I was afraid and angry at the same time. Afraid I'd never love anyone as much as him. Angry he had that power, and I could do nothing about it. I couldn't choose not to love him, as hard as I tried.

Riley's words from last night were weighing heavy on me also, the way he accused Stephen of knowing something I didn't. It had me almost calling Stephen to find out, but things had been strained with Stephen and me since he left California.

It turned out Rhett was right about Stephen wanting more with me. We spent a few weeks together in California. I was continually suffering from the pain of losing Rhett and my father. Stephen tried comforting me. After holding me in his arms one night, he leaned in and kissed me.

At first, I kissed him back, wanting to feel anything but grief. But I quickly pulled back, because none of it felt right. My grief was combined with guilt, instead of the pleasure I'd been desperate for. I was in no place to start another relationship so soon, and I was afraid of losing our friendship. I didn't exactly have a great track record, and my heart couldn't handle another loss.

He poured his heart out to me, trying to convince me we

were right for each other. I couldn't reciprocate his feelings, though. He went back to Wellesley a few days later with a bruised ego, and no matter how hard we both tried to stay friends, things had never been the same.

I poured myself another glass, letting the wine flow through my body to warm and numb me. I remained outside on the balcony, finishing the bottle over the next couple hours. I had a pretty good buzz when my phone chimed. I picked it up, staring at the screen.

R: Goodnight, beautiful. Be back as soon as I can.

I knew his words were a promise. I just wasn't sure if they were a promise I wanted him to keep. I didn't respond to his text. I put the phone down and closed my tired eyes. I let the sound of the ocean waves lull me to sleep as I dreamed of another life where I could be his girl.

～

Sunday morning I woke and headed into the office to work. I needed to focus on anything but my disastrous love life or lack thereof, so I threw myself into my work. I spent the whole day at the office and made a lot of progress on my projects. I was more productive than I'd been in a while.

At the end of the day, I stopped to pick up some sushi to take home, then planned to relax for the evening. I'd barely finished eating, while catching up on some shows, when my phone rang. I picked it up off my coffee table, expecting it to be Lizzie finally returning my call, but it wasn't.

Owen's name and phone number lit up on the screen. I hesitated for a moment, not sure if I wanted to answer it. Moments before it rang off, I made my decision.

"Hello."

"Ava, hey. It's Owen… The guy who took you home the other night."

I laughed inwardly. "Yes, I remember you, Owen," I replied, the amusement coming through my voice.

"Oh. Good." He sounded relieved. "Well, I thought I'd call and see if you wanted to go to dinner this week. Or we can just do coffee, whatever you're more comfortable with."

I fought back a giggle; his nervous babble was kind of cute.

"I would like that Owen. How about dinner? Wednesday night?" I suggested.

"Perfect. I'll pick you up?"

His approach was so different from Rhett, who always just made decisions for me. It was obvious he didn't have the same confidence as Rhett, but not many men did.

"Yes, how about eight? That'll give me time to get home from work."

"All right. I'll see you at eight on Wednesday." I heard the smile in his voice.

"See you then. Bye, Owen."

"Bye, Ava."

I hung up the phone with a mixture of emotions: a little excitement and a little nervousness, followed by guilt. I ignored the guilt and finished watching my shows before heading off to bed.

CHAPTER 4

Miraculously, I made it into work early Monday morning. Tom was already at the office. I'm sure he was anxious to get started on the contract for Rhett.

I popped my head into his office. "Good morning, Tom."

He looked up at me from his desk. "Ah, Ava! Good morning. I didn't expect to see you here this early."

I smiled sheepishly.

"How was your weekend? Did the meeting with Mr. Blackwood go well?"

"Yep," I replied, intentionally leaving out any details. Technically, it *had* gone well, up until the kiss on the beach. "I was about to upload the photos and type up my notes."

"Great. I'm wrapping up the proposal and contract to send over to him, then I plan to start reviewing the field information you gathered."

"Sounds good. I'll do that now." I dismissed myself.

I went back to my desk and got to work on transferring the files over. My phone chimed as I checked my emails.

L: Change in plans. I'm coming in this Friday. Hope that's okay?

A: Of course! Send me your flight information.

L: Will do. See you soon!

I put my phone back down, excited Lizzie would be here at the end of the week. By the time I wrapped up responding to a few emails, Drew and Joce had arrived at the office. Joce was in an extremely chipper mood as she walked through the door to her desk. I assumed it had a lot to do with Riley. I looked over at her expectantly as she put her things away and took a seat at her desk.

"I take it Friday night went well?" I inquired with a smirk.

She looked at me ruefully. Her pink cheeks brightened.

"Yes...*and* Saturday *and* Sunday morning," she whispered dreamily, lost in her reverie. "Well, that was at least after Rhett left on Friday. He had Riley's attention temporarily distracted." She turned, studying me. "I think our new, sexy client was hoping you'd stick around. He spent most of the night brooding after you left with that other guy. Even though he looked dangerously hot, it still kind of killed the mood," she teased.

I immediately started to panic that Riley or Rhett might've said something to Joce, revealing our history. I hoped she still had no clue.

"Don't be silly, Joce. He's a client and that would be completely unprofessional," I replied, giving nothing away.

She shrugged her shoulders, giving me a nonchalant smirk. "That's too bad. He really is gorgeous. I don't know how you're going to work with him. I wouldn't be able to control myself," she said, grinning wickedly as she teased me.

Annoyance and jealousy suddenly churned in my stomach. I didn't know how I was going to manage to work with him either, but I was suddenly glad I didn't turn the project over to Joce after all. I needed to steer the conversation away from Rhett and me.

"Will you be seeing Riley again?" I asked, my question with an ulterior motive.

Rhett never told me exactly when he'd be back, and I didn't want to be caught off guard again. I figured if Riley had made plans with Joce, it would give me somewhat of an idea.

"I hope so. It figures when I finally find a guy I really like he'd live on the other side of the country," she huffed. "He promised to call me when he got settled back in New York and that he'd be back here soon, but didn't really say when. He could've just been saying that though..." Her face fell.

"Well, I'm sure you'll hear from him." I gave an encouraging smile.

I really did hope she would, and not only for my benefit. I knew Riley was a good guy and Joce deserved someone good. I just hoped he wouldn't break her heart. The long distance would be a major hurdle for them to overcome if they wanted to pursue this.

Our conversation was interrupted by someone coming through the door. Both of us turned our heads to see who'd arrived at the office. A delivery guy stood with a huge bouquet of white roses in a shiny crystal vase. There had to be at least two dozen stems. They were extravagant and beautiful.

My heart sank, knowing who they were from immediately. I looked over at Joce, whose eyes lit up. I knew she was hoping they were from Riley. I kind of hoped so too, for both of our sakes.

"Looking for a Ms. Ava Conner?" The delivery man peered around the ungodly large bouquet.

Joce sat back in her chair, deflated, as I hesitantly stood from my desk. "That's me." I waved my hand timidly as I walked toward him.

"Here you go," he said smiling, passing the roses off to me. I took them back to my desk as he left out the front door.

"Wow! Who are they from?!" Joce asked nosily before I could even read the card. I took the card out of the bouquet, nervously pulling it from the envelope.

Ms. Conner,

Thank you for joining me Saturday.

I'm looking forward to our next "business"

meeting.

-RB

"Well?" Joce asked impatiently. "Are they from the guy at the bar?"

"What?" I asked, distracted from my thoughts. "Oh, yes," I lied. "We have a date this Wednesday. I guess this is his attempt at courting me," I added, not sure why I felt the need to expand on my deception. I felt terrible about lying to Joce, but I couldn't very well tell her they were from Rhett.

"Lucky girl. He must be smitten already. It looks like we both found our perfect guys Friday night!"

She had no idea. I gave her a half-hearted smile in response and quickly hid the card so she wouldn't see it.

Turning my focus on my computer, I attempted to bury myself in some work, drafting up some final drawings for Tom's review. I mindlessly worked, glancing back and forth between the flowers on my desk and my monitor.

The more I looked at them, the more aggravated I was he sent them to me. I had a hard enough time putting him out of my mind. Now, I had a constant reminder of him sitting on my desk. I'm sure that was exactly what he wanted. I contemplated sending him a warning text when my thoughts were interrupted by Tom.

"Ava, I just finished going through everything on the Blackwood residence and didn't see any mention of deed restrictions or property lines. Do you happen to have this information?"

I immediately felt terrible and embarrassed. I'd been so distracted by Rhett I'd forgotten to ask for both.

"I'm sorry, Tom. It completely slipped my mind," I apologized for forgetting something so fundamental. "I'll contact him now to get the information."

"Thank you, Ava. Let me know when you've received it. I'd like to get started on some design sketches right away," Tom added before walking away.

I turned back to my computer, frustrated. Rhett was already affecting my work. I needed to focus, and I needed to draw the line. I couldn't allow him to be sending me flowers and trying to kiss me during business meetings. I started to write an email to tell him just that before deciding against it. I'd text him later. For now, I'd keep the email professional.

Mr. Blackwood,

I apologize. I forgot to request the deed restrictions and survey of the property. Please forward to me at your convenience.

Sincerely,

Ava Conner

I hit send and went back to working, but was immediately distracted by his response arriving in my inbox.

Ms. Conner,

No apologies required. I should have provided you the information. I apologize. I was distracted by the beauty around me. Please see attached.

Did you get the flowers?

Sincerely <u>yours</u>,

Rhett

He was maddening. He insisted on making this impossible for me.

Mr. Blackwood,

Yes and it was completely inappropriate. <u>Especially</u> sending them to my office.

Thank you for the files.

Regards,

Ms. Conner

There. Hopefully he'd get the hint. After sending the files to Tom, I tried refocusing on the project I'd been working on. But not even two minutes after I'd sent my email, Rhett responded.

Ava,

I will send you flowers when and where I damn well please. And you're welcome...for both.

<u>Still yours</u>,

Rhett

Bastard. Screw professionalism.

You're impossible! You arrogant ass!

Ava

What is wrong with me? I needed to focus and stop arguing via my work email.

You're unreasonable. Watch that mouth, beautiful.

Always yours,

Rhett

Seriously? I sat back in my seat with a huff, frustrated with the man. I was trying to decide how to respond when my thoughts were interrupted by the phone ringing. I ignored it, hoping Joce or Drew would pick up. I was too infuriated to sound cheerful in greeting the person on the other end. I decided not to respond at all. It was a rock and a hard place. I was letting him win by not responding, but I was also letting him win by responding.

I attempted to work as I seethed. A few minutes later Tom stopped at my desk, again.

"Ava, that was Mr. Blackwood."

Oh. Shit. Did he say something to Tom? Surely not. He wouldn't want to get me fired.

"He'd like to see some preliminary concepts Thursday morning. I should have some sketches to you tomorrow afternoon."

Even worse. He'd found a way to ruin my work life *and* my dating life.

"We'll need to draft up the floor plans and do some rendered elevations, creating some presentation boards for the meeting." Tom looked at me apologetically.

We both knew it was a lot of work to turn around in a short timeframe. I was going to be working late Wednesday night. I'd either have to cancel my date with Owen or reschedule. If I didn't know better, I'd think Rhett somehow found out about my date with Owen. That was impossible, though. *Right?* I glanced suspiciously over at Joce, who was the only person I had told. She was blushing, her fingers moving furiously over the phone hidden on her lap under her desk.

"No problem." I forced a smile.

"Thank you, Ava. I knew I could count on you." Tom flashed his smile as he walked away.

I put my forehead down on my desk, lightly banging it.

"Everything okay?" Drew approached me with an amused and quizzical expression.

I looked up at him, shaking my head. "Not really. But it'll be fine," I responded, not wanting to discuss it.

"Joce and I were about to head to lunch. Did you want to join us?"

I was glad he didn't bother to question me any further. I liked that about Drew. He always avoided our "girl drama," as he referred to it. I looked over at Joce, gathering up her purse, then back to Drew.

"Thanks, but it looks like I'm going to have to work through lunch."

I hated I had to skip. Lunches with Joce and Drew were always comical, and I could really use some humor to get my mind off things.

"Next time, then."

"You're not coming?" Joce asked, coming up behind Drew.

"Nope, you guys have fun."

"Okay, see you in a little bit." She waved as she and Drew walked out of the office.

I went back to work, trying to get as much done as possible on my other projects. It was a good thing I went to work yesterday, or I would've been even worse off. I needed to text or call Owen to see if we could reschedule.

I decided on a text, not wanting to hear his disappointment. I also didn't want Tom to overhear me calling him.

A: Have an unexpected work deadline. Can we reschedule for later in the week?

He responded a few minutes later.

O: Last-minute business trip came up. I leave Thursday evening and won't be back until the following Thursday. Can you do lunch Thursday?

That worked perfect. I'd be done with my deadline by then. I typed out my response.

A: Lunch Thursday works. See you then!

∾

The last couple of days went by quickly. Rhett continued to respond inappropriately to any business emails I sent. At least, in my opinion they weren't appropriate. Anything that could make me suddenly flush by simply reading it was *not* appropriate.

I gave up on arguing with him about what was appropriate and what wasn't. It seemed any time I argued, it only encouraged him more. I kept picturing his devilish smirk every time I read one of his emails. Instead, I only responded when I had to and kept it completely professional...mostly. I couldn't help it. The man knew how to get under my skin.

I'd worked late Wednesday night to make sure the presentation boards were perfect for today's meeting. I didn't know why, but I was somewhat nervous about Rhett seeing them. I got in early Thursday morning to make sure I didn't miss anything, still trying to make up for my rookie error from our previous meeting. I knew Tom wasn't holding it against me, but I still felt ashamed.

"Good morning, Ava." Tom passed my desk as he arrived at the office.

"Morning, Tom! I was just adding final touches to the boards, then I'll print them for your meeting. What time are you leaving to meet Mr. Blackwood?"

"Actually, we'll be meeting here. He should be here around ten."

"Oh." I tried hiding my distress.

This day was not off to a good start. I didn't want to see Rhett before my lunch date. Plus, Owen would be picking me up at my office. I only hoped Rhett was gone by then.

"I figured you should sit in the meeting with us. This way you have all his comments firsthand," Tom said, smiling proudly.

I knew he thought this was a way to reward me for all my hard work and had no idea it was doing the opposite.

"Great!" I tried for feigned enthusiasm. Instead, my voice came out high pitched and cracked at the end.

I spent the rest of the morning nervously watching the clock. Knowing I'd be seeing Rhett had my stomach in knots from anxiety. Joce asked me more than once if everything was okay. I just nodded my head, brushing her off. I kept an eye on the door the closer it got to ten, on the verge of a nervous breakdown.

At a quarter till ten, I couldn't sit still at my desk any longer. As I stood to set up for the meeting, the front door opened. Rhett walked in wearing a sexy grin and a dark navy suit that enhanced the color of his eyes. He stopped just inside the door, casually tucking his hands in his pockets as he stared at me.

My heart raced, and my eyes instinctively started to scan his body, taking in every inch of masculine perfection. By the time I reached his face, his sly grin had turned into a knowing smile, his eyes darkening. It was no secret I'd been admiring him as we stood across the room from each other. And from the look in his eyes, he'd been doing the same to me.

My hands were clammy from nervousness, my body already responding to his presence. I wiped my damp hands down the sides of my fitted gray Ralph Lauren dress. From the look on his face, the act was more seductive than I intended. I stood frozen, until Tom's voice thawed me.

"Mr. Blackwood, I'm glad you found the place," Tom said, walking past me to greet Rhett.

"Mr. Willis," Rhett shook hands with Tom, barely taking his eyes off me.

"Ava, grab the presentation boards and join us in the meeting room," Tom directed.

"Sure," I agreed as I tried to convince my body to move.

"Ms. Conner, it's a pleasure seeing you, again," Rhett said with a wink as he walked past me, following Tom.

I rolled my eyes, glad Tom's back was to us.

When I walked into the room, Rhett's eyes instantly went to me, making me conscious of the hunger growing inside. I fought the craving of my body, taking a seat next to Tom, putting him between myself and Rhett, who sat at the head of the table. Tom started going over each design as Rhett studied them. Tom had come up with two concepts, both of which I thought were fabulous. He was talented, and I hoped Rhett could see that.

After about an hour of Tom going over each one and his thoughts behind them, the two men went back and forth between the concepts, discussing what they liked and didn't about each. I sat silent, watching them as they talked, occasionally glancing at the clock, hoping the meeting would be done soon.

Owen was picking me up a little before noon. I anxiously glanced at the clock, again. It was already half past eleven. A slight panic rose inside me. I needed time before my lunch date to recover from the onslaught of emotions Rhett's presence had brought on.

"Ava," I heard Rhett's addictive voice say, warm and inquisitive. "What do you think?"

I looked between him and Tom. I didn't want to answer. I wanted this meeting to end.

"I think they're both great designs." I gave my noncommittal response.

I wasn't going to critique my boss's work. Plus, it was the truth. I did like both of Tom's designs. He'd done a brilliant job taking the notes from Saturday and coming up with two good designs meeting the specifications.

"I agree. Which one speaks to you more, though?" Rhett leaned forward to draw me into the conversation, watching me intently.

He was not going to let me out of this meeting until I gave him an answer. I looked at both of the concept boards. There was one I instantly fell in love with when I was drafting the floor plans and putting the presentation together. It had a very Cape-Cod feel, reminding me of my home back East and my time in the Hamptons. The other was a very modern, minimalistic design with a little more edge.

"I, personally, prefer this one." I pointed at the Cape Cod-style home. "But as I said, they're both great designs."

"Well Tom, I think we will go with the one Ms. Conner has selected. I couldn't agree more with her."

"Perfect. I'll begin finalizing the designs, and we'll work up some preliminary drawings for you to review. We'll also need to discuss your thoughts on the interior."

"Let's discuss over lunch. I'm sure you're both hungry," Rhett suggested.

"That sounds good. Let me grab my cell from my office, and I'll meet you two out front."

"Actually, Tom," I interrupted, more calmly this time, "I apologize, but I have prior plans. Would you mind if I missed lunch?" I asked nervously, avoiding eye contact with Rhett, grateful for Tom's presence. I could feel the tension emanating from his body.

"Of course, Ava. Enjoy your lunch." Tom dismissed me.

I hurriedly exited the room without looking back at Rhett, leaving him alone to brood. As I made it to the front, I saw Owen already waiting for me. Joce was talking to him while he stood near the door. I don't know how long he was waiting. I only hoped she hadn't mentioned the flowers to him.

"Oh, there she is!" Joce said, seeing me approach.

Owen turned to face me. "Ava." He smiled in greeting.

"Hi," I responded shyly. "Let me just grab my things, and we can go." I rushed to my desk, wanting to leave before

Rhett saw us, ignoring the fact I felt the need to hide my date.

I snatched up my purse and walked toward Owen. As he put his arm out for me, I took it, trying to rush us out the front door. It was too late. Rhett and Tom were already coming toward the main area, and his eyes immediately went to me and my arm linked with Owen's.

I could see the pain and anger spread through his body like wildfire. The recognition on his face made me instantly feel guilty. I have no idea why. I had no reason to. Rhett started to step toward us. I turned quickly, moving Owen out the door into the street. I was gambling on the hope Rhett wouldn't try to stop us in front of everyone. Owen helped me in his car with a peculiar look on his face. I just gave him a big smile, as if nothing awkward had just happened.

The whole lunch I was distracted. I did my best to focus on Owen as he talked and asked me questions. He was genuine and kind, but all I could think about was Rhett. I was annoyed with myself for letting Rhett get in my head, ruining my date.

Owen was what I thought I always wanted. He was exactly the kind of guy I'd have fallen for before Rhett. But that was the problem. He was post-Rhett, and no matter how much I wanted to feel things for him, I couldn't.

"You seem distracted," Owen said, watching me intently as the server cleared our plates.

I casted my eyes downward, feeling ashamed he'd

noticed. "I'm sorry, Owen. I just had a really busy week. Work has been keeping my mind pretty occupied, even when I'm not there," I said apologetically, feeling remorse for my distracted mind, and my lie.

"I see... Does this work have anything to do with the gentleman there when I picked you up?"

I stared at him, surprised by his perceptiveness.

"I recognized him from the other night. At the bar. He had the same expression that night as he did today."

I turned my head from Owen, not wanting to meet his eyes. Discussing my ex on a date was not something I wanted to do.

"Ava, I like you a lot, but if you aren't in a place—"

"No!" I interrupted, panicking. "I am," I said unconvincingly.

He gave me a small smile. "Okay." He didn't sound convinced, but he didn't challenge me further.

We left the restaurant, and he took me back to work. I was thankful to see Tom was back with no sign of Rhett. We stood on the sidewalk outside my office.

"I'd like to see you again, when I'm back from my trip."

"I'd like that, too," I said, not sure I meant it.

"Great. I'll call you when I get back." He hesitated before leaning in, giving me a lingering kiss on my cheek. I was relieved he didn't try to kiss me on the lips. "Bye, Ava," he said with a small smile before walking away.

~

The rest of the day was uneventful. When I got home that night, I half-expected Rhett to be waiting for me. Or maybe I hoped he would be. I'm not really sure. My brain and heart were constantly confused these days.

I made myself dinner and got ready for bed. I tried reading a book to distract myself from checking my phone. Rhett had been texting me goodnight every night since our day in Malibu. He didn't text me. I closed my eyes, trying to convince myself it was for the best.

CHAPTER 5

It was finally Friday. I couldn't be more excited. I was picking Lizzie up after work. It'd been months since I'd seen her last, and I could really use my best friend at the moment. I still hadn't heard from Rhett, but I wasn't going to think about that today. It's what I wanted, after all, and nothing was going to ruin my weekend with Lizzie.

Halfway through the day, Tom called me into his office. "Ava, I have some exciting news for you."

I groaned internally. Lately, Tom's idea of exciting news for me was anything but.

"During our lunch yesterday, Mr. Blackwood mentioned he'd like some of the marble and other materials we'll be using on the interior to be sourced directly from Italy. He suggested we make a procurement visit to select the items. He'd like you to join him. You'll be there for a few weeks."

I sat there speechless. *What the hell? Did I hear him right?*

"I can see you're shocked with excitement," Tom offered as he looked at me questioningly, his eyebrow raised.

I finally found my voice. "Yes. Shocked." More like infuriated, though, rather than excited. And confused. "I don't understand. Shouldn't you be going instead of me?"

"Well, as you know, Mr. Blackwood is in a bit of a hurry for this project. He's arranged for the trip to happen next week, and there's no way I can leave Marie to go overseas."

"But what about my other projects? And you don't have enough people to get all the work done if I'm gone."

I searched for excuses to stay. I thought about lying and saying I didn't have a passport, but Rhett knew I did. He'd made me get it right after he gifted me with a trip around the world.

"Don't worry, Ava. Joce, Drew, and myself will all look after your other projects. And Mr. Blackwood has given me a very hefty retainer to make all this happen quickly. It's enough for me to hire another person on if needed."

"Right," I replied, still sitting there dumbfounded.

Somehow, Rhett managed to talk my boss into this absurd idea. Though, I knew it probably didn't take much convincing on Rhett's part if he was paying Tom upfront.

"When do I leave?" I asked quietly, trying to control the agitation in my voice.

"Monday."

"Monday!?" I squeaked.

"Yes, I know. Like I said, short notice and all…" Tom had the decency to look remorseful as he delivered the information. "I figured you could take the rest of the afternoon off to start preparing for your trip. Paid, of course," he said, trying to soften the blow. "Mr. Blackwood has arranged for the two of you to fly out Monday morning. A car will pick you up and take you to the airport. I'll email you the details."

"Right. Okay, then." I stood, feeling like my world just turned upside down. I turned to leave Tom's office.

"Ava," Tom called after me.

"Yes?" I spun around.

"Try to have fun and enjoy the experience. This really is a great opportunity for you," he said with a concerned smile.

I responded with a feeble smile of my own. If Tom only knew what I already knew—this was not about a procurement trip.

~

I arrived at LAX airport a little early, thanks to Tom letting me off for the rest of the day. I texted Lizzie to let her know I was there. She'd barely landed. I waited at curbside pickup for her. As soon as I saw her, I almost cried. Okay. I did cry.

I sprinted to her, too excited to wait for her to make it to my car. We hugged, jumping up and down as we turned in circles, screaming like two teenage girls who just won back-stage passes to a Justin Bieber concert.

"I missed you," I said, finally calming down, pulling back from our embrace.

"Missed you, too. Now, let's get out of here. I only have the weekend with you, and I don't want to spend it at the airport."

I linked my arm through hers as we walked to my car, putting her luggage in the trunk.

~

We stopped at my apartment to change before going to dinner after deciding to walk to one of my favorite seafood restaurants located near the Santa Monica Pier. It had a beautiful view and excellent food.

"I'll have a martini, extra dirty," I ordered with our server, feeling adventurous and ready to kick off the weekend with my bestie.

"Only water for me, thanks." Lizzie returned her focus to the menu, ignoring my confused stare.

Lizzie was not one to pass up a drink on a girls' weekend. About two seconds later my mouth fell open.

"Oh my God. Are you?" I couldn't even finish saying it.

Lizzie looked up at me, grinning ear to ear.

"Oh my God. You're freaking pregnant! Aren't you!?"

She laughed, nodding her head. "Yep, you're going to be Auntie Ava."

I squealed with excitement, jumping out of my seat. "Oh my God! Oh my God!" I repeated as I hugged her.

"Calm down, Ava. People are going to think you're having an orgasm over here." She laughed wholeheartedly.

"Congratulations! I had no idea you guys were even trying," I said, sitting back down in my seat, still a little stunned.

"We weren't exactly trying. In fact, it probably couldn't have come at a worse time, with him opening up his restaurant, but he assures me it'll all work out."

"Of course it will! This is so exciting. How far are you?"

"Only ten weeks. I barely found out the day I called you, but decided I couldn't tell you over the phone. I had to do it in person," she said, smiling at me. I was so glad she did.

"Wow. I'm so happy and sad at the same time. I hate that

we're so far apart," I paused, wishing I wasn't on the other side of the country from my friends and family.

I loved California and it had helped me heal, but a huge part of me wondered if I should move home. It felt like I was missing so much of my friends' and family's lives.

"I want to be the one to throw your baby shower."

"You better! There's no way I want my mom handling it. She's already driving me nuts," she said, rolling her eyes. "If I thought she was an overbearing, unbearable woman before, she's even worse now that she has a grandbaby on the way."

I laughed, knowing Lizzie had always preferred to be around my family, rather than her own. The waiter returned with our drinks and took our food order.

"Well, I guess I'll be drinking for two, while you eat for two," I goaded her.

"Ugh. Don't remind me. That's going to be the worst part. I will be fat and sober for the next few months." Her nose scrunched up with disgust.

I chuckled as I sipped my martini.

"Enough about me. Anything going on with you?" she asked nonchalantly, but there was caution in her voice.

I eyed her suspiciously as I placed my martini back on the table. "You know," I said, looking at her in disbelief.

"Know what?" She attempted innocence.

I tilted my head at her while crossing my arms, giving her a look that told her I didn't believe her charade.

"Okay. I know he was here," she surrendered.

"Did you know, before?"

"No."

I narrowed my eyes.

"I promise, Ava. I didn't know until recently. That was

one of the reasons I decided to come early. That and I couldn't wait to tell you about the baby. I wanted to make sure you were okay." She waited for me to answer as I looked out at the Santa Monica Pier, all lit up in the dark sky. "So... how are you?"

"Confused," I said honestly, turning back to look at her.

"What are you confused about?"

"Everything. I have no idea what he's doing here. I have no idea why now. I have no idea how I feel about it. As much as I tell myself it's in the past and I've moved on, I can't help how he makes me feel every time I see him."

We were silent for a moment before she spoke. "Do you still love him?" She leaned forward, studying me.

I didn't want to answer. Saying it out loud hurt too much. A tear rolled down my cheek before I could stop it.

"Oh, Ava...have you told him? Have you talked to him about everything that happened?" She sat back, her face full of sympathy.

"There's nothing to talk about," I replied flatly.

She gave me a look that told me she disagreed, but she knew better than to push it. Suddenly I felt the need to know why she'd always been so adamant about me talking to him. Riley's words seeped into my thoughts at the same time.

But before I could ask her, our food came, and she changed the subject to lighter topics. She filled me in on what Mike's plans were for the new restaurant and things that'd been going on back in Litchfield. I told her about my date with Owen. She pretended to be happy for me, but I knew she was only doing it to be a supportive friend. She was Team Rhett. By the time we finished dinner, we were both exhausted and decided to call it a night.

~

The next morning, we went shopping. She wanted to buy maternity clothes, and I needed some clothes for my trip to Italy. I could tell she was excited for my upcoming 'business trip,' but she pretended to be indifferent about it as we picked out clothes. We stopped in a few baby stores, and I bought her a tiny, cream, knitted baby blanket as a congratulatory present.

Saturday night we stayed in, hanging out on my balcony, eating Chinese food, and laughing about old times as we listened to the ocean.

"It's so peaceful here. I'm jealous you get to fall asleep to this sound every night." She looked out at the ocean.

"It does beat the sounds of New York traffic and sirens."

We both leaned back, listening to the waves roll onto the shore.

"How's Stephen?" I asked, breaking our comfortable silence.

She turned to look at me as I stared out into the darkness. "He's good. He started dating Amber earlier this year," she responded carefully, knowing what happened between Stephen and me.

"Really? That's great!" I was genuinely happy to hear the news.

"Yeah. She's finally getting him to straighten out and grow up."

I waited a moment before bringing up my next question. "Lizzie...when Rhett first showed up, Riley was with him. He mentioned something to me about Stephen. He accused

Stephen of knowing something and not telling me. Do you know what that'd be?"

She took a deep breath, letting it out before responding, "Yes." She sat up, twisting her body toward me. "Ava, Rhett was at the hospital that night." She delivered the words slowly, allowing them to sink in. "Stephen wouldn't let him see you."

My heart beat faster as she spoke, and I was suddenly having a hard time breathing. "What?" I could hear my pulse beating in my ears, making it hard for me to focus on what she was saying. "No. That doesn't make sense. If Rhett were there, he wouldn't have let Stephen stop him from getting to me. How would he have even known to go there?"

"Because I told him." She dropped her eyes, looking at her feet remorsefully. "I didn't tell you before because, at the time, I knew you'd kill me. But I also knew you needed him. I didn't know he actually showed up, though. I thought he'd chosen Serena by not coming. I was angry at him for a long time, until we ran into each other in New York. After I chewed him out for being an ass, he told me everything."

I sat there, my head and hands shaking, not believing everything I was hearing.

"As far as Stephen, Rhett thought it would've only made things worse for you, if he did anything to Stephen."

This can't be true. None of it. But Lizzie wouldn't lie to me. The tears were coming as I started to realize how different things could've been for us.

Why didn't anyone tell me? Why would Stephen do that to me?

I already had my answers. I just didn't want to accept them. I wouldn't let anyone talk to me about it, especially not Rhett. I refused to listen to what anyone had to say. I was too hurt and grief stricken. Stephen had his own reasons, but I needed to hear it from him.

Lizzie moved to sit with me on my lounger, hugging me as I struggled to hold myself together. "It's not too late, Ava," she whispered as she held me.

She kept her arms around me until I calmed down and assured her I was okay. I told her to head to bed and get some rest. I needed a few more minutes alone with my thoughts.

I lifelessly stared into space, reliving that moment in my Wellesley apartment. Hating myself. I never even gave Rhett the chance to explain. It still didn't explain why he wasn't at the funeral, or why it took him so long to come to me.

I picked up my phone, staring at it, needing answers. I needed to hear it from his mouth. I scrolled through my contacts, looking for his name. I knew it was late there, but I didn't care. I listened to the ringing on the other end of the phone, hoping he'd answer.

"Hello?" his gruff, sleepy voice answered.

"Is it true?" I tried to hold back the anger in my voice.

"Ava?"

"Yes, Stephen, it's me. Is it true?" I asked a little more harshly. "Did you keep Rhett from me in the hospital the night my dad died?"

He let out a heavy sigh as a ruffling commotion sounded in the background. He didn't answer for a few seconds, but it felt like an eternity. "Yes," he finally responded. That one word was like a dull knife twisting into my heart. "Ava, I'm sorry. I thought it was what was best for you at the time."

I didn't respond. I just hung up. Suddenly his excuses didn't matter. The damage was done. The years lost.

As we stood outside the airport, I hugged Lizzie tight, not wanting her to leave.

"Ava, if you squeeze any tighter, I may pass out from lack of oxygen," she laughed, breathless.

"Sorry," I apologized, letting her go as she took a deep, exaggerated breath. "It was just too short of a weekend."

"I know. I'll try to come back out before the baby comes. And you'll be home soon for the baby shower."

"Yep! Pick a date. I'll start the planning."

"Okay, one more hug." A tear fell down her cheek. "This damn baby is making me sappy." She wiped it away.

I hugged her happily. "Call me when you get back home to New York. And give Mike a hug for me."

"Will do"—she grasped the handle of her roller luggage —"as long as you do something for me." She paused, making sure she had my attention. "Give Rhett a chance to explain. Hear him out."

I nodded my head at her, giving her a reassuring smile. I'd already decided I would last night, so it was an easy thing to promise her. I wasn't sure I could give us another chance, but I at least needed to know what happened after I left him at his home in Boston. She squeezed my hand before turning to leave. I watched her walk away, part of me wishing I was going with her.

I went for a run along the beach after dropping Lizzie off at the airport. I attempted more than once to call Rhett, but every time, I chickened out. I wasn't sure what to say when he answered...*if* he answered. I knew him seeing me leave with Owen the other day had to hurt him more than anything.

I hated myself for being the one to hurt him like that. No matter how angry I'd been with him, I realized hurting him wouldn't make me feel any better. Only I realized it too late. The pain had been inflicted. Both of us had burned each other deeply. I didn't know if we'd ever be able to recover.

I rested on my favorite bench on the pier, pulling my knees into me. I studied the world around me. Everyone seemed so happy, enjoying their Sunday on the sunny Santa Monica beach. It made me feel hope for the first time in a long time as I watched all the smiling faces.

Whether Rhett and I ended up together, I knew our pending conversation would at least bring some closure— the closure I think I've needed for a long time in order to move on with my life.

The sun began to set, and I realized I'd been sitting there entirely too long. I still needed to finish packing before I left for my trip tomorrow. I walked home, savoring the beauty of the sunset.

After I finished packing and eating, I lay in my bed, contemplating my phone as if it held all the answers. In a way, I guess it did. I navigated through my phone to my blocked voicemails. In the past, I had deleted most of his blocked messages without listening.

I saved the last one, though. After they stopped filling my voicemail, I was too afraid I'd never hear his voice again. I knew it wasn't healthy, but for some unknown reason I liked to inflict pain on myself in my weakest moments.

I pushed the button to play the voicemail, needing to hear it for the first time.

"Ava." He sighed. "I'm not going to call anymore. This doesn't mean I'm giving up on us," he said, his words slow and deliberate. "It's just too painful to keep calling you with no response. I don't even know if you're listening, but if you are, please know this is not over for me. It will never be over. I'll always be yours and I'll be waiting, until you're ready." He released another heavy breath. "I miss you, beautiful."

I hung up the phone as a tear rolled down my cheek. For the first time, I wished I hadn't been so stubborn over the last three years. I scrolled to our recent text message conversation and stared at his last message from Wednesday night. I typed out my message to him, my finger hovering over the send button. I took a deep breath then pushed it.

A: Goodnight.

I turned my phone to 'do not disturb,' not wanting to know if he responded or not. It would hurt too much if he didn't. I rolled over, forcing myself to sleep.

CHAPTER 6

I ran through my packing list, making sure I didn't forget anything for my trip. My stomach was twisted in knots, knowing I'd see Rhett soon. I didn't know how things were going to play out. We had a long flight ahead of us with nothing but time to talk about everything and no escape. As much as I wanted the conversation to happen, I couldn't help feeling nervous about the outcome. I didn't even know what I wanted at this point, and I wouldn't know until after we talked.

There was a knock at my door. Assuming it was the driver Rhett had sent to pick me up, I zipped up my luggage, pulling it off the bed, rolling it behind me as I picked up my purse. I opened the door to find Rhett wearing a perfectly tailored business suit and a stoic expression.

My body wanted him immediately, but my heart felt hollow from the way he regarded me—emotionless, as if we were strangers. The guilt paralyzed me. I'd hurt him to the point that he'd shut down, closing himself off to me.

Everything was said in our silence as we stared at each other. Without a single word, he took my luggage from me before turning to walk down the hall, expecting me to follow. I sighed, locking my apartment before slowly trudging behind him.

A black town car was waiting for us at the curb. Rhett handed the luggage off to the driver to put in the trunk. He held my door open, allowing me to get into the car first, still saying nothing and giving me nothing but coldness. I slid into the car. He closed the door behind me, striding around to the other side, climbing into the backseat with me but being sure to stay on the other side of the car.

The noticeable distance he was putting between us hurt more than anything. Rhett had never been the one to try and distance us. It made me realize how much it must have pained him every time I pushed him away or forced us apart.

I wanted so badly to crawl into his arms and tell him I was sorry, but I couldn't. Maybe it was too late for us. I remained silent, looking forward as the car moved onto the road headed for the airport. The silence transformed into my own personal hell. I fought back emotions, trying to remain as resigned as he was.

Rhett pulled out his phone and scrolled through it, making a few business calls as we drove. He looked straight ahead the whole time, not glancing over at me once. I wanted to be anywhere but where I was—trapped in a car with tension so thick it was palpable.

As we pulled up to the private-jet tarmac, he hung up his phone, ending his conversation with whoever was on the other end of the line. He got out of the car, making his way around to help me out, but I didn't wait for him. I opened the door, rushing out of the car before he reached me. I immediately boarded his private jet, leaving him to deal with our bags. The tears were swelling. I needed a minute alone to gather myself.

I took a seat in one of the captain chairs toward the back. The flight attendant brought me some water as Rhett talked with the pilot in hushed voices. He took a seat across from me. I was surprised he didn't choose the farthest seat away.

The pretty flight attendant approached him. He smiled at her, asking for a water. It was the first emotion I'd seen on his face since he picked me up. I instantly felt jealous and hurt his smile was directed at her instead of me.

I chided myself for my insecurities, looking down at my water glass, fidgeting, spinning it in my hands. The flight attendant returned, giving him his water and letting us know we were ready for takeoff. She moved toward the front of the plane to the flight-attendant area. He watched me as I watched her leave us, closing the door behind her, giving us privacy.

"We'll be stopping in New York to fuel up before heading on. I've arranged for lunch to be brought on the plane before we take off again," he said, his voice still giving nothing away.

I stared up at him, studying his eyes, pleading with him to give me something.

"So you're talking to me now?" I asked, more harshly than I'd meant to. This was not how I wanted to start this conversation.

He sighed heavily before standing to remove his suit jacket, laying it on the chair he was sitting in. "I have some work to do, Ava. If you need anything during the flight, Amanda will get it for you."

"I'm fine." I glanced up at his beautiful eyes, noticing for the first time that they looked like they hadn't rested in days. I worried it was because of me, but not wanting to add that to my own personal guilt that seemed to be piling up, I hoped it was actually from work.

He nodded his head once, moving across the aisle, where he set up his laptop to work.

I watched him for a few moments before getting up to move toward the front seats to watch a movie. Amanda helped me navigate the menu, then I sat back, trying to ignore the huge hole in my heart that could only be repaired by the man who sat a few feet from me.

~

"Ava." I heard Rhett's soft, caring voice. *I must be dreaming.* "Ava, wake up." I felt his hand rubbing gently down my arm.

I blinked my eyes open, staring at Rhett's handsome face. He had an affectionate look on his face as I woke, giving me a glimpse of hope. But as soon as I rubbed my eyes open and looked up at his face again, the emotion I thought I saw was gone.

"We'll be taking off again in a few minutes. There's lunch on the table. You should eat before we do. I'm going to step outside to make a few calls." He stepped forward to leave.

"Rhett," I hastily shouted, desperately wanting to stop him. It came out of my mouth before I even knew what I wanted to say.

He halted, looking back at me expectantly. I sat there, overwhelmed by insecurity.

"Thank you."

That was it. The only words I could summon. He gave me a semblance of a smile before leaving the plane.

I collapsed back into my chair, defeated. I watched him for a few seconds outside the plane on his phone. He was so utterly handsome. I wished he were still mine. I got up from my seat to use the bathroom before eating my lunch.

He re-boarded the plane as I finished. Amanda took my food plate, disposing of it and closing the door behind her after telling us to prepare for takeoff. Rhett returned to the chair where his laptop sat.

Once we were in the air, I decided to move to one of the couches to read a magazine while he continued to work. I took my heels off and pulled my feet up under me as I sat on the farthest end of the couch in front of him.

I could see him watching me from the corner of my eye as I flipped through the magazine. His gaze sent a buzz through my body, causing my stomach to do a series of flips. I wanted him closer to me. As if sensing my longing, he stood from his seat, removing his tie. He unbuttoned the top buttons of his shirt and rolled up his sleeves to his elbows, getting more comfortable. He picked up his laptop, moving to the opposite end of the couch from me.

He looked sexy, refined, and rugged all at the same time, sitting in his ruffled suit with stubble growing on his jaw line. I watched him, admiring the man before me, wanting to crawl into his lap and make him mine again, even just for one more time.

I didn't hide my blatant perusal of him as he worked. I

saw the light in his eyes return and a mischievous grin start to spread across his face.

"Ms. Conner, you're making this hard on me. I won't be able to keep things professional if you keep eyeing me like that," he said, a smirk tugging at his lips.

"Is that what you've been doing? Trying to keep things professional?" I asked, curious if that was what all this was about. The coldness. The silent treatment.

"Isn't that what you wanted?" He looked at me, studying my face.

"Yes," I hesitated. "Maybe...I don't know," I finally answered honestly.

He closed his laptop before setting it aside. Leaning forward, he rested his elbows on his knees as he rubbed his hands over his face and up through his hair, releasing a frustrated sigh.

"Ava. You're driving me mad, woman. We need to talk. I need to know what you want."

"I know," I sighed, momentarily looking away from him.

"Is *he* what you want?" He looked back over at me, the agony crystal clear in his blue eyes. He was struggling to control the hurt and anger as he watched me closely.

"No," I stated simply, without hesitation, because it was the truth.

Owen was not what or who I wanted. I watched the stress slowly leave his body as he relaxed back into the couch, his head falling back to look at the ceiling of the plane.

"What I want is answers."

"That's what I've been trying to give you for the last few

years, Ava." He rolled his head to the side to look at me once again.

"I know. I'm sorry. I'm sorry for pushing you away. I just…"—I tucked a strand of hair behind my ear, letting out a heavy sigh—"I know you were there that night. At the hospital. I didn't know until a few days ago, and I wish I'd known then. I wish Stephen hadn't stopped you. And I feel terrible about everything. For blaming you and accusing you of not being there when I needed you."

Rhett's body hardened.

"I should've listened to you about Stephen. You were right," I admitted quietly, wondering, had I listened, whether we'd be in this position.

He sat up, his body angling toward me, staring into my eyes. "Did he touch you?" His teeth clenched, anger and hurt seething below the surface.

I lowered my head, not wanting to look at him when I told him the truth. I didn't want to see him hurt more from my response. "We kissed. Once."

He stood abruptly, moving across the plane, putting distance between us again, his back a shield.

"When?" He gritted his teeth, the utterance more a growl than a word. He turned to face me when I didn't respond immediately.

I swallowed the lump in my throat. "A few weeks after we got to California."

"Did you kiss him back?"

"Rhett, don't do this. We have enough to deal with. Don't do this," I begged.

"Answer me, Ava," he commanded.

I locked my eyes with his. I needed him to see I was

telling him the truth. "Yes, but only because I wanted to feel again. It didn't *mean anything* to me. And I stopped it as quickly as it happened. I was hurt, Rhett. You hurt me. Then I lost my dad. I was numb and just wanted to feel something. I know it's not an excuse, but it's how I felt. We were over with."

"No, we weren't, Ava."

"You kept choosing Serena over me. You believed her over me. I can't go back to feeling like she'll always be between us." The tears I'd been holding back escaped.

"Ava." He shook his head, coming toward me.

I looked down at my hands, trying to fight the falling tears, so damn tired of crying.

He knelt on the floor below me. "Look at me, beautiful."

I shook my head no.

"Ava, I need to see your eyes. I need you to understand."

When I didn't move, his hand nudged my chin gently, raising it the way he always had, the familiar gesture making my heart skip a beat.

"Ava, I didn't believe her over you."

"You—"

"No," he stated firmly. "It's my turn to talk, beautiful. I need you to listen."

He waited for me to nod my understanding.

"I believed *you*. I just lost control when I saw Adam and you alone on the patio with your hands on him. I lost my freaking mind. And I thought I lost *you*." His brow furrowed, twisting in pain as he relived the moment.

"I didn't expect you to leave. I only let you go to give myself time to calm down, so I could hear you out. I'm sorry. I never want to lose control like that again. But sometimes you make it hard for me." He gave me a weak smile.

I blushed, knowing we were each other's weaknesses as much as our strengths.

"I knew you wouldn't lie to me. I went after you as soon as I knew you were gone. I searched all over Wellesley for you until Lizzie sent me a text, telling me where you were. I went straight to the hospital. I guess you know that part already."

I nodded my head.

"After I left the hospital, I went to Adam's. He told me everything and so did Val. I flew to New York to confront Serena. She tried denying it. I cut her out of my life. I was cutting her out whether she admitted it or not. I went to my father to make sure she had no way to interfere in my life. In *our* lives, ever again."

The tears poured as I sobbed, wishing the whole night had played out differently. He pulled me close, hugging me to his strong chest with the arms I missed being in so much it made me cry harder. He continued to hold me, letting me soak his shirt. I reluctantly pulled away, needing to know the rest.

"I don't understand. Why didn't you come to the funeral? Why did you wait weeks, until I was leaving, to come find me?"

"I wanted to be there, babe. I did. I hadn't planned on missing it. But I hadn't slept in days. I only went to New York to hunt Serena down. I fell asleep. By the time I woke it was too late to make it. By that point, I knew I just needed to fix things. It took some time to make arrangements with my father to get out of business deals I had with her family. I came as soon as I could. I'm so sorry I wasn't there. I wanted to be. I regret it more than you'll ever know."

Even without the regret and sorrow on his face, I knew he was telling me the truth, which only made it worse. Years together were lost over a stupid misunderstanding. I hated myself for allowing it to happen. Serena made me feel insecure. I never should've let her get in my head.

"At my apartment in Wellesley..." I said, my voice shaking, strained from nerves and crying. There was one thing I still needed to hear. I tried looking away to gather the strength I needed.

He turned my head back to him, holding his hands delicately on each side of my face. "Ava. I need you looking at me. I need to see those beautiful eyes when I tell you this."

I bit my bottom lip, nodding my head, scared and hopeful.

"I know what you wanted me to say in your apartment, but I wasn't saying it when you wouldn't let me touch you and wouldn't look at me"—the pads of his thumbs brushed the tears from my cheeks—"Ava, there's only you. There has only ever been you. You're my beautiful girl, and I'll never let you go. I love you, Ava Conner."

My chest deflated with the breath I'd been holding. My eyes dropped to his lips as my hands instantly gripped his hair, slamming his mouth to mine. He deepened the kiss, probing my lips with his tongue, begging for entrance. Our tongues collided as I let him into my mouth, my heart, my soul.

Our kiss was desperate and demanding, both of us needing each other. I hastily stripped him of his shirt, wanting to feel his skin on mine. He moved quickly, pulling me to the edge of the couch, lifting me without breaking our kiss. I wrapped my legs around his hips as he turned, sitting us back on the couch. I straddled his thighs, pushing my skirt up to my waist.

Our reunion was no fairytale. We'd been starved and greedily devoured each other, our kisses frenzied and frantic. He undid his pants, freeing himself while moving my panties aside. He lifted me, slamming into me, not wasting any more time.

I needed him inside me as much as he needed the same. A raw and unadulterated need. His hands held onto my hips as he guided my movement, working us both to the release we'd waited way too long for. I moaned my pleasure loudly as my body detonated. He placed a hand over my mouth, muffling my breathy cries.

"Shhh, babe. You don't want Amanda to hear you," he whispered with a chuckle, pulling my mouth to his as my body went limp, relaxing into him.

Oh. Crap.

I'd totally forgotten she was on the plane with us. I broke from our kiss flushed with embarrassment. "Oh my God. What if she walks in?" I panicked, searching for my shirt.

He laughed. "She won't. I put the 'do not disturb' light on before I sat with you on the couch."

I looked at him with a disapproving eyebrow. "That was a little presumptuous of you."

He shrugged his shoulders, looking at me unapologetically with his wicked smirk.

I smacked him on the shoulder while trying to climb off him. "Rhett Blackwood. You had it all planned out, didn't you?" I chastised.

He laughed his deep baritone laugh I'd missed, still holding me tight to keep me from moving from his lap. "Not exactly. I didn't expect *this*, but I knew I didn't want to be disturbed, either way." He smiled, giving me a chaste kiss on the lips. "I'm not complaining, though. This is better than I expected. I thought I was going to have to wear you down over the next couple of weeks. And I was one hundred percent prepared to do that."

I shook my head at him in disbelief. I loved him more in that moment than ever before. He was never going to give up on us, no matter how hard I made it for him. I'd been fighting a losing battle and didn't know it. I was glad I was on the losing side, because it meant I won him in the end. I smiled at him, my arms wrapping around his neck, giving him a lingering peck on the lips.

"I need the bathroom."

"I don't want to let you go, yet. I barely got you back in my arms."

"I'll be back. I promise. Besides, there's nowhere else for me to run. Not that I want to…" I brushed a hand through his thick hair. "I love you, Rhett Blackwood."

He kissed me then smacked me on the ass as he released me. "Hurry up, beautiful."

∼

I returned to the main cabin to find Rhett had converted one of the couches into a fold-out bed. He was sitting on the edge of it with his shirt still off and only his pants on. He was a magnificent manly sight as he sat forward with his forearms resting on his knees. His sculpted upper body made the Statue of David look like a scrawny school boy.

I felt my body go weak with desire, losing my footing.

Or maybe that was turbulence?

Either way, I wanted him again. I couldn't have him only once. I ungracefully made my way to him as he stood, catching me before I fell over.

Okay. Definitely turbulence.

I was still half-dressed, shirtless, with nothing but a bra and skirt to cover me. He helped me to the side of the bed where I sat, removing my skirt. He handed me his button-up shirt. I pulled it on. "I figured we'd eat a little then try to get some sleep."

"You have food?"

"Yes. I had Amanda set it up on the table while you were in the bathroom."

A sudden wave of possessiveness passed through me when I realized she'd seen him with his shirt off. I screwed up my face at the thought. Rhett, knowing what was running through my head, chuckled. Pulling me back up and into his arms, he gave me a sweet kiss on the lips. "Only yours, babe. Remember that."

"I know, but I still don't like other girls ogling you."

He smiled fondly at me, pushing my hair behind my ear. "Come on, beautiful. Let's eat. I need to be back inside you."

"Why don't we skip the eating then?" I suggested seductively, running my hands down his firm chest.

"Tempting, but you need to eat. And *don't* argue. You're going to need your energy. I plan to make up for lost time." He gave me his sexy smile, failing miserably at calming my libido.

"Fine," I pouted, making my way over to the table with food. I was kind of hungry anyway.

Rhett sat across from me, removing the lids covering our food. I couldn't believe my eyes or my nose. The food looked and smelled delicious. This wasn't your typical plane food. I felt like we were dining in a five-star restaurant as we ate.

We talked and flirted, constantly touching each other as we enjoyed our food. Rhett finished eating before me. Pulling my feet into his lap as I finished, he began massaging them, relaxing me into a further state of bliss. Between the food and his tantalizing hands on my feet, I thought I was going to have another orgasm.

I leaned back in my seat, closing my eyes, reveling in his touch. His hands made their way up my calves to my thighs, manipulating my body. He stood, removing his hands from me. I groaned my displeasure at the loss of his touch. I opened my eyes to his smiling face. He put his hand out to help me up.

I took it, standing slowly. He lifted me into his arms, carrying me steadily over to the bed. He laid me on my back as he moved over me, deliberately keeping his movements slow as his eyes penetrated mine. I widened my legs, letting him settle between them. He kissed me gently on the lips, moving to my neck as his hand sailed up my thigh, lifting my shirt. He showered my body with soft, warm kisses as he slowly undressed me, causing my body to spasm with anticipation. He groaned as my hips lifted, pleading for him.

"Ava," he whispered my name desperately as he kissed between my thighs. "Always so responsive," he breathed. "That's how I knew you were still mine." He continued to torture my body into submission. It was always willing to comply with his demands.

I moaned with desperation, but he was adamant about taking his time, working me up. A radical contrast from earlier. Just when I didn't think I could take it anymore, he towered above me, taking my lips with his as he pushed inside me. He made love to me slow and gentle, but with a force that told me I was his. It was more passionate than any other time we'd been together, and with all the emotions attached to our reunion, I found myself wanting to take my time loving him back.

～

I relaxed in his arms afterward, feeling like everything was finally right with the world. I listened to his heart beat as I rested on his chest, knowing for the first time in years, my heart was beating again too. He dragged his fingers lightly up and down my arm as I closed my eyes.

"Goodnight, beautiful," he whispered, kissing the top of my head. His voice was the last thing I heard before drifting off into a deep, satisfied sleep.

CHAPTER 7

I awoke to soft kisses being sprinkled across my skin while Rhett's strong arms held me tight. I opened my eyes, rotating my head to stare up at a pair of striking blue eyes.

"Hi," I said, smiling up at him, a giddy feeling inside.

"Hi, beautiful." His smile spread across his face and he gave me a peck on the lips.

I stopped him from pulling back, moving my hand to the back of his head, fortifying his lips to mine. He moved over my still-nude body, settling between my legs. His hand skimmed up my side, tickling me with excited suspense. I was ready for him, humming my eagerness through our kiss.

"Mr. Blackwood," the captain's muffled voice interrupted over the speaker system, "we'll be arriving at Heathrow in thirty minutes, as scheduled. Please prepare for landing."

"Shit," Rhett groaned, breaking our kiss, irritated that we wouldn't be finishing what we started.

"Watch your mouth, Mr. Blackwood," I mocked him, biting my bottom lip to contain my laughter.

He was not amused. He responded to my wisecrack with a stern look as he tickled my side, releasing the laughter I was holding in as I squirmed beneath him.

"Get dressed, beautiful. We'll finish this at the hotel."

"The hotel?"

"Or the limo, seeing as how you seem to have a transportation fetish," he said with a self-satisfied smirk, trailing kisses up my neck again.

"Wait. What?" I was even more confused.

"Okay. Fine. Limo *and* hotel."

"Rhett!" I exclaimed, exasperated, lightly smacking his butt.

"What?" He pulled up to look at me, his brow furrowed.

"What are you talking about?"

"You, seeming to enjoy sex in limos and planes."

"Ugh!" I sighed in frustration. "That's not what I'm asking about. And *I* am not the one with the fetish. That is all *you*." I poked him in the shoulder as he smirked at me. "Why would we be headed to a hotel right now? Didn't he say Heathrow? That's London. Not Carrara, Italy."

His face remained impassive as he watched me. I could see the wheels turning in his head, trying to figure out how to respond. His silence only ignited my fury.

"We're making a quick stop. I have some business to take care of. We'll be staying a few nights in London."

"What about the business I have to take care of?"

"I am your business."

"You know what I mean, Rhett"—I rolled my eyes—"I

have a job to do. I can't just be frolicking around London as if I'm on vacation."

"You can, and you will," he ordered me with a hardened face.

"No! I'm being paid for my time here."

"And I'm technically the one paying for your time, so if I require part of it to be spent at your leisure, or at mine, then you're doing your job."

"So, now I'm your whore." I hid my smirk, making a point I knew he wouldn't like.

His mouth opened and then snapped shut as his brow furrowed.

Ha! Point for me.

"Ava, damn it. You know that's not what I was implying."

"Fine. Then don't manipulate me or try to force me into situations. Besides…I know what we're *really* doing here." I grinned. "You're trying to make good on your gift."

His half-attempt to hide the smile forming on his face told me I was correct. "I wouldn't have to manipulate you if you would stop being so defiant and argumentative all the time," he stated unapologetically.

"I'm not—" I stopped short as he arched an eyebrow at me, making me realize I was about to argue that I wasn't argumentative. *Crap. Point for him.* "Fine. I'll try to be less argumentative if you try to be less manipulative," I offered.

"You like when I manipulate you," he teased, dropping kisses on my collar bone, working his way up the side of my neck. He was right. I did.

"Okay," I breathed, desire rebuilding inside me. "No manipulation outside of the bedroom."

"Just the bedroom?" He cocked his head back at me questioningly. "There goes the transportation fetish," he said with another smirk.

"You know what I mean!" I laughed.

"Agreed. Now, let's move, beautiful. We need to get dressed and seated." He gave me a final kiss before pulling us both out of bed.

～

Once we made it through customs, Rhett escorted me to a limo waiting for us at the airport. It was early morning in London, and as we drove through the city, I watched it come alive with people, cars, and the famous red double-decker buses I'd always wanted to ride on. Rhett would probably think it was silly, but it was on my bucket list if I ever made it to London.

I stared out the window, in awe of the city. Rhett sat close, holding my hand on his leg. I could feel his eyes regarding me. I'm sure he'd prefer to be doing other things on the drive, besides watching the passing city. I glanced over at him, beaming my excitement, inciting a big smile to spread across his face. He winked at me, gently squeezing my hand tighter.

"What do you think?"

"It's beautiful and thrilling. It reminds me of the liveliness of New York City, but with an older sophistication. The buildings and bridges are"—I looked back out the window —"I don't even have the right words for them. They're enchanting. I almost feel like I'm stepping back in time, with the exception of the modern transportation." I glanced back over at him. "Is it weird to have nostalgia for a place you've never been before? I have this crazy urge to make this home."

He wore a fond smile on his face as he listened to me ramble on. "We could, you know."

"We could what?"

"Make this home."

"Don't be absurd, Rhett. I can't move to London."

"Why not?"

"Because," I responded like an adolescent.

"Because isn't a reason, Ava." He prompted me to expand on my answer.

I sighed with annoyance. "Because, that'd be crazy! Because I have a job I love. And friends and family who I have a hard enough time living on the other side of the country from. I couldn't imagine being on another continent."

"It's only a couple more hours of flight time than where you live now."

"Says the man with a personal jet at his disposal," I mumbled inaudibly, shaking my head at him in frustration, turning to look back out at the city.

He chuckled lightly and kissed the back of my head.

The limo stopped outside the Mandarin Oriental near Hyde Park, only blocks from Harrods and across the street from Harvey Nichols. I couldn't contain my excitement. I immediately decided I'd be taking a run through Hyde Park in the morning. I packed my running clothes, thinking I'd get in a morning run at the hotel gym, but running through Hyde Park was way more appealing.

After getting out of the limo, I spun slowly, looking around, taking it all in. I was already in love with the city and

I hadn't even really experienced it. I felt Rhett's hand at the small of my back as I stared up at the massive, enticing, red brick-and-stone Edwardian-style building that towered before me. It exuded elegance and sophistication, screaming opulence. The façade was enhanced by the balconies projecting from the face along each story as it rose into the sky.

I wasn't surprised by his choice of hotel. He was a Blackwood, after all.

"Should we go in, or would you like to stand out here a little longer?"

I heard the hilarity in his voice that was complimented by the smile he revealed when I tilted my head to look up at him. I playfully nudged him with my elbow as he wrapped his arm around me to guide me inside.

The interior was just as sumptuous. I walked through awestruck, trying to process where I was. It was a good thing Rhett was guiding me, because I hadn't bothered watching where I was going. It was a visual overdose. There was so much to look at, and I indulged greedily. I didn't even realize we'd made it to the reception desk until my inattentiveness was disturbed by Rhett's voice.

"Which room would you prefer, Ava?"

"Huh?" I responded ignorantly, confused as to what the question had been.

"I booked the suite facing Hyde Park, but would you prefer a Knightsbridge suite?"

I looked at him with a furrowed brow. *He only booked one room?* That was a very bold move. Of course, at this point, I guess it wasn't. I mean, we barely made it across the Atlantic before he had me naked and panting.

"Ava, it's a two-bedroom suite," he interjected, as if knowing my inner turmoil.

Oh.

"Hyde Park," I finally answered.

He shook his head with amusement, then turned back to the pretty English woman, giving her a nod to proceed with the check in.

When we crossed the threshold to the suite, Rhett released his hold on my hand. He walked toward one of the bedrooms while removing the wrinkled suit he'd been wearing on the flight. "I'm going to shower, and then I have a meeting to get to. Would you like to join me in the shower?" He smiled playfully.

"You're leaving?"

My question came out more needy and desperate than I'd intended. I immediately chided myself, not wanting to be that girl. His statement had just taken me by surprise. I thought he was only claiming he had business here in London. I didn't think he'd truly be leaving to attend business meetings.

His smiled dropped as he processed my reaction. He moved back toward me, taking me in his arms. He tilted his head down, touching his forehead with mine as I gazed up at him. "Babe, it'll only be for a few hours. I figured you could explore a little."

"I thought we'd be doing that together," I replied, disappointed. *What was wrong with me?*

"We will, after my meeting. Maybe you could check out the shops. Then we'll meet back up," he suggested. I could see the remorse on his face, and I felt terrible for making him feel bad. This was technically a business trip for both of us.

"Of course. Don't worry about me." I smiled weakly at him.

He kissed my forehead. "Shower? We have some unfinished business of our own to attend to." His devilish grin reclaimed his face.

"Yes." I smiled wide this time, the thoughts of a naked, wet Rhett instantly lifting my spirits.

～

I lay on my side in the oversized, plush hotel bed of soft, twisted sheets, admiring Rhett as he readied himself to leave for his meeting. My body was sated, my mind was blissful, and my heart was filled with love and adoration. His hands moved efficiently as he knotted his black, silk tie around his neck into perfection.

Everything about my man was perfect—*that's right, he was mine*—his tie, his suit, his muscular body, his intense blue eyes, his soft demanding lips, his chiseled jaw with the light stubble, and that voice. That voice that was breaking my concentration on God's masterpiece standing before me.

"Ava."

"Huh?" I shifted my eyes to his, coming out of my trance.

He smirked confidently at me. "I asked what your plans were today."

"Oh." I sat up in the bed, pulling my sheet-covered knees to my chest as I hugged them with my arms. "I'm not sure. I may window shop some. I've always been curious about Harrods and Harvey Nichols."

"You don't have to window shop. You can actually shop."

I snorted sarcastically. "There's no way I can afford

anything in those stores." *Except maybe a small souvenir at Harrods.* "I'll stick with window shopping."

He moved to his wallet laying on the bedside table. "Here"—he handed me the credit card he pulled out—"Take my card. Get whatever you like."

"Absolutely not!" I swatted his hand away. "I'm not spending your money."

"Ava." His tone was warning. "How many times do we have to go over this?"

"As many times as it takes for you to understand I'm not comfortable spending *your* money."

"I thought you agreed not to argue anymore." His eyebrow raised as he cocked his criticizing head to the side.

"This is not an argument. It's not even debatable. It's the end of the conversation," I retorted, with as much confidence and authority as I could.

He let out a frustrated sigh as he sat down on the bed next to me. "Okay, beautiful." He tucked some of my wild bed hair behind my ear. "I'll text you when my meeting is done. I hope to be finished by lunch. Order some breakfast before you go," he gently commanded, giving me a parting kiss. "Call or text me, if you need me. I'll leave the local number to the office on the coffee table."

He stood from the bed and walked toward the door, turning back to look at me, his eyes becoming intense as he burned the image of me into his mind. Seconds later, he shook his head to knock himself out of his own musings. "Promise me you'll be careful wandering around alone." There was worry in his eyes as he made his request. One I didn't understand.

"Always," I promised.

He gave a quick nod of approval and then he was gone. I threw my body backward onto the bed, spreading my arms and legs out like a starfish. I slid them opened and closed, as if I was making a snow angel in the plush mattress.

The bed was entirely too comfortable. Maybe I'd just stay buried in the sheets and fluffy pillows instead. I could read a good book and indulge on ridiculously good room service. *Who am I kidding?* I was in freaking London for the first time. I was not spending it in this hotel, as luxurious and tempting as it was.

I looked around the room—with its feminine English elegance of creams, light grays, and various shades of mauve to accent the space—taking it all in now that Rhett wasn't here to distract me. The walls were adorned with white wainscot and crown moldings. It reminded me of Vivian, Rhett's mother. I could picture her staying here and admiring the décor.

I stared up at the shimmering, antique chandelier hanging over the bed as I stretched my limbs one more time before forcing myself to fall out of the bed.

It was a warm—by London standards—June day. I searched through my suitcase for something classy but casual to wear for my mini tour around the city. I decided on my short black dress with my white vans. The dress was a loose T-shirt material, making it comfy and lightweight. I wrapped a blush-colored cardigan around my waist in case I got chilled during my walk. I pulled my thick hair into a loose pony tail and applied minimal makeup.

I went into the main living area linking the two bedrooms together to find Rhett's office number and my brown, leather purse. I draped the purse across my body as I left our suite.

Walking slowly through the lobby once again, I took it all in, popping my head into some of the different bars, lounges, and restaurants before heading to the exit. An older, distinguished gentleman was entering as I exited. He stepped aside, allowing me to pass first.

"After you," he said with a smile and an obvious English accent.

I gave a small smile in return as I walked out.

Harvey Nichols was directly across the street and my first stop. I spent all of thirty minutes perusing the store and admiring the beautiful scarfs before leaving to keep from blowing my next month's rent on one individual item. I pulled out the city map Rhett had graciously left on the table for me, determining where to head next. I knew I looked like a typical, lost tourist. After ten minutes of trying to figure out where to go, I folded up the map and slipped it back into my purse. I'd take my chances.

I strolled down Brompton Road at a leisurely pace, stopping at a Starbucks to grab a latte and pastry. I'd forgotten to order breakfast before I left, too thrilled to get out and see the city. I found an open table in the Starbucks and sat to eat and drink as I studied the map some more. There were so many places I wanted to go and see. I wasn't sure how much time I had or how long it would take to get to each, making it difficult to decide.

I considered buying a pass for the double-decker buses, but I wickedly wanted to save that experience for Rhett and me to do together. I figured he wouldn't be as amused with the public transportation as me. The thought of torturing him with it tickled me for some reason, though.

I finally made it to Harrods and immediately knew what all the fuss was about. It was enormous. I could get lost in the vast floor plan, spending hours on each floor. I figured it would take me at least two days to cover the whole store.

I'm not sure how long I'd been in the store when I finally stumbled upon the grocery. The prices were steep, as I expected. I found some mini English jam jars that would make perfect souvenirs. They came stacked in a clear plastic tube as a pack of four in various flavors. The lids were adorned with the English flag, and I knew my mom and Nana would get a kick out them, so I grabbed a couple for my family and myself.

I placed them on the checkout counter while digging through my purse for my wallet. As I pulled it out, a credit card and paper fell to the ground. I picked it up, not recognizing it until I read the name imprinted on it. I huffed my aggravation, reading the note.

Buy yourself something. A gift from me.
Enjoy London, beautiful. x
-RB

As sweet as his sneaky sentiment was, I still didn't feel right about it. I tucked his card safely in my wallet and pulled out my own, paying for my items. I checked my phone as I walked out of Harrods. It was already a quarter past noon, and I'd missed a text from Rhett.

R: Meeting taking longer than expected. Should be done in an hour.

A: No problem. Picnic in Hyde Park for lunch?

His reply came within seconds.

R: Sounds perfect. I'll have the hotel make us something to take. x

A: Got it covered. Meet you at the hotel. x

I dropped my phone back in my purse and headed back into Harrods' food hall to pick out some items for our picnic.

~

I walked rapidly on my return to the hotel. I'd spent way too much time sampling the charcuterie before selecting what to buy. Rhett had already texted to say he was on his way back to the hotel. Luckily, I was only a few blocks away.

As I approached the exterior of the hotel, Rhett stepped onto the sidewalk from the limo. His face was stressed and weary. He saw me immediately, and I went from a fast-paced walk to a full-on sprint with my bags in tow. Dropping the bags to the ground, I slung my arms around his neck to pull him in for a wet kiss. He laughed at my shameless greeting, lifting me from my feet as he kissed me back.

"Did you have a good day?"

"Yes! I love this city. How was your meeting?"

"Boring. And long. I'm starved. Should we head to the park?" He placed me back on my feet.

I pulled back slightly, assessing his attire. "Did you not want to change?"

"No. If we go upstairs, we won't be leaving that bed. And *I* don't want to be the one responsible for you missing out on anything in London."

He dropped his forehead to mine with a sheepish smile. I kissed my appreciation before taking his arm as he picked up my bags to carry them to Hyde Park.

The park was filled with picnickers and sunbathers, lounging on the lush green lawns throughout the park. We found as secluded of a spot as possible before staking our claim to our little piece of lawn.

"I didn't think about a blanket." I looked at Rhett in his expensive tailored suit. I feared he was going to ruin it with grass stains.

"Here," he said, taking off his jacket, spreading it out on the grass for me like a gentleman. "Sit."

"Rhett"—I laughed at his cluelessness—"I was more worried about you and *your suit*. Not me and my twenty-dollar Old Navy dress."

He stared at me, baffled by my statement.

"Never mind." I shook my head at him with astonishment, picking up his suit jacket and folding it delicately before setting it aside.

We both sat on the grass as I pulled out all the food for our picnic. We ate and chatted idly as I people watched and Rhett "Ava watched," as he called it.

"Did you buy anything other than our picnic?" Rhett looked over at the Harrods' bags resting near us.

I eyed him suspiciously. "Yes. Jam."

"Jam?"

"Yep. I got my family and myself some English jam souvenirs." I pulled one out of the bag to show him.

His eyes twinkled with amusement, the corner of his mouth curling with a restrained smile. "That's it?"

"Yes. Oh...and well...I decided to pay for everybody's purchases for the two hours I was in Harrods with your credit card," I deadpanned, restraining my own smile.

It was no use. The grin broke through. He tackled me

108

into the grass, tickling my sides until I begged and pleaded through my unceasing laughter for him to stop.

"I should punish you further for your defiance." His sexy smile spread across his face, his eyes full of mirth.

"And *I* should punish you for your relentlessness."

"What's wrong with me wanting to buy you a gift?"

"Nothing…I just don't want you to feel like you have to, especially not ridiculously expensive things. *You* are all I want. Not your money." I wrapped my arms around his shoulders as he towered above me.

"And *you* are all I want. But I'd like to be able to spoil you a little, beautiful." His face softened as his eyes penetrated mine.

How could I deny those enchanting blues? "Compromise?"

"Sure. What do you suggest?"

"I'd like to check out Camden Market tomorrow. I'll allow you to buy me something there."

I watched as his face contorted in deep thought, wondering if he was scheming something up in his beautiful mind. Of course, he was. I just wasn't sure what.

"Agreed. What would you like to do for the rest of today?"

I smiled mischievously at him. "I want to take a double-decker bus tour."

"We don't need a bus. We can have the limo take us around the city."

"No! I *want* to ride the bus."

He stared at me in disgust and disbelief, as if I'd just said the most absurd and repulsive thing he'd ever heard.

I pushed playfully against his shoulder. "Don't be such a snob, Rhett. We're in London! It's about the experience! I want to see the city from the open-air top deck. I can't do that in a limo. Besides, this way you'll be forced to control your fetish. You can't very well have your way with me on a public bus."

"Exactly. All the more reason to take the limo." He grinned ruefully.

I rolled my eyes at him.

"Okay, beautiful. If it's what you really want to do, we'll take the dirty, crowded bus."

"It is." I gave him a triumphant grin. "Thank you."

"Anything for my girl." He grazed his fingers down the side of my face before dropping a soft, sweet kiss on my lips. "Let's get on with it." He rolled off of me, pulling me to my feet.

~

Rhett purchased our hop-on hop-off bus passes before we boarded the first double decker. I grabbed his hand in mine, excitedly tugging him up the steps to the open-air deck to find our seats.

As we drove through the city to our first stop, I pulled out my phone to take pictures. I even convinced Rhett to do a few selfies with me as we drove past the Marble Arch and Buckingham Palace. He was being a good sport, even though I knew he'd much rather be in the limo. Yet, he still seemed to be amused, if only by my own enthusiasm.

Looking between Rhett and the other passengers, it was glaringly obvious his distinguished appearance and manner-isms didn't quite match the average passenger on the bus. Their worlds were miles apart, and it made me realize our two worlds were too. But somehow, we had found each other and fallen in love.

We arrived at our first stop, St. Paul's Cathedral. Rhett's hand was clasped with mine as we toured the English Baroque church. It was surreal, seeing firsthand so many of the masterful pieces of architecture I'd studied in school. I walked silently, running my hand along the surfaces as I appreciated every inch of it.

I'd read about the massiveness of the building, but didn't quite comprehend it until I was actually standing in the middle of the vast space. I stared at the colossal cathedral ceilings towering over me, taking in the impressive, intricate details.

As I stood there with my head tilted back, enamored with it all, I felt Rhett's warm embrace slip around my waist as he pulled me into him, looking up at the ceiling himself.

"I would love to know what's going through that beautiful mind of yours," he whispered.

"Awe. Inspired. Disbelief."

I gave my one-word answers slowly, without taking my eyes from the ceiling. I felt the grin of his mouth on the back of my head as he pressed a kiss on it.

"I'm amazed how they did all of this without the technology of today. It's more than impressive to think about." I dropped my head and rotated into his arms to gaze up at him. "Thank you."

"For what?' His brow furrowed in confusion.

"For bringing me here. To London. To see all this."

He responded with a firm, searing kiss on my lips. I felt both of our arousals as warmth streamed through my body, pooling between my legs. I broke the kiss before we got too carried away in God's house. I blushed. He chuckled.

"I want to see Big Ben," I said, trying to distract myself with a change in topic.

He looked at me with boyish glee. "Is that what you're calling it now?"

"Rhett Blackwood!" I whispered loudly, pushing his chest, flustered and embarrassed by his brashness but still acutely aware of our surroundings.

He laughed harder.

I threw my hand over his mouth, trying to muffle it. "Let's go, before I'm sentenced to hell."

"Sorry, babe. You left that one wide open." He draped his arm around my shoulders, guiding me out with a smug grin on his face.

～

We spent the rest of the afternoon viewing the city from the bus. Rhett held me tucked firmly in his side. I took pictures as we passed the London Bridge, The Shard, Tower Bridge, and many more sights. We switched buses to head to Big Ben and Westminster Abbey.

By the time we were done touring, exhaustion over-whelmed my body from the traveling and activity of the day. We headed back to the hotel to rest, ordering in room service for dinner and having each other for dessert.

Best.

Dessert.

Ever.

My limp, sated body laid in Rhett's arms, ready to fall

asleep when I felt him shift below me. He rolled us, so I was lying back on the pillow, him hovering over me.

"There's somewhere I want to take you," he spoke softly, moving my hair from my face.

"Okay."

"That means you'll need to get dressed."

"Now?" I glanced toward the windows. It was dark and late.

"Yes. Now," he muttered into my neck, planting a kiss.

"It can't wait for tomorrow morning?"

"No." He refused to waver. "It's something I prefer to do at night. Don't argue, Ava."

"I'm tired, though," I whined like a toddler.

"I promise it'll be worth it. It's my favorite thing to do in London." He smiled hopefully at me.

I couldn't resist that smile, nor the chance to know what his favorite thing to do in London was.

"Okay," I conceded with a grin.

He gave me a quick peck on the lips before dragging me to my feet. I groaned my displeasure of leaving the comfort of his arms in the heavenly bed.

"Get dressed, beautiful." He held me upright, giving my bare bottom a final squeeze before releasing me.

The limo was waiting for us outside the hotel when we exited. I climbed in, sliding across the seat, making room for Rhett to slide in next to me. He held me in his arms, occasionally kissing my head as we drove.

"Where are we going?"

"You'll see," he responded, revealing nothing.

A few minutes later, we pulled up to the London Eye. I smiled up at Rhett as the driver moved efficiently around the car to open our door. Rhett climbed out, offering his hand to me.

I stepped out of the car, and he pulled me into his side with his arm around my shoulders as he walked us to the London Eye.

"I think it may be closed, Rhett."

"It is. But not for us."

There was a man waiting at the gate, who allowed us to walk through to the platforms. There was nobody else, just a few guys who obviously worked the famous tourist attraction.

We stepped into one of the glass capsules, where a bottle of champagne and flutes were waiting for us. I looked up at Rhett, who grinned, releasing me to pour us each a glass.

He handed me a champagne flute as the massive wheel started to move us up into the dark, cool air. He grabbed my hand, pulling me to the far end of the capsule overlooking the Thames. I observed the city as we got higher in the sky. The view was breathtaking. Seeing the city lit up at night made it more enchanting than it already was in the day.

The wheel stopped, stranding us at the highest point of view. We both stood silently, staring out over London. Rhett put his glass down, returning to wrap his arms around me and rest his chin on my shoulder as we both admired the city.

"Worth it?" Rhett asked, interrupting the silence.

"Yes," I breathed, not removing my gaze from the twinkling lights of the city. "I can see why it's your favorite thing. Thank you for sharing it with me."

"Any time, beautiful." He squeezed me tighter to his chest.

I relaxed in his arms, feeling content and somehow more in love with the man than I'd been before. He had a way of making me fall deeper and deeper, to depths I didn't even know existed.

CHAPTER 8

The rush of water hitting the shower floor woke me. I stretched my tired limbs before rolling up to a sitting position on the bed. I picked up my cell phone from the bedside table. I had a few missed calls and texts from my mom, Lizzie, and Owen.

Shit. Owen.

I hadn't even thought about him since our lunch date. I scrolled through the text messages first. Lizzie was curious how things were going with Rhett and me. My mom was asking to Skype today, explaining Nana wanted to know what the hell Skype was and the only way my mom could make her understand was if we did it. Owen wanted to know about dinner Friday night.

I responded to Lizzie, telling her things were going well and I'd try to call her later. I agreed to Skype with my mom, suddenly aware I hadn't even told her I was in London—or that Rhett and I were here together.

My fingers hovered over the phone as I tried to decide what to say to Owen. I couldn't tell him things weren't going any further through text. It didn't seem right. I needed to at least call him and explain. I sent him a quick text saying I was out of town for the next couple of weeks on business, and I'd call on my return. I hoped it would buy me some time to figure out how to explain things. Before I could contemplate it any further, Rhett's naked body distracted me as he strode brazenly across the room with a boldfaced grin.

"Morning, beautiful," he crooned, slipping on some gray boxer briefs.

Damn.

"I figured you'd be out longer. I was going to take care of a few work things while you slept."

I set my phone aside and stood from the bed as he walked toward me, taking me in his arms, his forehead resting on mine.

"Don't let me keep you from work. I was thinking about going for a run in Hyde Park."

He pulled back, watching me carefully. "I'd prefer you wait. I'll go with you."

"Rhett, I want to go now. Besides, you have work to do. What else am I going to do in the meantime? I'll be fine on my own."

I watched his face contort with different emotions as he contemplated whatever it was in his sexy head until finally, his face dropped with defeat, followed by a stern expression. I wish I knew what ran through that brilliant mind of his.

"I won't be long. Be back in an hour. We'll head to Camden afterward." His tone was exacting.

I nodded my agreement, knowing I'd be back when I was

back. But I wasn't going to argue with him. Better to ask forgiveness later. He pressed his soft lips firmly to my forehead before releasing me.

He pulled on some jeans over his boxers.

I about died.

Rhett with no shirt, in jeans that hugged his firm ass, would have any woman keeling over with desperation. I didn't bother disguising my lust as I ogled his ass. It wasn't until he pretended to clear his throat that my concentration on the toned curves beneath his jeans was broken.

"Huh?" I blinked twice, staring blankly up at him. *He said something, right?*

He stalked toward me like a conniving cat about to pounce a tiny, unknowing mouse. "I didn't say anything." He gave me his sly grin. "But that look on your face has me thinking maybe you should skip the run." He leaned in. His body inches from mine. His lips grazing my cheek as they traced a path to my ear before releasing that alluring, whispering voice on me. "If you stay, I promise to have you panting and sweating."

My body fizzled. My brain malfunctioned. My face turned into his instinctively, wanting those addictive lips on mine. Without warning, my hands flew to his hair, pulling him to me as my mouth attacked his. His hands immediately went to my body as he scooped me up into his arms, moving us back to the bed.

He moved swiftly, removing the T-shirt I'd slept in, stripping me bare. I hastily worked at the zipper of the jeans that started it all. His lips worked their way down my collar bone, taking my breast into his mouth while his hand massaged the other one in a slow rhythm. I tried pushing the waist band of his jeans down his hips when the ringing of his phone halted my progress.

"Shit," he clipped, pausing momentarily from his manipulation of my body.

"Leave it," I panted, lifting my hips to him, my body begging him not to stop.

The phone rang a couple more times before ringing off. Rhett went back to obliterating me with ecstasy. His lips moved farther south, coasting over my belly. His phone rang again. He stopped.

Damn it!

Breathing heavily, he dropped his forehead on my stomach, rotating it slowly from side to side with disappointment.

His warm breath skated across my navel. Both of us struggled to breathe as we fought our bodies' urges.

"Babe." The word oozed desperation and regret. I wanted to scream. "I have to get that," he continued, his forehead still resting on me.

His phone rang off again. I slid my fingers through his hair, loosely gripping to pull his head up to look at me. "It's fine," I said, smiling half-heartedly.

I lied. It wasn't.

He groaned, moving back up my body, stopping when his face met mine. "I'm sorry. I'll make it up to you."

"I know you will," I quipped cheekily.

He devoured my lips one more time before reluctantly moving from the bed. He zipped his pants, his bulge ever present, and grabbed his phone, moving into the living room suite to return the call. I buried my face in the pillow, screaming my sexual frustration. It didn't help.

I dragged my deprived, hormone-laden body from the

bed and pulled on my running clothes and shoes. I freshened up in the bathroom before picking up my phone and headphones for my morning run in Hyde Park.

I walked into the living area, where I found Rhett at the desk with his laptop as he talked to whoever was on the other end of the phone. I didn't know who it was, but I unreasonably hated them for robbing me of an orgasm.

His back was to me. I listened to his commanding voice as he talked. Watching and listening to him, I wanted to climb on his jean-cladded lap and run my hands up his strong, bare chest, just to torture him the way I was being tortured.

I fought my compulsion and instead dropped a kiss on the back of his head to let him know I was leaving. I turned to walk away when his hand gripped my wrist, stopping me.

"Hold on," he demanded to the person on the phone. He buried the phone in his chest, looking up at me. "Be careful, beautiful."

"Always." I leaned in to give him a soft peck on his lips. I smiled reassuringly.

He nodded, releasing his hold before placing the phone back to his ear. "Proceed," he commanded the person on the phone as I left the suite.

~

My feet pounded the pavement as my body pushed forward, relieving the pent-up energy from earlier. It wasn't as exhilarating as an orgasm from Rhett, but running still had a way of putting my body into a euphoric state. I fell into pace like I was on autopilot, listening to my playlist, focused on the path ahead, only occasionally glancing around me to enjoy the beauty that was Hyde Park on a cool, summer morning.

I ran along the Serpentine after doing the half-lap around the park. I'd already run three miles. My heart rate elevated, beating powerfully in my chest. I kept my breathing at a steady rhythm, picking up my pace as "Starlight" by Muse started to play. The beat of the music motivated me to push harder.

I completed the loop around the Serpentine, collapsing in the damp, cold grass. I lay on my back, looking up at the sky, letting my rapid breathing slow. My chest felt heavy as it expanded and contracted. I was energized and spent at the same time. I knew I needed to stretch, but I couldn't move. I'd gone close to five miles. I lay there for a while longer, feeling dizzy as my heartbeat calmed. Peeling my back off the ground into a sitting position, I watched other runners as they passed by.

As I people watched, an uneasiness came over me. The hairs on my nape stood. My heartrate started to pick up, despite my resting state. I glanced around at my surroundings, feeling eyes on me. I didn't recognize anyone—not that I would in London—and there was nobody even remotely close to me, other than the joggers running past.

My phone vibrated with a new text, snapping me out of my sudden insecurity.

R: Where are you?

My hour was up.

A: On my way back now.

∿

I walked into our suite and saw Rhett where I'd left him more than an hour ago: still at his laptop, still on his phone. The only difference was now he wore a gray T-shirt. I rolled my eyes, annoyed he cut my recovery time short when he wasn't even done working.

He twisted as he heard me enter, his eyes locking on me as he listened to the phone. I didn't bother greeting him. I headed straight to the shower, ignoring his glare that followed me as I walked.

The warm spray poured over me, relaxing my muscles as I washed and conditioned my hair. I squeezed some soap onto a loofah and started to wash my body when I felt the tingling of nerve endings course through me. I sensed his presence before I saw him move into the bathroom from my peripheral.

I wondered if he planned on joining me. He didn't. He leaned against the bathroom counter, his arms and ankles crossed, smoldering as he glared at me through the glass shower walls. I knew he was angry about me defying him, once again.

I didn't care. In fact, I was hell bent on driving him crazy mad. If he wanted to watch, I would give him a show. I ditched the loofah, favoring my hands. I worked a lather of soap between them before placing them on me. I dragged them slowly and seductively down my body, taking my time and moaning my exaggerated pleasure as I massaged.

"Shit," he muttered gruffly under his breath.

I bit my lip, holding in a laugh.

He shifted to adjust himself, his body revealing he was affected, even if he held his face impassive.

I rinsed the soap from my body, taking my time before

shutting off the water. I opened the shower door, lifting my towel from the hook, pretending he wasn't there. I dried myself and wrapped the towel around my body before training my eyes on his.

I moved to leave the bathroom. Before I could exit, he was on me, scooping me up into his arms and over his shoulder like a sack of potatoes. I squealed. He slapped my ass, playfully.

"You're driving me crazy, woman," he growled as he took determined strides to the bed. He tossed me onto the pillowy mattress as I laughed. "I told you one hour." His voice was stern, but his face was fighting back a grin.

"I lost track of time." I shrugged, unapologetically.

"You're going to cause me to lose my shit. I worry about your safety."

"Rhett, I'm fine. I was fine. And I'll be fine. Stop worrying so much," I assured him, despite the fact that I'd had my own moment of paranoia in the park. It was probably just him getting into my head.

He'd always been possessive and concerned about my wellbeing, but it seemed like this Rhett was more paranoid than the Rhett I'd known three years ago. I had no idea where this was coming from. At some point, we would need to have a conversation about it.

I appreciated his concern, but at the same time, I was used to my independence. I required it. I didn't want to bring it up right now, though. Everything was too fresh, and we were barely getting back on track, making up for lost time.

He stared into my eyes as I brought my palm to his cheek, trying to reassure him. He turned his head, kissing the palm of my hand, before pressing his lips to mine. His hands moved diligently, discarding my towel and his clothes. This time...there were no interruptions.

～

We spent the rest of the day perusing Camden Market after arriving by the tube. I'd twisted Rhett's arm, once again, to take public transportation. I told him I'd never forgive him if he didn't allow me to experience the tube and "mind the gap."

It wasn't true. I'd forgive him, and he likely knew that. But he didn't want to disappoint me. I think he enjoyed it less than the bus, but he humored me, nonetheless. He held me tight to him the whole ride, guarding me from anyone who dared to get too close.

We ate some lunch and had a few pints of beer before we strolled the stalls of Camden Market. Rhett followed closely behind me. I browsed while he patrolled. We came across a booth with various accessories and a few London souvenirs. I sorted through some keychains when I came across a round, button-shaped keychain with a night shot of the London Eye. I smiled inwardly, picking it up.

Facing Rhett, who was eyeing some cheap, knock-off watches suspiciously, I held it up into his view with a wide smile.

"I found what I want you to buy me."

"A keychain?" he asked with incredulity.

"Yes," I sighed, exasperated. "A keychain. It's what I want." I swung my hips to one side, resting my hands on them, daring him to argue with me.

He shook his head in amusement. "If that's what you *really* want." I could hear the doubt in his words.

"It is."

He put his hand out to me, silently asking for the keychain. I placed it in his hand. He held it up, studying it as if he were inspecting a rare diamond. A slow smile spread across his face as he lowered it. He turned to the grungy man working the booth and gave him the cash to purchase it. He handed the keychain back to me, and I slipped it into my purse. I wrapped my hand around his arm, leading us out of the open-air stalls.

"I think I'm done shopping for the day."

"As you wish. Should I call for the limo to pick us up?"

I laughed, shaking my head in disbelief at his persistence. He'd been such a good sport, I didn't have the heart to deny him.

"Yes."

"Really?"

"Yes, babe. Call your precious limo. I may even let you satisfy your fetish, for being such a trooper on the tube." I winked at him.

He chuckled before planting a kiss on my head and pulling out his phone to call the limo driver.

"Ava? Honey, are you there? I don't think it's working."

"Yes, Mom. I'm here, but I can't see you." I giggled, looking at the ceiling of my home in Litchfield live on my laptop screen. "You need to adjust the webcam, so I can see your face and not the ceiling."

"Oh! One second...here we go."

Her smiling face appeared moments later, with Nana looking over her shoulder. My heart filled with happiness, seeing the two of them.

"Hi, Mom! Hi, Nana!" I waved at them as I grinned.

"Well, I'll be damned. Look, Sarah! It's Ava." Nana's face lit up, full of amazement and delight.

"Yes, Mom...I know. That's what I've been trying to tell you." Mom's annoyance with Nana was evident.

"How is she on here? Is this a recording?" Nana's face inspected the screen.

I couldn't help but laugh.

"No, it's live. In real time."

"I don't believe it."

"Well, talk to her. Ask her a question."

"What's two plus two?" Nana asked seriously.

"Really, Nana?" I asked through my laughter as Mom rolled her eyes with a sigh. "Four," I answered her trivial question.

"It's really you, Ava?"

"Yes," I said, the laughter now causing my stomach to ache. "I'm here on a live feed. Almost like I'm right there with you."

"Ava," Mom said, moving her face closer to the screen, while squinting her eyes. "Where are you? That doesn't look like your apartment in the background and it looks dark outside."

"Oh," I said, glancing behind me at the hotel suite. "Well, I didn't get a chance to tell you. It all happened rather quick-ly..." I stalled, trying to decide how much I wanted to tell them at the moment.

"What did, honey?"

"Well, I'm on a business trip. It was last minute. They sent me to London. Well, Italy really—"

"London!" Mom screamed excitedly, cutting me off before I could finish.

"That's wonderful, Ava," Nana chimed in.

"Yes, well—"

"I can't believe you didn't tell me!"

"Like I said, it was kind of a last-minute trip."

"Wait—Ava, there's a man in your room!" Mom's eyes widened as her face turned from excited shock to fearful shock. I turned around, seeing Rhett's back as he moved across the room, hanging up his phone call.

Crap. "Right. Umm..." I hesitated, unable to find the words to explain everything.

"Are you okay? Who's that man?"

I gave Rhett my death glare for walking across the room in my webcam's view. He didn't seem concerned. He pocketed his phone and walked toward me. I tried shooing him away, but it was too late.

"Honey, is that Rhett?"

"Move aside, Sarah, let me see," I heard Nana say in an impatient voice. I turned back to the screen to see Nana pushing Mom out of her way, her face magnified as she tried to get a closer look.

"It is! It's Rhett! Hi, Rhett!" Nana waved, overly enthusiastic.

"Hi, Nana," Rhett said with a smirk as he squatted so his head was in view of the webcam with mine. "Mrs. Conner," he greeted my mom.

"Rhett, it's good to see you." Mom smiled her confusion at his presence. "So, you're both in London?"

"It appears that way." Rhett grinned, not giving my mother any further explanation. "I'll let Ava fill you in. It was good seeing you both." He kissed my temple before standing and walking back to the bedroom.

Great.

He couldn't just be incognito until I had time to figure out what I was ready to tell my family. I watched him walk away, not wanting to face Mom and Nana.

When I finally turned, Nana's face was ecstatic, as expected. Mom's had a questioning eyebrow raised, also as expected.

"So, Rhett's here..." I forced a tight, toothy smile.

"Well it's about damn time," Nana said firmly. "I thought I'd be six feet under before you put your damn stubbornness aside."

"What's going on, Ava?" Mom lightly shoved Nana aside, her face stern demanding an explanation.

"Honestly, I don't know. It's all new and unexpected. And kind of a long story. Can we talk about it another time?"

Her face softened. "Sure, honey...just tell me one thing... are you happy?" The concern was present in her voice.

"Yes," I replied without a thought. "I'm very happy." I smiled at her.

"That's all that matters," she said, smiling back.

"Thanks for understanding, Mom."

"Of course. Well, it looks like it's late there, and I need to get Nana home and fed some dinner. We'll talk to you soon, okay?"

"Yep. I love you both."

"Love you too, honey."

"Love you, Ava! Give Rhett a squeeze on his cheeks for me," added Nana.

"I'm hoping you mean the ones on his face, Nana." I playfully narrowed my eyes disapprovingly.

"Both, dear. Both," Nana responded, unashamed and grinning ear to ear.

"Mother, I swear," Mom reprimanded Nana as she shoved her out of view of the webcam.

I chuckled.

"Sorry, honey. Give Rhett our love. Talk to you soon."

"Will do. Bye." I waved one last time before the screen went black. I stared at it for a little while longer, missing them already, a piece of my heart aching.

I'm not sure how long I was staring at my laptop when I felt Rhett's hands on my shoulders. His head moved down next to mine, kissing me behind my ear. "Are you okay?" he asked.

"Yes. I just miss them."

"Understandable." He moved to my side, offering his hand to me. "Are you ready for bed?"

I nodded at him as I placed my hand in his. He guided us both to the bedroom. We lay in bed facing each other as I studied all the details of his face. He moved his hand to my cheek, brushing his fingers downward and then behind my neck, where his hands weaved into the hair at my nape.

"Where do you want to go next?"

I let out a sigh, not having even thought about our departure tomorrow. "Next? Are we not going to Carrara?"

"Yes. We will. I just didn't know if you wanted to make a stop or two before then."

I rolled to my back, thinking about where I really wanted to go. Only one place came to mind. He shifted, resting his head on his elbow.

"I want to go to Carrara next."

His face dropped, not liking my answer.

"Then...I want to go home."

"When you say 'home'..."

"I mean Litchfield...and maybe New York. I'd like to see my family and friends."

"I think we can manage that." He smiled down at me.

"Good. We have plenty of time to see the rest of the world. I just want to see them right now."

He kissed me, rolling on top of me as he settled in *his spot* between my legs. I moved my hands to his butt, giving his cheeks a squeeze. I giggled through our kiss, unintentionally disrupting it. He pulled his head back, looking down at me, confused.

"That was from Nana." I grinned, only moderately embarrassed.

He chuckled, completely unembarrassed. He brought his lips back to mine before moving inside me, ruining me for any other man, making me his forever.

～

Our first day in Carrara, we toured the ancient and colorful town of Baroque architecture as we strolled along the old stone streets. We sat in the main piazza of the town, people watching and sipping our cold coffees the locals called shakerato. The relaxed, unhurried vibe of the Italians had me wanting to sit there all day, soaking in the sunrays.

The small Tuscan town was not your typical tourist attraction. The people were friendly and buoyant, excited to share their town with us. They knew little English, but we were able to communicate well enough, since Rhett knew more Italian than I expected.

We were standing in a local shop specializing in expensive, tailored formal wear. Rhett insisted we make the stop. I tried to avoid it, afraid he was trying to trick me into allowing him to spoil me with lavish attire I would likely never wear. When he promised he wouldn't, I relented.

The shop was impressive, covered in marble and exquisite works of art. It had a historic elegance to it that could only be achieved over time. They served us tea as they measured Rhett. Thankfully, it was a man taking all the measurements, otherwise my jealousy would have reared its ugly head, considering the precision they took and the proximity they were to every inch of his body.

While they busied themselves with Rhett, I meandered through the shop, eyeing a beautiful black and white, wide-striped shoulder wrap that would be perfect to wrap myself up in when I sat on my apartment balcony. I moved closer to run my hands over it. Lifting the tag, I gawked at the price, dropping the expensive material and stepping away as if it had burned my hand with its exorbitance.

I looked over at Rhett—who was speaking to the tailor—impressed and even more turned on as the Italian vocabulary flowed freely from his lips. When he noticed the yearning I'm sure was written all over my face, he gave me a garish grin.

"I may never stop speaking Italian, seeing you look at me

that way," he said as the older Italian gentleman left the room.

"Promise?" I goaded him, thinking it was the best idea he'd ever had, despite me having no idea what he'd been saying. It didn't matter. He could say whatever he wanted to me, as long as he said it in Italian. The language only enhanced the effect his deep, sexy voice had on me.

He laughed wholeheartedly, snaking his arms around my waist, kissing me.

~

The morning of day two in Carrara, I finally felt like I was doing my job. Tom had already emailed me a few times during the trip to see how things were going, wanting a status update. I gave him vague responses like "everything is great," "making lots of headway," and "excited to show you." Every time I responded to one of his emails, the guilt from lying to my boss amplified.

We were on our way up the Marble Mountains in an off-road vehicle snaking up the narrow, steep, dirt roads leading to the quarry. I peered down out the window once and immediately regretted it. I gripped the sides of the vehicle as it climbed. The edge of the mountain was a mere foot away, and I suddenly had visions of plummeting below.

Making it to the top of the mountain was worth the gut-wrenching drive. The breathtaking view revealed marble as far as the eye could see. In the distance, our eyes were rewarded with the gorgeous view of the Apuan Alps, along with the Tuscan coastline. I watched in awe as the men working the quarry moved the massive marble that would be worked into masterpieces.

After our tour of the mountain, we met with the head foreman of the manufacturer turning our selected marble into the final product that would be installed in Rhett's Malibu home. We spent a couple hours going over all the details and specifications, promising to email him final measurements once we got further along in the design process. We finished our day enjoying the local summer festival and open-air markets of the charming little town.

Our last day and night in Italy we spent at a seaside hotel twenty minutes from Carrara. The seaside resort had marvelous views of the mountains and sea, and food that left my taste buds wanting more, despite my stomach being past capacity.

I sat between Rhett's legs on a lounger on the beach. The cool, night breeze blew across our bodies. His warm, strong embrace enveloped me as we gazed at the soothing sea. I was pretty sure this was where dreams were made, at least, *my* dreams.

I only prayed nothing would ever come between us again. Yet, I couldn't help but feel things may be too good. I didn't know what was going to happen when we returned to the reality of our lives.

Before I could get carried away with my doubt, Rhett squeezed me tighter, kissing the top of my head. "We should get some sleep, beautiful. We have an early flight home tomorrow."

He held me a few more seconds, before shifting us both and guiding me back to our room for the night.

CHAPTER 9

I texted Lizzie as soon as we landed in New York. We made plans to meet up the following day, after I'd had time to sleep off the jet lag. Jim was waiting for us at the airport when we arrived in New York. He gave me a jovial smile as we approached the limo.

"Hi, Jim!" I beamed as I rushed toward him. I had an urge to give him a big hug but stopped myself. Unsure if it would be considered inappropriate, I gave him an awkward pat on the arm instead. Sensing my discomfort over how to greet him, he chuckled to himself.

"Ms. Conner"—he bowed his head— "always a pleasure to see your smiling face." He held the door open as I climbed in. Rhett followed behind me after greeting Jim.

I laid my head on Rhett, wanting to fall asleep for the night, even though it was only midday in New York. Rhett scrolled through his phone, checking and responding to emails with one arm around me as we drove into the city.

I felt the limo slow and pull to the side to a stop. Rhett kissed the crown of my head. I sat up sleepily, expecting to be outside Rhett's parents' penthouse. I was caught slightly off guard when the building in front of us was not one I recognized.

"Where are we?"

"We're home."

I looked at him, then back outside the limo as he gauged my reaction. He wasn't simply stating our location; there was something more behind his words. "This is your place," I confirmed, more for myself.

He turned away from me as Jim opened the door for us. Rhett stepped out of the limo and offered his hand to assist me with my own exit.

With his hand at my back, he guided me through the lobby of the modern steel-and-glass building, nodding at the concierge sitting at the front desk. The elevator was already waiting for us at the ground floor. He stepped us both inside, punching a key code to take us to his penthouse.

Thoughts of our elevator ride in L.A. had me grinning from ear to ear as he stood behind me, holding my back close to his chest. His arms were loosely snaked around my waist. My mind ignited my body with the thought of him pinning me to the elevator wall again. My cheeks heated. My hips pressed backwards into Rhett, my subconscious taking over. I felt his body go rigid, responding to mine.

"Ava." His tone was warning but pleading.

"Hmm?" I hummed, feigning innocence.

I moved to grind my ass into him once again. His arms moved quickly, planting his hands firmly on my hips, stopping their seduction. Milliseconds later the door dinged open. A big, burly man with a stoic expression and impenetrable stare stood facing us.

Crap.

He acknowledged Rhett with his eyes only, as we approached a large, black, steel door. To say he was intimidating was an understatement. Rhett unlocked the door and pushed it open, stepping aside for me to lead the way. His face was expressionless in front of the large security guard, but I knew he was affected by my little stunt in the elevator. He was fighting to control himself. And I wasn't done teasing him.

I sauntered by with a sway to my hips, biting the corner of my bottom lip with a grin as I passed him. I'd barely made it through the threshold when the door slammed shut and locked. I turned with a gasp, startled by the slamming door. My feet left the floor before I had a chance to fully turn. I was dangling like a ragdoll over Rhett's shoulder, laughing as he slapped my ass, carrying me off to what I assumed was his bedroom.

He dropped me on the bed with a small bounce as he crawled over me with his wicked smile. "You, Ms. Conner, need to learn to control yourself."

"You like me out of control," I countered, pulling at the edges of his shirt collar to bring him closer to me.

He hovered over me, his forearms caging me in, our heads touching as I stared at his kissable mouth. I licked my lips, inviting his to dance with mine.

"Only when I'm the one making you out of control," he said with a smirk.

He moved devastatingly slowly, bringing our mouths together, his hands caressing and stimulating every inch of my body...slowly...torturously. He was evil—pure, intoxicating, delicious evil. He was teaching me a lesson, schooling me on the art of seduction, teasing me until I was at the brink of losing my ever-loving mind.

"Rhett," I breathed, begging him to take me already. Just when I thought he couldn't possibly make me feel needier and more desperate, I felt a vibration on my inner thigh. "Mmm..." I moaned.

What is that? Does he have a vibrator in his pocket?

"Damn it," Rhett cursed, pulling away from me to reach into the pocket of his pants.

His phone. His bloody damn phone, once again. I'd prefer it to remain in his pocket, vibrating on my leg, if it was going to continue to interrupt my reawakened sex life.

He pulled it out, glancing at the screen, an apologetic expression taking over his face.

"Don't you dare!" I warned, wide-eyed.

"Sorry, babe. It'll only take a minute," he promised, moving his finger to answer the phone—the phone I wanted to yank from his hands, throw against the wall, smash with my heel, then light on fire.

Wow. Where did all this aggression come from?

He answered with an abrupt greeting, pinning me in place when I tried to move out from underneath him. His eyes warned me to sit tight. I watched and listened to his direct, short responses.

He hung up within minutes, but I could tell by the look on his face, we wouldn't be continuing our little cat-and-mouse teasing game.

"I have to go into the office, beautiful. I won't be long.

Then we can finish what we started here," he assured me, pushing a wild hair from my face with his sexy smirk.

Frustrated by all the hot and cold this week, I responded like any sexually deprived woman would. "What if I don't want to?"

"We both know you do, so don't even try to argue otherwise."

He's right. *I hate him. I love him. Damn him.*

"Get some sleep while I'm gone. You'll need your energy for when I get back." He winked and gave me a cheesy grin. I rolled my eyes at his presumptions.

"Why are you going in? You weren't even supposed to be back from Italy yet. You need your rest, too." I struggled for ways to convince him to stay, concern for him filling my heart.

It seemed like he always had to work, even when he wasn't at work. Taking over the Blackwood Industries empire was going to run him into an early grave.

"I'm fine. I'll rest when I get back. There are some things I need to take care of that are more easily handled at the office than from here." He gave me a quick kiss before removing himself from the bed to shower.

I rolled to my side, listening to the spray of water hitting the shower tile, wanting to join him, but not wanting to delay him any further. The sooner he was done with work and back in my arms, the better.

He walked back into the bedroom in a fresh, fitted suit that had me salivating. He straightened his tie before looking up at me. His eyes roamed up and down my body as I lay in the bed. I watched his face as his mysterious mind worked.

"What are you thinking?"

"I've envisioned you in that bed so many times. But nothing compares to seeing the real thing."

My heart faltered. Regret drowned my senses.

He moved closer to me, trailing his hand on my cheek, knowing the guilt I was feeling. "All that matters is we're here now."

I knew he didn't blame me for the years we lost, but I couldn't help blaming myself. He gave me a soft but firm kiss before putting space between us. He turned back to look at me one more time, hesitating at the door frame.

"Make yourself at home. Call me, if you need anything. I'll leave my office number and address on the counter. I love you, Ava Conner." His smile was bright and youthful.

I couldn't help the corny grin pulling at my cheeks. "I love you too, Rhett Blackwood. Think about me while you're gone."

"Always," he promised before winking and disappearing from my sight. I rolled my face into the pillow, once again, letting out a scream of frustration. And once again, it didn't help.

～

I passed out in a deep sleep after Rhett left. When I awoke, it was dark. The only illumination in the room was the city lights coming through the floor-to-ceiling windows opposite the bed.

Wow. I sat up, looking forward. How had I not noticed this view before? One word. Rhett. His presence was like blinders for me. He gave me tunnel vision, my focus always on him.

I shifted my body backwards to lean against the head-board as I stared out at the city. The penthouse was silent. Rhett still wasn't home. I checked the time on my phone sitting on the nightstand. It was barely past eight. After a few minutes of staring out at the view, I decided to explore. I hadn't had a chance to even look at his home, plus my mouth was dehydrated.

His bedroom was basically empty, besides the very large and very comfortable bed, flanked by dark wooden night-stands, and one leather armchair near the windows. There was a balcony outside of the windows. Upon closer inspection, I noticed two of the frames of glass were actually doors opening onto the balcony.

I stumbled through the dark into the en-suite. I flipped the light switch and was momentarily blinded. Rubbing my eyes open, I was graced with the sight of a modern, mascu-line restroom retreat of large gray tiles, white fixtures, and dark brown woodwork. It was all man. All Rhett. A white, porcelain free-standing tub was framed by a large window boasting another picturesque view of the magical city of New York.

There was a massive walk-in closet off the bathroom the size of my apartment bedroom. Only half of it was filled with Rhett's clothes and shoes. The other rods, built-in shelves, and drawers sat empty. I maneuvered my way back out of the closet, bathroom, and bedroom, stepping into the hallway that led to the rest of the penthouse. I turned away from where I knew we entered, finding two more bedrooms and bathrooms, both basically empty other than beds.

I started to wonder how long Rhett had lived here. It lacked the hominess I was used to in his previous Boston home. In fact, as I moved back down the hallway into the large, open floor plan of the main living areas, it was blaringly obvious that this whole penthouse was an extreme contrast to his home I'd fallen in love with in Boston.

It still had the air of wealth, but it was modern, minimalist, and cold, versus historic, warm, and inviting. Where his old residence had touches of comfort, the penthouse looked like it had barely been touched at all. Looking at the bare, expansive walls extruding to the high ceilings above made me feel sorrowful. It was as if the space reflected the state of mind Rhett had been living in for the last three years. Empty. Hollow.

I quickly shook the thought from my head, hoping that wasn't the case. Surely, he just moved in and hadn't had the time to make it a home.

I stepped down into the living room, where minimal furnishings faced a fireplace with more floor-to-ceiling windows on each side of it. I moved to the mantle of the fireplace, where a few framed photos caught my eye. The only personal touch found in the massive floor plan.

There was a photo of Rhett with his family, huddled in front of their lake house. It was an older photo. One I recognized from his childhood bedroom. I picked up the other photo, studying it closely. It was a candid shot of Rhett and me at my sister's wedding. I sat in his lap, laughing at something as he stared up at me with the biggest smile and adoration in his eyes. A sharp pain ripped through my chest, knowing this photo was one of the few personal items he'd chosen to display.

I hadn't seen the photo before. I assumed he got it from Jackson. They had purposefully hidden any photos of Rhett from me at my request. My selfish, stubborn request. I placed the photo back down on the mantle, looking at it one more time, before turning around to look at the rest of the space.

Behind the living room area was the industrial-style kitchen, with a long island of white and gray granite. To the left of the living area, across from the entrance to the penthouse, was a dining area. The whole open floor plan had a view of the city and tall ceilings, except the dining area. There was a metal spiral staircase leading up to a loft area above the dining area. I placed my bare foot on the cold metal steps as I slowly took the stairs.

At the top was a home office. The loft area was edged with a simple, clean, metal railing, and looked down on the rest of the penthouse. It was the only area of the whole home that seemed lived in.

I made my way around the desk, finding another framed photo placed off to the side. It was of the two of us dancing at his parents' New Year's party. We held each other close, my head lying on his chest with my eyes closed. I could see the contentment and happiness on my face. I remembered the moment and the way I felt during it.

Before I could be overrun by guilt again, I rushed back down the stairs into the kitchen in search of a glass. I shut the cabinet doors a little harder than necessary, frustration building inside me. I told myself it was due to the lack of glassware, but I was lying to myself.

I swear I went through every cabinet before I gave up, sinking to the floor with my back against the lower cabinets, wanting to cry. I heard the front door open and footsteps coming toward me. I rushed rubbing the tears away that had unwillingly formed in my eyes.

Rhett's tall figure loomed over my tiny frame. His face dropped with concern, finding me on the floor with my knees pulled into my chest.

"Ava? Are you okay?"

Not wanting him to worry, I nodded and gave him a semblance of a smile. "I couldn't find the glasses in your oversized kitchen."

He studied me for a moment before setting down a brown paper bag he'd been holding on the kitchen counter. He offered his hands out to me, pulling me to my feet, kissing my forehead. He walked to the upper cabinet beside the fridge, pulling out a glass, then opened the fridge, grabbing a large bottle of water.

After filling the glass, he handed it to me, watching me as I took a much-needed drink. I gulped it down, wishing it was something stronger than water.

"What's in the bag?" I nodded toward the paper bag giving off a delicious aroma, attempting to distract him from probing me for what was really going on.

"Dinner. I picked up some Chinese. Figured you might be hungry."

"Starved," I said, smiling salaciously.

He laughed, shaking his head at me.

"Food first. Then dessert," he ordered.

He moved, opening more cabinets, pulling out plates and silverware and another glass for himself. He set up two place settings at the island before pulling the Chinese takeout from the bag.

We ate, while stupidly grinning at each other like two

inexperienced teenagers, finding ways to flirtatiously touch each other. As if we really needed to find ways. He could brazenly take me now on his counter, and I wouldn't refuse him.

I looked around the nearly empty space, needing answers for my own peace of mind. "How long have you lived here?"

He took a bite, not responding to my question immediately. He finished chewing, considering me carefully. "A little less than three years."

My hand halted its movement to my mouth, lowering the fork back to my plate. That was not what I wanted to hear. My face and eyes instinctively dropped, not wanting him to see the shame and sorrow in my eyes.

He moved his hands under my chin, lifting it. "Ava, look at me."

I shook my head no, closing my eyes as he held my head up with his fingers.

"Let me see those eyes. Don't deny me of them."

I exhaled, not wanting to ever deny him again, and opened them. "Why does it look like you barely live here?"

"Because I do barely live here. I spend most of my time at the office or traveling."

Another answer I didn't want to hear.

"Okay..." I let out a sigh, "still it seems unlikely your mother wouldn't try to help decorate and make this a home for you."

"She did try. I told her no."

"Why?"

"Because there's only one woman I want to turn this into a home for me. I want her stamp on it. Not my mother's. And until she came back to me, I didn't need this to be a home."

His words overwhelmed me. He'd left it a blank slate for me. He wanted this to be *our* home. *Our home.* Us. The thought had me filled with determination. His unwavering confidence in us, even when we weren't an us, had me feeling I didn't deserve him but selfishly refusing to let him go.

"There's my beautiful girl." He returned a grin in response to a smile that had unknowingly crept across my face. "Come on. I need you in *our* bed."

He pulled me from my barstool, wrapping his arms around me to lift and carry me to the bedroom. We spent the rest of the night wrapped up in each other. In our own little world.

~

I met Lizzie for brunch, before we headed to a little hole-in-the-wall nail salon where we got manis and pedis. We'd barely hugged our greeting before she demanded I "spill it" and fill her in on all the details.

"I'm so happy for you, Ava," she said, looking over at me with a tear in her eye as a woman filed away at her toes. She really was super emotional these days. "Are you happy?"

"More than ever." My face displayed the happiness I was feeling, but my tone revealed the worry clouding my heart and mind.

"Why did that sound like you aren't?"

"I am. I…"

"You what?"

"I can't help feeling like this is too good. It's great. And I *am* happy. And I want to be with Rhett. But we live across

145

the country from each other. His life is here. Mine is in L.A. I'm not sure how all this is going to work."

"Have you talked to Rhett about it?"

"No. I'm not ready to deal with reality. I just want to enjoy our time together for the next week, live in our little bubble before the world comes along to burst it."

She smiled at me reassuringly as she reached over to squeeze my forearm with her one free hand. "Something tells me Rhett won't let anyone burst your little bubble ever again."

I forced a small smile at her, not convinced Rhett could control it from happening. Wanting a lighter topic and not to think any more about what may or may not happen with Rhett and me, I changed the subject to her baby shower.

~

After my reluctant goodbye with Lizzie, I grabbed a cab headed to Rhett's parents' home. We were meeting there to have dinner with his family before we left the following day for Litchfield to see mine.

I was anxious and nervous to see his family. Mostly his parents. I knew Valerie would be more than stoked about Rhett and I being back together, but I had no idea how his parents felt.

Do they hate me for pushing Rhett away? Do they know I broke his heart?

"Miss, we're here. Should I keep the meter running?" came the gruff, annoyed voice of the cabbie.

"Right. Sorry," I responded, distracted from my fearful

thoughts. I handed him his money and stepped onto the curb as the building doorman held the cab door open for me.

I stared up at the building that still made me feel inferior. I took a few steps toward the door and it flew open barely missing me. I halted, startled by the woman exiting before me. I'd hoped to never see her stupid button nose and beautiful blond hair ever again. She strolled up to me confidently, not as startled by my presence, smirking at my discomfort.

"I didn't expect to see you here." The snarky tone in her voice told me otherwise. "I thought the two of you were finished."

"What are you doing here, Serena?" The edge in my voice was spurred by both fear and rage.

I thought Rhett had said she was cut out of his life. My clammy, cold fists clenched at my sides. My heartrate picked up. It was taking everything in me not to attack her in the middle of the sidewalk in front of this swanky building. In front of Rhett's parents' building. *Do they still have a relationship with her? Did they forgive her for everything?*

"I don't have to explain myself to you."

"You do to me." Rhett's authoritative voice interrupted us.

I looked behind me. Barely arriving to his parents', he stepped between us, protectively pushing me behind him. I wasn't the one who needed protecting. Had he shown up two seconds later he'd have found me pounding my fists into her pretty face. Okay, maybe not. But I was visualizing it. I peered around him to continue glaring at her.

"Rhett," the desperation in Serena's voice had the hair on my body standing like the hackle of a protective, growling dog, "I didn't know you'd be here. I swear it."

"I don't want to hear your excuses, Serena. Leave."

147

"I'm sorry, Rhett. For everything. I came to apologize to your parents." Her pleading became more desperate with every word she spoke.

"Leave!"

His harshness and dismissive tone had her startled, with tears swelling in her eyes. His coldness toward her almost had me feeling sorry for her. *Almost.* His body was rigid, showing no emotion or sympathy for her nearly sobbing state.

She took one step toward him, reaching out for his shoulder. He shifted us both back, avoiding her touch. He glared at her warningly. She dropped her hand before reluctantly stepping past us. I didn't look at her as she passed me, but I could feel her angry glare on me.

Rhett turned to me, pulling me into his chest in a strong embrace. He held me for a second before pulling back to look at me.

"Are you okay?" Concern and fear etched his face.

I was confused by the worry in his voice. He asked as if I'd suffered the most traumatizing event ever. I mean, it did catch me off guard, but I was fine.

"I'm fine, Rhett," I assured him, bringing my palm to his cheek.

He took a deep breath and exhaled, letting whatever crazy thoughts were running through his head out. "Stay away from Serena. Don't talk to her. Don't engage in her games."

"It's not as if I sought her out!" I huffed defensively, pushing off his chest, trying to break his hold on me.

"Ava. Stop." He held me tighter, thwarting my struggle from his arms. I relented. "I don't want her near you."

"What was she doing here? She's had three years to apologize to your parents. Why now?"

"I don't know. But I have my suspicions. She's been living overseas the last three years. Rumors spread among her social circle of why I shut her out of my life. I never told anyone or confirmed them. I have too much respect for her parents. But it's not like our smaller circle didn't know. I don't see Riley ever saying anything, but I can't say the others wouldn't. She ran to Europe to escape the gossip. I'd heard she was back, but didn't expect to find her *here*. Promise me you'll keep your distance. If she approaches you again, tell me."

"What do you think she's going to do, Rhett? Why are you so worried?"

"I don't know what she'd do. I'm not saying she'd harm you physically, but I'm not putting anything past her anymore. She's done enough things I would've never expected." He lowered his forehead to mine, our lips inches apart. "Promise me."

"I promise." I stood on my toes, closing the few inches between our lips, and kissed him, sealing my promise.

∼

When we finally made it inside his parents' home, I was smothered in hugs and kisses from his family. It seemed my fear that his parents would not be thrilled to see me was unwarranted. They kept gushing how happy they were I was there and wanted to know everything about my time in L.A. and my new job.

By the end of dinner, I was exhausted from all the

conversation and laughter. We said our goodbyes and I promised to visit them again soon. They mentioned visiting me in L.A., once Valerie moved out there. I could sense the subject of Valerie in L.A. was a touchy one for Charles, but he agreed with Vivian they'd be visiting often, which earned an eyeroll from Valerie behind his back.

I curled up in Rhett's lap in the back of the limo as Jim drove us back to Rhett's home. He rubbed my back, occasionally dropping kisses on my head. I listened to the steady rhythm of his heart as I pressed the side of my face to his chest.

"I love you, beautiful." His voice broke our comfortable silence.

I rotated my head, looking up at his strong, stubbled jawline. I'd never get tired of hearing those words from his lips. I kissed his jaw, not bothering to say the words back. He'd always known I loved him.

CHAPTER 10

The remainder of the week in Litchfield was more than I could ask for. It wasn't London or Italy or even New York, but it was home. I was surrounded by my family, and Rhett was with me. Nothing could compare to that. We spent a lot of nights with my extended family, drinking, playing games, and laughing into the early morning hours at Nana's house.

By the end of the week, the reprieve from the chaos was welcomed. Our last couple of days were spent with only my mom, Nana, Emily, and Jackson. It was already Thursday, and we would be headed back to L.A. in the morning. We debated on staying until Sunday, but I needed to take care of some things over the weekend to prepare for work on Monday. I had a lot of emails to sort through. I also knew Rhett and I needed some alone time to discuss how things were going to work between us.

Rhett and Jackson were in the living room talking, while Mom, Emily, and I were in the kitchen going over a grocery list for tonight's dinner. Mom had planned to make my favorite, her homemade lasagna, for our last dinner at home. Nana would be joining us for the evening.

"I think that should do it." Mom skimmed the list one last time to make sure she didn't forget anything. "Would you mind swinging by the bakery, also, to pick up some French bread? I'm not sure I'll have time to make homemade bread."

"Of course, Mom. Anything else?"

"Nope, I think that's it." She handed me the list. "Let me get you some money for the food."

"I have it covered."

"Ava, you don't need to pay for all that food. Besides, I added extra items for the house." She jabbed her debit card at me.

"Put it away. I'm not taking it." I swatted her hand away from me, smiling at her. "Just lend me your car keys."

She let out a heavy sigh and rolled her eyes to demonstrate her exaggerated frustration. Walking back to her purse, she put her card away and pulled out her keys.

"Do you want me to go with you?" Emily offered.

"Nope. I plan to drag Rhett along. Teach him how normal people grocery shop. I'm not sure he's ever even been inside a grocery store."

"Ah...I get it." She nodded her head in understanding. "You're needing a little quickie in the backseat." A naughty smile reminiscent of the Cheshire Cat's slithered across her face as she wiggled her eyebrows up and down.

I flushed with embarrassed annoyance, flipping her the bird.

"Emily! For heaven's sake!" Mom gasped. "Don't say things like that." She paused in thought. "I guess that means I need to schedule for my car to be detailed this weekend." Her voice strived for seriousness, but her giggle broke through the grin she was failing to contain.

"Mom!" Emily and I yelled in unison, our eyes and mouths wide open, Emily shocked with pride, me mortified. My mom had always been modest and easily embarrassed like myself. I came by it honestly.

Flustered and unable to respond, I grabbed her car keys from her hand, stomping out of the kitchen. I could feel the warmth in my cheeks, knowing my face was beet red when I walked into the living room.

"Everything okay, babe?" Rhett asked, a smile tugging at the corner of his mouth. He likely overheard the whole conversation in the kitchen.

"You." I pointed at him. "Car. Now." I couldn't even form complete sentences.

"Who would've thought Ava was the domineering one in the bedroom?" Emily laughed, coming up behind me with Mom, both of them still giggling at my back. Jackson's deep laugh joined in.

I swear. This family. *Why do I love them again?*

I glared at Rhett as amusement spread across his face, warning him, his laughter about to erupt. His face straightened with my glare. I walked past them all, straight out the door, not bothering to look back. Another fit of laughter exploded as I crossed the threshold.

Jerks.

I continued my determined march to the car. I was feet away from the shelter it would provide from their torment when I felt Rhett's strong arms wrap around me, derailing my progression. My body was airborne as he pinned me over his shoulder.

"Put me down, Rhett!" I yelled, kicking my legs and smacking him on his butt.

"No." His voice was calm and firm, and he responded with a slap of his own to my bottom as he walked us the rest of the way to the car.

"You're such an unreasonable ass," I said as I tried to wiggle out of his strong hold.

"Ava," he warned.

"Ugh!" I screamed my frustration. "I hate my family."

"No, you don't. Don't ever say those words." His tone was firm with warning.

"Fine. I don't hate them. But I strongly dislike them right now."

He chuckled, sliding me down his rock-hard body as he placed my feet back on the ground, sandwiching me between him and the car.

"Give me the keys. I'm driving."

I started to open my mouth to say I was driving, when he silenced me with a cock of his head and a raised eyebrow.

"Don't argue, Ava."

I rolled my eyes. "You don't know where you're going."

"I'm sure I'll manage to navigate your little town. Besides, you can give me directions."

"Fine," I said, placing the keys a little too forcefully in his palm. He kissed me on the tip of my nose and stepped back, opening the passenger door for me as I plopped into the car, defeated.

We stopped at the bakery first. I ran into the shop while Rhett waited in the car. It was going to be a quick stop, and Rhett needed to respond to a few work emails.

After we parked at the grocery store, Rhett took my hand, walking us through the parking lot. It was silly how much I was enjoying running errands with him. I admired his handsome face as we walked across the hot black pavement. Besides his GQ looks, wearing his jeans and gray T-shirt, he oddly appeared to fit in with the other shoppers.

He was at ease with our little shopping trip, as if it was something we did regularly together. I have no idea why the naturalness of him doing every-day, normal tasks always surprised me. He was confident no matter what it was he was doing. It's what attracted me to him.

I grabbed a shopping cart when we walked through the first set of sliding glass doors. He followed me as I led us through the store, going over the list, checking off items as we placed them in the cart.

I was familiar with the store and where everything was located, having grown up shopping here with my mother on a weekly basis—sometimes twice a week. I'd adopted her methodology of maneuvering through the store, starting at the dried goods and ending at the frozen foods and fresh vegetables.

As we neared the end of our route, I realized I'd missed toothpaste on the list. "Crap," I grumbled, annoyed I'd have to circle back to the other side of the store.

"What?" Rhett asked peering over my shoulder as I studied the list, making sure there was nothing else I missed.

"I forgot toothpaste."

"Do you want me to run and get it?"

"Would you?"

"Of course, babe. Be right back." He kissed me on the head before leaving me to pick through the fruit and vegetables.

I grabbed the ingredients for the salad and then moved to the fruit to select a cantaloupe for my mom. I picked through them, thumping and smelling them to find a ripe one.

"Nice melons." A deep voice I'd know anywhere sounded behind me. The bile in my stomach rose as I turned to face him.

"Really, Chris?" I asked, irked by his stupid comment, wondering what I ever saw in him.

"Sorry." He shifted his eyes down toward my chest momentarily before looking back up at my narrowed eyes. "They're nice, from what I remember," he said with a smirk.

The nerve of this guy!

"You're about two seconds away from my fist landing on your face," I threatened.

"Whoa!" He threw his hands up in surrender as he stepped closer to me, chuckling. "I come in peace, Ava."

"What do you want?" I asked, not hiding my annoyance as I stepped back to restore the space between us.

"I just wanted to say hi. See how you were. I never had a chance to talk to you after your dad…" He shifted uncomfortably, his face softening. His concern had my contempt for him momentarily subdued.

I let out a relenting sigh, temporarily looking away from him. "I'm good."

"I'm glad. I heard you finished school. You're in L.A. now?"

"Yes."

I kept my answers short, but was feeling ashamed at my coldness. He was trying to be nice. We'd gone through a lot together in the past. It didn't matter how it ended. I was over it and happy now. I should give him a break.

"How about you? How's your wife and daughter?"

My words came out more accusatory than I'd intended. He flinched. Maybe conversation with him wasn't a good idea.

"We, uh...we're divorced," he answered, watching me carefully.

"Oh. Sorry...I didn't know." I was sorry, but not for him. For his little girl.

"Don't worry about it. It's for the best."

"Right, well...I should—" I started to end our conversation, not wanting to talk to him any further.

"Ava, can we have dinner or a drink?"

"I'm leaving tomorrow." *Why didn't I just tell him no?*

"It can be another time. I can come to L.A. Visit you for a weekend." He stepped closer.

An irrational fear heightened my senses. The smell of alcohol lingered in the air. *Had he been drinking?*

"I don't think—"

"Come on, Ava. We were good together."

His hand was on me now. Ice coursed through my veins.

"No, Chris." I tried to remove his hand.

He gripped tighter.

"Let me go," I said, my voice shaking as I looked up at him, a coldness slowly seeping.

"Ava." Rhett's protective voice carried from a few feet behind me.

Chris looked past me, glaring at Rhett, and then turned his enraged eyes to me. "I thought you two were broken up."

He squeezed tighter, pain radiated through my arm. His voice intense, harsh. I could hear the disgust and accusation in his words. An uneasiness rushed through my body. My stomach sank. He'd never looked at me with so much hatred. I shook my head no, not able to say the word aloud.

Chris's hand reluctantly dropped as Rhett approached. Rhett's protective embrace surrounded me as he trained his own intense gaze on Chris, warning him to back off. Chris scowled back at him, sizing him up. A malignant smile spread across his smug face. He took a step back.

"See you soon, Ava," he said, smirking at Rhett before turning and walking off.

My hands were unreasonably shaking. I had no idea what I was so scared of. He wouldn't be seeing me soon. He wouldn't be seeing me ever again, if I could help it.

"Babe?" Rhett rotated me gently to face him.

I threw my arms around his strong body, hugging him to me, burying my face into his chest. I let his warm, strong body calm my irrational fear.

After a few moments, I lifted my head from his chest to look up at him. He hadn't said anything while he held me, but I could see the stress all over his face.

"I'm okay."

"What did he say?"

"Nothing. Let's go. We need to get home."

He didn't release me immediately. He held me a few seconds longer, debating whether to push me for answers.

My body relaxed when he decided not to. He took my hand while pushing the cart to the checkout.

~

I was relieved to be back at my parents' home, surrounded by my family's easy-going demeanors. I put Chris far out of my mind, never wanting to think about him again.

We ate Mom's homemade lasagna and drank wine as we visited, enjoying one more night together. The only thing missing was my father. He never said much during our family dinners. He mostly listened to the rest of us, chuckling to himself at our antics. But his presence had always filled the room and would forever be missed.

As the conversation settled and the night fell, Emily and Jackson used the lull in conversation to make their departure. "I guess we should head out. We need to get Nana home." Emily stood.

"Don't use me as your excuse, dear. I'm happy right where I am." Nana linked her arm with Rhett, who sat between us.

Of course, she was. She'd barely let Rhett out of her sight all week.

Emily rolled her eyes. "Fine. I'm tired and ready to go home. If you want a ride, you old biddy, then you better kiss your beloved Rhett goodbye."

We all laughed as Nana pouted, not ready to say goodbye to Rhett. He patted her hand resting on his forearm, placing a platonic but loving kiss on her wrinkled forehead. "Come on, Nana. I'll walk you to the car."

"Such a gentleman. The rest of you should take some

lessons. Learn to respect your elders, instead of pushing me around." She turned her judging eyes on us.

We all snickered. Rhett stood, helping Nana from her chair to escort her out. I hugged Emily and Jackson goodbye.

"When are you guys coming to L.A.?"

"Soon. I want to get out there before the summer ends. I'm just waiting for Jackson to determine when he can take vacation from work." She gave him an accusatory glare.

"I'll put in the request Monday. Promise."

"Great! Let me know the dates. I'll take off work, too." I gave them one last hug, walking them to the door where Nana and Rhett were waiting.

Nana released Rhett momentarily while she squeezed me into a bear hug. "You and Rhett come back to see your feeble old grandmother soon."

I chuckled. Nana was hardly feeble. "Will do, Nana. I love you. Take care of Mom for me."

"Of course, dear. Love you, too."

She gave me one last squeeze and kiss on my cheek before looping her arm back with Rhett's. He moved to escort her out, and we all followed behind. Rhett, Mom, and I stood in the front yard, waving them off until they were out of sight.

~

I helped Mom clean up the kitchen while Rhett took care of some work upstairs in my childhood bedroom.

Mom put away the leftovers, and I worked silently at scrubbing the dishes and loading them into the dishwasher.

"Everything okay, Ava?" Mom came up beside me, taking the plate from me to load it into the dishwasher.

"Yes. Just not sure I'm ready for this time to be over."

"Me neither. It's been nice having you home. This house is too quiet these days."

I looked up at my mom, hating how lonely she must be, since my father passed away. I watched her as she placed another dish in the rack.

"I'm thinking about selling the house. Moving in with Nana."

My hands stopped, my eyes turning to her. "Really? But this is our home."

It was selfish of me to want to guilt her into staying. But the thought of not having the home we grew up in anymore, where my dad spent the last of his days, suddenly made me upset.

"I know, honey. I'm not sure if I will or not. There are so many memories here...but Nana is getting older, and it would be easier to take care of her if we lived together. Her home has more room and is our family estate, so I couldn't ask her to sell it."

I didn't know what to say. Anything I said at this point would only make her feel worse. I didn't want her to sell it, but I didn't want her to be lonely, either. She was right. Selling Nana's house was not an option. I would be just as upset about that, anyway.

"How are you and Rhett?" She changed the subject.

Like selling the house, Rhett was a topic I'd have preferred to avoid.

I shrugged my shoulders, scrubbing food from the plate once again.. "Things are great..."

She looked at me expectantly, waiting for me to continue, knowing I wasn't telling her everything. I focused on scrubbing the lasagna pan.

"What is it, Ava?" she asked, urging me to go on.

I let out a heavy sigh, shaking my head. "How can we make this work, Mom? We're on opposite sides of the country."

"You wouldn't move to New York?"

"No," I said without thinking, not sure I even meant it. "I mean...I don't know...I love my job. L.A. has been good for me."

"I can understand that."

"I'm not sure I have the strength to be part of his elite world. I don't exactly fit in. The one time I was surrounded by paparazzi, I had a panic attack. And now, he's even more in the public eye than he used to be. My life will be under constant scrutiny. Our life."

"Forget about the rest of the world for a moment. What does your heart say, Ava?"

"Obviously, I want to be with Rhett. Unfortunately, it's not that easy."

"Maybe it is," she concluded.

I shook my head at her, baffled she could push my concerns aside so easily.

"Ava, if there is one thing I know about Rhett, it's that he'll do everything in his power to be with you and give you everything you need and want. That's not something you should dismiss."

"What if it isn't in his power?" I faced her, both of us stopping our work at the dishes.

She gave me her signature motherly look, grabbing my

hands to pull me away from the sink. She held them in hers as she spoke, "Honey, every relationship has its hurdles. And not one thing you said to me is something I can't see you two overcoming together. That man loves you. I knew it the day I met him. And so did your father. He'll move heaven and Earth for you, so being across the country is not something I see standing in his way."

I hugged my mom to me, breathing in her scent and letting her words and familiar warmth calm my nerves. I knew she was right. Rhett had proven that to me time and time again.

"Thanks, Mom," I said, still holding her close.

"Of course. I want you to be happy, Ava. I know Rhett will make you happy, so don't let your fears keep you from him. I love you, honey." She released her hold on me, stepping back to look at me again.

"Love you, too."

"Now, head upstairs. I'll finish up here." She squeezed my hands before turning back to the sink.

"Are you sure?"

"Yes, you need your rest before your flight home tomorrow."

"Okay," I agreed, unwillingly. "Goodnight." I gave her one last hug from behind her shoulders as she worked at scrubbing a dish. She patted my hands as I hugged her.

Rhett was at my desk when I walked in the bedroom. He was focused on his laptop, with his back to me. I approached him, sliding my hands over his tense shoulders, massaging them to relieve the stress. He moved his hand to mine, pulling me around his body and onto his lap.

"Hey, beautiful."

"Hey," I grinned at him. "Are you almost done?"

"Yes. I need to finish reviewing this last contract, then I'm taking you to bed."

"Well, in that case, don't let me keep you"—I smirked, kissing him—"I'm going to change and brush my teeth." I stood from his lap, walking toward my luggage to pull out my pajamas and toothbrush before heading to the bathroom.

I changed and readied myself, taking my time to allow Rhett to finish his work. Exiting the bathroom, I heard my phone ringing downstairs in the living room where I'd left it. I rushed down the steps, reaching for it before it rung off.

"Hello," I answered hastily without checking the caller ID. Nobody responded. "Hello," I tried again. Still nothing. *Maybe I missed the call.* I pulled the phone away from my face to look at the screen. The call was connected.

I moved it back to my ear to listen, "Hello?" I tried one more time. Heavy breathing broke through the silence.

What the hell?

"Ava?" Rhett's voice called from behind me.

I turned to face him, pulling the phone away from my ear. He was coming down the stairs shirtless in his pajama pants.

"You coming to bed?"

"Yeah. Sorry. One second." I glanced down at my trembling hands holding the phone. I pushed end and scrolled through the history to figure out who'd been calling. A blocked number.

"Who was that?"

"I don't know. Must've been the wrong number." I joined Rhett on the stairs, ignoring the dread the call had provoked. *What is wrong with me lately?*

He took my hand, leading us back up the narrow staircase as I followed. Rhett climbed in my bed. I crawled in behind him. He pulled me into a spooning position. Taking a deep breath, I inhaled his calming scent before closing my eyes.

"Goodnight, beautiful." His lips pressed against my head before I fell into a restless sleep.

CHAPTER 11

"I'm so tired," I complained through the muffling of my pillow as I belly flopped face first onto my bed. My internal clock was beyond confused. All I wanted to do was sleep when we finally got back to my Santa Monica apartment.

"Come here, babe."

The bed dipped as Rhett crawled onto it, rolling the dead weight of my body onto him like a blanket. My body melded into his as I lay limp across his large frame. My mind was on the verge of sleep as his fingers traced imaginary patterns on my back.

"This is my favorite spot. With you in my arms, pressed against me. I don't ever want to leave it."

A smile crept across my face, hearing his words. "Good," I mumbled into his chest, "because I don't think I can move any time soon. You may be stuck there awhile until my body and brain recover."

His body shook beneath me as he silently chuckled, before kissing my head. "I need to get some work done."

"You work too much," I groaned. "How are you not tired right now?" I forced my head to lift and look at him.

"It comes with the territory. You get used to the traveling and time changes."

"You need to rest, Rhett. It worries me how much you're working. It's non-stop."

"Don't worry about me, beautiful." He tucked some rogue hairs behind my ear.

My brow wrinkled as I gave him my best look of disapproval.

"How about I lie here with you until you fall asleep?"

"I'm not sure that's much of a compromise."

"Take it or leave it." He shifted our bodies so we were on our sides, spooning.

"I guess, if those are my only options, I'll take it." I didn't have the energy to argue with him. I closed my eyes, drifting off.

I awoke from my nap, missing the comfort of Rhett's arms. I sat up, looking around. Discovering he was no longer in the room, I got up in search of him. I could hear the wind and waves coming through the open balcony door off my living room. Rhett was sitting on a lounger with his laptop. The sun was setting over the beach, painting vibrant shades of pink and orange across the sky.

A relaxed Rhett, framed by the beautiful ocean and sunset, was an image that would be imprinted in my memory forever. I stood, absorbing the whole scene for a few moments, not wanting to disturb him or the thoughts taking hold of my mind. I wanted this. Every day. Him. Here with me. I didn't want him to go back to New York.

"Are you going to stand there all evening or are you going to get your cute ass over here in my lap?" Rhett's amused voice broke me from my revelation. He hadn't even turned around to see I was there.

I smiled sheepishly as I walked out onto the balcony. Rhett set his laptop aside. I shivered as the cool evening breeze hit my body. He pulled me down in between his legs on the lounger, wrapping me in his strong embrace. Warmth flooded me from inside out.

"Did you sleep well?" he asked, raining kisses down the side of my neck to my shoulder, causing my insides to tingle.

"Yes. Did you sleep at all?"

"No. I'll sleep tonight. Are you hungry?"

"A little, but I don't think I have much in my kitchen. I'll need to go to the store this weekend."

"Do you want to go out to eat?"

"Not really…I can order a pizza if you're okay with that. I mean, I know it's not your usual caliber of food," I teased him, looking over my shoulder at his straight face.

He pinched the ticklish spot on my side, triggering a giggle from me. "Watch it, beautiful," he warned playfully, a smile pulling at his mouth. "Pizza is fine."

I turned my head to look back out at the ocean, neither one of us moving to order the pizza. We remained silent as we watched the sun descend behind the horizon. My mind was racing, trying to decide how to broach the subject of us and what would happen after this weekend when he returned to New York.

"Talk to me, beautiful. I can hear the wheels spinning in that sexy mind of yours."

I let out a small sigh, not responding. I gave a slight shake of my head.

"Ava." My name was a command to speak. He was not letting me avoid my thoughts.

"I'm not sure how this is going to work."

His body hardened with my words. Afraid he was misunderstanding me, I turned in his arms, seeing the concern written all over his face.

"Let me rephrase that. I want this to work. I want to be with you. I just don't know how we're going to make it work...with you in New York and me here. I don't want to leave California. I love my job, the friends I've made—"

"Then I guess we should probably make sure that boss of yours makes our house a priority." The tension left his body as he smiled slyly.

"What do you mean?"

"What do you think I mean, Ava?"

I stared at him, dumbfounded. I think I knew what he meant, but I needed him to say it.

When I didn't answer, he proceeded to explain, "I have every intention of moving here. I never expected you to move to New York or leave your job. And there is no way in hell I'm being apart from you more than I have to be."

"But...your company? Your family? Your life is in New York."

"No. My life is you. And you are here, which means my life is here. As far as my family, Valerie will be moving here

169

at the end of the summer. My parents are relieved I'll be here with her. They are retired, and both of their kids will be here. I'll see them plenty."

"And your company?"

"Well, there *are* perks to being the boss," he said, grinning at me. "I opened an office in downtown L.A. —the office where we met. I'm relocating the headquarters here. It's been in the works for months. I have a few loose ends in New York to take care of, like getting someone in place to run things there. I'll still have to travel back to New York occasionally, but for the most part, things will be run from L.A."

I looked at him in disbelief. He said months. He's been working on moving here to be with me for *months*. Before he even knew if I'd take him back.

"Months?"

"Yes, Ava. I should've done it fucking years ago. But I wanted to give you the space you needed. You weren't exactly making it easy on me, either. You kept going on dates. It was driving me crazy mad to the point I wanted to kill every single one of those bastards. The thought of them touching you—"

"How did you know about my dates? Were you spying on me?" My anger began to manifest.

"No. Your family and friends threw it in my face every chance they got, telling me I was being a damn idiot for waiting. And they were right."

I looked away from him, the guilt suffocating me, once again. "Why now?" That was the one answer I didn't know. *What changed?*

When he didn't respond, I looked back at his face and saw

him struggling to answer. Different thoughts and emotions appeared then faded from his face like a mood ring.

"Rhett?" Concern grew inside me.

His face straightened to impassiveness, but I could see the emotion still in his eyes. "I couldn't allow it any longer. I couldn't be without you." His tone was matter of fact, demanding me to accept his answer.

I knew there was more he wasn't telling me. I could see it in his eyes. Not that I didn't believe his answer was true. I just knew it was only part of the truth, and he was avoiding the rest of it.

I started to push him to tell me the whole truth, but was interrupted by the ringing of his cell phone. He retrieved it from the side table, answering before I could tell him not to. He shifted, turning his body away from me, wanting privacy for the call. Hurt by his obvious dismissal and avoidance, I stood and left to order the pizza.

Since he was still on the phone, I killed some time going through a couple work emails after ordering dinner. When it seemed like he wasn't getting off the phone any time soon, I jumped in the shower, giving Rhett space to finish up whatever work he still had to do, and me space to process everything he'd told me.

I was relieved to know he'd be staying in California with me, but it was being overshadowed by the thought he was keeping something from me. The warm spray of the shower pelted my skin as I closed my eyes to rinse the conditioner from my hair.

I felt Rhett's hands settle on the hips of my naked body, causing me to flinch from the surprise of his touch. I kept my eyes closed as the warm water continued to stream down me. I stood motionless, only wanting to feel him.

He glided his hands from my hips to my lower back, moving at a steady pace upwards. I felt the heat from his body radiating inches from me.

"So beautiful." His husky whisper forced my body's craving to take over.

My heart pounded with anticipation, my breathing erratic. I inhaled a small gasp of air when I felt the warm sucking of his mouth on my breast, then sighed my displeasure when his mouth released me, only to be immediately silenced as his lips moved up my collar bone to my neck before finally landing on my lips.

He pulled our bodies together, where I could feel his hard length pressed against me. He was ready and so was I. His hands tangled in my wet hair, deepening our connection. His kiss was aggressive, using my lips as a punching bag to take out a frustration. I didn't question it. I couldn't. He was rendering me incapable of a single coherent thought.

Not able to remain idle any longer, I flung my arms around his neck. His hands moved to grasp my ass, lifting me into his arms. My legs wrapped around his lean waist as he spun us, pressing my back into shower wall, our mouths still taking each other hungrily. The cool tile sent a shiver up my spine.

He broke our kiss, breathing heavily, resting his forehead on mine. He held me in place as he tried to steady his breath.

"Open your eyes, beautiful." His voice was gruff, demanding.

I opened them instantly, desperate for him to continue the pleasure he was bringing to my body.

His magnetic eyes locked with mine. I moved my hand down the side of his jaw, trying to read him like braille with my touch. Before I could decipher his coded face, he shifted, slamming his hard length into me. My head fell back from the gratifying pain.

"Eyes, Ava," he demanded once again.

My head snapped forward, watching him as he continued to move inside me, milking the pleasure from my body. He kissed me gently. His rough assault from seconds earlier tamed. Our bodies remained fused together until our harmonious climax exploded through our gasps and heavy breathing.

~

"Do you want to talk about it?" I asked Rhett as we lay in bed after we ate. My head was on his chest as he traced his fingers over the bare skin of my back.

"There's nothing to talk about, babe."

I sighed, shifting to stare up at him. "Don't shut me out, Rhett. I know something is bothering you."

He studied me, contemplating whether to say anything. I gave him a comforting look, hoping to encourage him to open up to me.

"It's nothing you need to worry about, beautiful. I have to leave for New York early Monday morning. It'll only be a few days, and then I'll be back."

"Okay," I relented after trying to read his eyes and finding nothing. I laid my head back down and traced figure eights on his chest. "Where do you plan to stay when you get back?"

"What do you mean?"

"You know...since the house isn't done...I mean, if you don't have somewhere..."

"Are you asking me to move in with you, Ms. Conner?" I heard the amusement in his voice; he obviously found my nervous discomfort entertaining.

"Don't be so arrogant," I huffed. "I'm only saying, if you need a place to stay. You could stay here. With me."

His movement was swift as he rolled us. I was on my back as he grinned cheekily above me. "I'd love nothing more than to fall asleep every night and wake up every morning with you."

"So you'll stay here? Until your house is built?"

"Yes, beautiful. If that's what you really want."

I wrapped my hands around his neck, bringing his grinning lips to mine. Yes. That's what I really wanted. Rhett in my arms. Every day. Forever.

∾

"Ava!" Joce screamed my name when I walked into the office Monday morning. She was up and running from her desk, throwing her arms around me before I made it two steps through the door. Drew followed sluggishly behind her.

I laughed, tickled by her excitement. "Did you miss me?" I asked sarcastically as she released me.

"Eh." She shrugged her shoulder, unconcerned, before flashing her smile at me. "Maybe a little. It's hard to have girl talk with Drew."

Drew approached, hugging me as if hanging on for dear life. "Oh, thank God you're back, Ava," he said, his greeting overdramatic. "I don't think I could take any more of Joce's girl dilemmas."

"I'm glad to know I was missed." I laughed at the two of them as we all walked back toward my desk.

"Ava, good morning!" Tom came up behind Drew and Joce, who were still huddled around me. "How was your trip?"

"It was productive." That wasn't really a lie, per se. "Did you get everything I sent you from the marble manufacturer?"

"Yes, I did. Thank you again, for going on the trip. I know it was a lot of time out of your personal life. Along with being sprung on you last minute. Mr. Blackwood emailed me this morning with nothing but accolades for you. Said you exceeded his expectations."

Of course he did...was that because he had me naked before we even landed? My cheeks flushed. *Shoot me now.*

"Don't mention it, Tom."

Guilt. Nothing but guilt. I turned my eyes away from Tom, having a hard time looking him in the eye, only to catch Joce's judging eyes. Her hip was cocked to the side, arms crossed at her chest, eyebrow raised and a knowing smugness on her face.

Shit. Does she know something?

"Well, we'll give you some time to catch up." He shooed Drew and Joce back to their desks. "We'll have our Monday-morning meeting in a few hours to discuss all current projects."

"Sounds good." I took a seat at my desk, trying to busy myself and avoid Joce's laser-beam eyes.

"Ava, stop trying to ignore me," she whisper-yelled at me from her desk after Tom had returned to his office.

"I don't know what you're talking about," I whispered back, full of innocence. At least, I hoped that's how it came across.

"We're going to lunch today, so don't make any plans. I want to know all about your little trip with the brooding, sexy Mr. Blackwood."

"There's nothing to tell." I continued to refuse to look away from my computer.

"Uh huh," she said, unconvinced. "Riley came to see me while you were gone."

Shit.

That had my head twisting over to look at her. "Oh, yeah?" I failed at keeping my voice steady.

Her eyes narrowed at me, but the smirk on her face told me she wasn't truly mad. "Yes. You and I are talking at lunch."

"Fine. Just keep your mouth shut," I hissed at her. It was obvious Riley had spilled my dirty little secret. I just didn't know how much he divulged to her. I was already plotting his murder in my head.

Dropping my head down, I got to work. I had a lot to catch up on. By mid-morning, I'd finished responding to all the necessary emails and voicemails. I was actually feeling good. I'd been stressed I'd be further behind and having to work long hours, but Tom had kept his word about taking care of everything while I was gone.

After our meeting, Joce demanded we take an early lunch. I reluctantly grabbed my purse and headed out with her. Drew looked more than ecstatic that we hadn't tried to drag him along with us. He'd obviously exhausted his tolerance for girl talk over the last few weeks.

~

We ordered drinks at our favorite little café, and I trained my eyes on my menu, pretending to be hyper focused on the specials, avoiding her expectant glare.

"Ava, seriously? We both know you're going to order the same thing you always get. Quit pretending to read the menu."

She was right. I always ordered the chicken salad sandwich here. It was my favorite. "I may want to try something new. Maybe my taste changed after traveling abroad and trying new things," I answered without lifting my eyes to her.

The menu was suddenly snatched from my view. Joce had swiped it from me and now held both menus hostage.

"Are you going to make me use brute force to get you to talk? Because I will."

Jeez, she's worse than Lizzie.

"Fine. What is it you want to know?"

"The truth. All of it."

I released a frustrated sigh as I watched the other customers sitting at the patio tables near us. That was one great thing about California. The weather was pretty much always great for having lunch outdoors. I turned back to Joce. "I don't know where to start."

"How about where you already knew Riley and Rhett the night we ran into them at the bar?"

"Yes, I already knew them...Rhett and I dated three years prior to that. It ended badly. I hadn't expected to ever see

177

him again. Or at least, at the time, I'd hoped I wouldn't. When he spontaneously appeared at the meeting and then at the bar, I panicked."

"Riley said things were pretty serious between you two before."

"Remind me to kill Riley the next time he's in town."

She laughed at my threat. "If it makes you feel any better, he didn't willingly tell me. I found a picture of you, Rhett, and some blonde in a tabloid article I was reading online. Something about a love triangle. You were standing on the street in New York when I knew you were supposed to be in Italy."

Shit. Shit. Shit. Nervous apprehension quickened my heart. "Does Tom know?"

"No. He has no idea. And I doubt he reads online gossip rags," she reassured me.

"Oh God. This is going to end up blowing up in my face." I dropped my head into my palms.

"It'll be fine, Ava. Tom won't care as long as he gets to brag about the house he did in Malibu. Don't stress about it."

I nodded, not sure I felt as confident in everything working out.

"So...what's the deal with you two? Are you back together? Why were you in New York?"

"Yes. We worked things out on the plane." I grinned as I thought about the plane ride over.

Joce raised a curious eyebrow. I suppressed my delicious, dirty thoughts.

"The whole thing was more of a ploy to get me to go on a trip he'd promised me years ago. He was only using work as an excuse. Tom can never know, Joce. I'll lose my job if he finds out."

"I doubt that, Ava." She chuckled, as if my concern was absurd. "Tom loves you. But either way, your secret is safe with me."

"Thank you."

"Just don't ever keep shit like this from me ever again. We're supposed to be friends."

"I know. I'm sorry. I just panicked that night. I didn't expect to see him and Riley there. I'd barely come to terms with the fact that he was our new client."

"You're forgiven." She smiled at me. "Oh, that reminds me, speaking of your love life…Owen stopped by Friday afternoon, looking for you. I guess he hasn't heard you're off the market?"

"Ugh. *Owen*." I threw my head back momentarily. "I feel horrible about him. I meant to call him when I got back to town to let him know. I completely forgot."

"Well, you should probably let him know soon. He seemed pretty disappointed you weren't back, yet."

"I'll call him later. For now, let's stop talking about my messed-up love life. What's the deal with you and Riley?"

Her cheeks blushed a bright pink at the mention of his name. "I don't know. I really like him. We talk pretty much every night. He came to see me last weekend and promised he'd come back out soon. He also asked me to come visit him in Boston"—she sighed, lost in her thoughts—"I don't know…I feel like this is all so crazy. I mean, how is this supposed to work?"

I gave her a sympathetic look, understanding her dilemma. I'd been there only a few days ago. Our server returned, interrupting our conversation. We ordered our usual entrees.

Once he was gone, Joce continued, "Sorry, to complain. I guess you're in the same boat as me. How are you and Rhett going to make it work?"

"Well…actually, Rhett is moving here," I replied cautiously, not wanting to rub it in her face. "I wish I could offer you some sage advice. I was feeling the same way as you a few days ago. The only wisdom I have to impart on you is to talk to him about it. I know Riley is a good guy. I also know, he's the type of guy who wouldn't go through all this effort to fly across the country if he didn't have true feelings for you."

"I hope you're right, because I'm already falling for him. I've only known him for a few weeks! I'm freaking out. I must be losing my mind."

I smiled, knowing exactly how she felt. I had no room to judge. Rhett stole my heart the same way. We spent the rest of our lunch with her filling me in on her time with Riley and things that happened at work, while I told her about London and Carrara.

We chatted about random things while we walked back to the office after lunch. The café was only a few blocks from where we worked, making it one of our frequent lunch spots.

We were only a few feet from the entrance of our office when my steps faltered, unease unsettling my stomach. From the corner of my eye, I saw a figure standing eerily still across the road. I turned to look at the person, but the passing traffic blocked my view. By the time the cars cleared, there was nobody, other than the normal, moving herd of people.

I must be seeing things. I absentmindedly rubbed the goosebumps from my arms.

"Ava, you coming?" Joce stood a few feet from me, holding our office door open.

My phone buzzed in my purse, causing palpitations in my chest, my mind going to the creepy call I'd received the other night. I pulled my phone out slowly, as if it were a grenade about to detonate.

I could feel Joce's questioning eyes on me as she waited. I looked at the screen of my phone. Rhett. My body relaxed.

I'm losing it.

I looked back up at her, "I'm gonna take this. I'll be inside in a minute."

"Okay." Without a care in the world, she disappeared into our office.

I pushed the green button, connecting the call. "Hey," I said, attempting to disguise the unease I'd felt seconds earlier. I was becoming a paranoid idiot.

"Hey, beautiful. Is everything okay?"

"Yep! I'm good," I said, exaggerating the state of my well-being. "Just getting back from lunch with Joce. How is your day going?"

"Terrible. I needed to hear your voice."

I smiled. "Same here. I miss you already."

"Miss you too, babe. I should be home on Wednesday night."

I loved the way he called my place home already. "I can't wait. What time? I can make us dinner."

"It may be pretty late. I'll let you know for sure on Wednesday."

I heard a female voice interrupting him in the background. Jealousy threatening to explode. *Calm down.*

"One minute, Celeste." He responded to the female before turning his voice back to the phone. "Beautiful, I have to go. I'll call you later tonight."

"Okay," I said, trying to hide my insecurity and disappointment.

"Ava. Only you," he reassured me.

"I know. I love you."

"Love you too, beautiful."

I ended the call, took a deep breath, then walked back into the office.

CHAPTER 12

I picked up my pace, the rush of a second wind coursing through me, energizing my already tired and burning muscles. Sweat beaded down my forehead, stinging my eyes. My feet sank into the dense, damp sand as I ran along the water's edge, underneath the pier where I typically stopped to rest. It was my usual turn-around point.

I didn't normally run past the pier. I didn't normally run at night. I didn't normally ignore every instinct I had. But tonight wasn't normal. Tonight, I needed to release the stress, jealousy, and anger I was filled with. Rhett hadn't come home on Wednesday. It was now Thursday night.

He was still in New York "working." I knew I was being irrational. I knew he loved me. I knew he'd never cheat on me. But I stupidly Googled him, looking through the latest tabloids, only to find him pictured with someone I assumed was Celeste at dinner in a restaurant.

He'd told me Wednesday he needed to stay another night

for a business dinner. And I'd believed him. I still believed him. I just couldn't get that stupid voice out of my head. The one that made me feel insecure. I hated that feeling, that voice.

In my defense, I only Googled to make sure there were no more incriminating pictures of me that had the potential to cost me my job. There weren't. Knowing that now, I wished I'd never Googled to start with. *Damn you, Google.*

My lungs tightened in my chest. My breaths were strained, my already-screaming lungs ready to burst. I pushed myself through the pain, surrendering myself to the angry pounding of my feet, letting the energy free from my body.

The cool, night air cleared my head. I was feeling better, and I knew I should turn around. I slowed my sprint, coming to a stop on the beach. I dropped my head between my legs as I folded my tired body forward. I stood bent over while I caught my breath.

After my breathing slowed, I raised myself back into an upright position, putting my hands on my hips, staring across the dark ocean as the moon glistened over it. The cool ocean breeze felt good on my sweaty, heated skin, helping me with my cool down.

I needed to get back to my apartment. I hadn't bothered bringing my phone, not wanting to be interrupted on my run. And, if I was honest, I was avoiding Rhett. I needed to get my head straight, and if he had called, I might have said things I didn't mean.

I turned back in the direction of my apartment. My body was aching. It was going to be a long walk back. I wish I'd brought my phone now...if only to call an Uber to take me home. I cut across the beach toward the paved trail. It'd be an easier walk than the sand.

It was late and there were very few people around—a drastic contrast to the normally busy, crowded beach and trail during the day. I continued to walk, my mind wandering. She was pretty. If she wasn't, I probably wouldn't have been as upset. I tried reasoning with myself. But the truth was, when it came to Rhett, I'd always feel unworthy of him. It was the one thing I was determined to change. I needed to talk to Rhett about Celeste, if only to ease my active imagination.

I was a few blocks from my apartment when heavy footsteps fell in behind me. I didn't look back, knowing it was likely someone going for an evening stroll.

My building came into view ahead of me. The footsteps picked up their pace, closing the distance between us. My blood turned cold and the hairs on my nape stood. My heart pounded in my chest. Instinct kicked in. *Run.* I bolted like a deer being chased by a hunter, letting the paranoia take over my body.

I didn't look back. My legs carried me, wild with fear. Adrenaline rushed through me, numbing my previously worn-out body. I hit the street pavement, headed for the safety of my apartment. Rounding the corner of my building, I looked back to see if they were following me, not slowing my stride.

I collided with a hard figure. Strong arms wrapped around me, trapping me. A piercing scream ripped through my throat. My arms instinctively thrashed out punching, fighting to get away.

"What the hell?! Calm down! Ava!"

My arms ceased. My body froze. My mind tried to catch up to what was happening. *Rhett.* Tears burst through as I clenched my fists on his shirt, burying my face in his chest, heaving and shaking. He continued to hold me close.

"Ava, what's wrong? What happened?" He forced his voice to stay calm as he interrogated me, but I could hear the stress.

My tears slowed. I shook my head as my breathing came out hitched. *I'm crazy that's what's wrong. I'm losing my freaking mind.* "Nothing," I mumbled, my face still pressed to his chest.

He peeled me away from his body, holding my shoulders as he peered down at my tear-stricken face. "That wasn't nothing. Tell me what happened."

I shook my head, no.

He looked over my shoulders, past my weak body, scanning the dark street. When he didn't see anything, he looked back at me, worry written all over his face. "Let's get you inside."

He picked up his luggage, which he must have dropped when I collided with him, then draped his arm around my shoulders to escort me into the apartment.

$\sim$

I leaned back on my couch after taking a shower. Rhett was in the kitchen, getting me a glass of water. I pulled my knees to my chest, wrapping my arms around them protectively. I was still shaken up, even though I told myself it was only my imagination. Nobody was chasing me.

He joined me in my tiny living room, handing me the

glass of water. He sat on the coffee table in front of me, still wearing his rumpled suit, minus the jacket and tie. He looked tired. I'm sure he came home wanting to go to bed, but instead, had to deal with me being an emotional mess.

"Are you ready to talk now?" he asked softly as he rubbed my arm, comforting me.

"Are you?" I accused him.

His hand stopped its movement. "What's that supposed to mean, Ava?"

"Nothing."

Everything. I needed answers. Answers and truths he'd been avoiding. He released a frustrated sigh as he rubbed his hands over his face and through his hair.

"Why were you running at night?"

"I needed to burn off some energy and clear my head."

"By yourself? You know I don't like you doing that."

"Well, maybe you should've been here," I snapped at him.

His face dropped with remorse. I didn't mean that. I was lashing out at him for no good reason. He ignored my comment.

"You should've at least had your phone with you. It wasn't smart or safe, leaving without it."

"I didn't want to be disturbed." I was being hateful. Defiant. I needed to let it go. I knew he was right.

"So turn it to silent. Damn it, Ava!" His aggravation broke through his calm, controlled façade. "What are you so pissed about? Tell me what's going on."

I turned my head away from him, angry tears making an unwanted appearance. I hated that I was an angry crier. I took deep breaths, getting them under control.

187

"I'm sorry. I'm being terrible. I know I'm being terrible. I'm mad at myself, not you."

"Why? Talk to me, beautiful." His deep voice softened. He moved his hand to my chin, turning me to face him.

"I saw a photo online of you and another woman having dinner last night," I sighed, defeated. He nodded his understanding.

"Celeste. She's the one I'm in the process of training to take over the New York office."

"It was just the two of you in the picture."

"Ava, babe. I haven't seen the picture, but I assume it was taken early in the evening before the guy we were meeting with arrived. She's working on a deal for me. He wanted us both present to discuss it. Otherwise, I would've come home and let her handle it on her own. You have nothing to worry about. You're the only one for me. I don't see anyone else." His thumb rubbed back and forth across my chin as he spoke. "Is that why you decided to run at night and leave your phone behind?"

I nodded.

"Will you tell me what had you scared?"

"It was nothing. Just my imagination."

His hypnotic blue eyes pierced my soul as he searched for the truth. He watched me as if he knew what I was hiding from him. "I don't want you running alone anymore. I'll go with you."

"And if you're not here?" I challenged.

"Then someone from my security team will go with you. I'll have someone permanently assigned to you."

"Rhett, no," I stiffened. "I don't need a body guard. You're being ridiculous."

"It's not up for discussion, Ava."

"It most certainly is!"

"No. It's not. Don't argue this," he warned.

"This is absurd! Why are you insisting on this?"

"Why were you running scared?"

Damn it. He wasn't going to let this go, until I told him. "If I tell you, will you call off the guard dogs?"

"I'm not making any promises until I know why."

"You're so fucking frustrating, you know that?" I rolled my eyes, looking away from him.

"Mouth, beautiful. Tell me."

I shook my head, exasperated with the man sitting in front of me, but so freaking in love with him. He'd do anything to protect me and keep me safe.

"I thought someone was following me."

"Why would you think that?" His question was expected, but there was a cautiousness in his voice, which told me he probably already knew. I turned my eyes to his, looking for answers while I spoke.

"I don't know...I think I'm probably just crazy." I hesitated, recalling the last few weeks. "I keep feeling like someone is watching me or following me. I haven't actually seen anyone. It's literally just a feeling. I'm being paranoid. It's nothing for you to worry about."

He stood, moving to the other side of the living room, one hand on his hip and the other rubbing the back of his neck as he paced the small area, deep in thought. My eyes followed him.

He looked so sexy, brooding across the room. My mind and body told me I was done with talking. I wanted to be distracted from the last few hours and forget they ever

189

happened. I wanted him in my bed. It'd been days since we'd seen each other.

Before I could make my move, he turned, facing me with a determined look. "I'm assigning a security detail to you."

"Rhett—"

"Ava, we aren't discussing it any further. I'm not willing to take risks when it comes to your safety."

"I'm not comfortable with a stranger following me around."

"What about Jim?"

"Jim? I thought he was a driver."

Jim had never come across as a security guard to me, unlike the other, more intimidating ones I'd seen at the Blackwood residences. Sure, he looked built and fit, especially at his age, but he was much more approachable.

"He's both." He smiled, knowing my thoughts. "Don't let his kind demeanor fool you. He's lethal. A former Navy Seal and MMA fighter. My father chose him to be my driver and security guard because of it. The others were a little too scary looking for a young child."

"I don't feel right about asking Jim to move across the country."

"He's already moving here with me."

"I feel like you're overacting to my paranoia."

He took a seat in front of me on the coffee table once again, grasping my hands with his, pulling them away from where they still wrapped around my bent knees. "Humor me, babe." A small smile pulled at his lips.

I couldn't help but smile back at him. His sexy smile had a way of doing that to me, no matter how infuriating he was.

"Is this only because of what I told you?" I opened the door for him to tell me whatever it was he knew.

"No. I always intended to assign Jim to you."

"Why?"

"Ava, being with me comes with certain exposure. There are a lot of crazy people out there. I know you like your independence, and I hate that us being together takes some of that away. But it's necessary. As much as I want to be, I can't always be with you to protect you at all times."

I didn't know if it was the only reason. I still got the sense he wasn't telling me everything. But I knew what he was saying was true. Everyone in his family had their own security detail.

"Will you at least give me some time to process?"

"Sure, beautiful. It'll take me a few days to get Jim moved here. Just promise me you won't go running at night by yourself."

"I promise." I hadn't planned to anyway, so the promise was an easy one. "Now will you take me to bed?" I grinned.

"That's a given." He tugged my arms forward until I was draped over his shoulder. I giggled with eagerness as he marched us to bed, where we put the night's events out of our minds, drowned in sensation.

～

Friday morning, we had another knock-out battle about him taking me to and picking me up from work. We finally compromised on him taking me to lunch, after I pointed out he could potentially be held up at work, stranding me without a ride.

I'd planned to wait for him on the sidewalk at lunch time, since it would look suspicious to Tom if I had an unexpected lunch with our new client—without Tom or his knowledge. My plan was foiled the moment Rhett sauntered confidently through the door, looking delectable as always. I was momentarily distracted from my discontent by the racy thoughts running through my head.

He showed no hesitation walking straight up to my desk to retrieve me. His eyes were husky with lust. My eyes widened. I silently pleaded with him not to kiss me, no matter how much I actually wanted him to kiss me.

"Beautiful," Rhett greeted me with his naughty, naughty smile.

Oh. God. He was going to have me melting into a puddle right here in my chair. I was already feeling needy.

"Mr. Blackwood?" Tom's voice came from behind me. *Shit. Get ahold of yourself, Ava.* "I didn't realize you were coming in today."

I straightened my back and looked away from Rhett, pretending to busy myself, because I had no idea what else to do. Rhett raised a curious eyebrow at me before turning toward my approaching boss.

"Tom." Rhett reached out his hand to shake my boss's. "My apologies for the unexpected visit."

I glanced past the two of them—praying Rhett didn't give me up—to look at Joce, who was watching the whole exchange like it was the best new drama on TV with a shit-eating grin on her face. All she needed was a box of popcorn to go with her blatant enjoyment of my discomfort. I glared at her, and she gave me a shrug of her shoulder, showing no sympathy. *Some friend.*

"I was in the neighborhood and stopped by to offer to take Ms. Conner to lunch. I wanted to thank her for everything."

"That's very generous of you, Mr. Blackwood. Ava, take your time at lunch. No need to rush back," Tom said, giving me his approval.

Of course, he did. All he saw was his children's private-school tuition when he looked at Rhett. I wouldn't be surprised if he billed my lunch time with Rhett as a business meeting.

"Thank you, Tom," I replied, keeping my gaze off Rhett. I didn't trust my body to not give me away.

"Ms. Conner, shall we?" Rhett offered his hand to help me up from my desk.

"Right." I nervously moved to grab my purse as Tom stood watching us. I ignored Rhett's hand, helping myself up, walking past him straight for the door, leaving him to follow.

He caught up to me, opening the door for me. He snatched my hand with his as soon as we hit the sidewalk outside my office. I glared at him before glancing back to make sure Tom hadn't seen. Luckily, Tom had already turned to walk back to his office.

"Rhett, you're going to get me fired. You should've waited in the car for me."

"That's ridiculous. I will not hide from Tom, Ava."

"Not even if it means costing the woman you love her job?" I asked hopefully as he opened the passenger door for me.

His brows pinched together. "He won't fire you."

"He might." I slid into the seat.

"Ava, you need to tell Tom. That's the last time I'm

pretending our relationship is purely professional."

"I can't. What am I supposed to tell him? What if he wants to take me off the project?"

"You can, and you will. I don't care what you tell him as long as he knows we're together. He won't take you off the project."

"How do you know?"

"Because I'll make sure of it." He leaned in, giving me a peck on the lips, before shutting my door and joining me in the car.

Arrogant bastard. What am I going to tell Tom? Maybe I can just avoid future lunches and meetings with Rhett. Who am I kidding?

"Can you at least pretend until after your house is built? I'll tell him as soon as we're done working on the project." I buckled my seatbelt.

"No. Either you tell him, or I will."

Well, shit.

～

"I need to go inside," I panted as I broke our kiss. My hair was disheveled, my lips swollen.

We were making out like a couple of randy teenagers in his car after lunch. I'd at least convinced him to park down the road from my office, slightly concerned Tom might come back from lunch and catch us. If I was honest, the thrill of getting caught made it a little more exciting as we kissed and groped.

"And I need to be inside you," Rhett said, pulling my lips back to his.

I didn't resist, allowing him to kiss and grope me a little longer. His hand coasted up my thigh under my skirt. My head fell back on the headrest as his fingers pushed inside me, and his lips found their way to my neck.

"Seriously, Rhett. I need to get back to work," I pleaded unconvincingly, heavy breathing escaping my lips.

"Hush, beautiful. I'm working."

I closed my eyes, letting him work—massage, rub, stroke—his fingers masterfully.

My moans increased as he brought my body to its precipice. My hands gripped his broad shoulders, needing something to hold onto as he took me over the edge.

"Oh...my...shit!" I gasped as my orgasm rolled through me.

Rhett released a throaty chuckle in my neck as I tried bringing my breathing to a normal pace. His relentless lips were not making it easy.

"I'll let that one slide." He flashed his wicked grin at me, referring to my foul language.

I slapped his shoulder weakly, my body still recovering from his exploitation. Opening the mirror of the visor, I checked my appearance before heading back into the office. It was worse than I thought. I looked like I'd been royally fucked—my hair a mess, lips abused, cheeks flushed.

"I look terrible."

"You look beautiful."

I rolled my eyes as I tried my best to fix my wild hair. All the while, Rhett watched, grinning at me proudly. After a few minutes of trying to straighten my hair, I dropped my hands, giving up. It was useless. This was his fault. He showed no remorse, laughing at my disgruntled face.

"Come on, babe. I'll walk you to the office." He took my hand, kissing my knuckles. Heat and tingles radiated from them like ripples in water. He released my hand, stepping out of the car. I watched him as he walked around the front, straightening his jacket, his confidence unshakeable. He opened the passenger door, helping me out.

He walked me to my office, grasping my hand tightly in his. I tried more than once to break free, with each step bringing us closer to the door. Every time, he gripped tighter.

"Stop it, Ava," he warned.

I huffed. "What if he sees us?"

"Good. Then you'll have no excuse not to tell him."

"Please, Rhett," I begged. We were only a couple feet from the storefront of my office, where we would soon be visible from inside. His movement was sudden, pulling me to the side of the building and into an alleyway. My back landed against the stucco wall, his body pressed against mine, holding me in place.

His eyes dropped to my parting lips. I instantly wanted him all over me, after moments ago wanting to separate us. *How does he do that?*

"Compromise?" he offered.

"What do you propose?" I proceeded cautiously. I knew his compromises usually ended in him getting his way anyway.

He hesitated.

"I need you to ask Joce to go out for drinks tonight."

The shock of his request had me less cautious and more confused. Rhett wouldn't normally ask me to go out for drinks, especially without him.

"Why would you want me to do that?"

"I don't necessarily want you to, but I owe Riley. He's coming into town tonight and plans to surprise her. He wants to make sure he knows where she is when he arrives. We both plan to meet up with you."

"So he wants me to keep tabs on her? Be his spy?" I smiled, straightening the lapels of his jacket, excited and thrilled for my friend. Riley really did like her if he was going through all this effort.

"Not necessarily a spy. He only wants to make sure nothing goes wrong."

"Okay. Though, I'm kind of surprised you're even getting involved in this little plan."

"What can I say? You've made me a believer. Plus, like I said, I owe him." His playful demeanor became more serious. "Promise me you won't drink until I get there."

"How am I supposed to ask her for drinks and then not drink? That'll look suspicious."

He contemplated this. "One drink."

"Okay," I agreed. He wouldn't know if I had more than one, anyway. It's not like I planned to throw them back haphazardly. "I should get back to work."

"Same." He pressed his lips to mine before stepping away, allowing me to push my needy body away from the wall. "Text me where you two decide to go. I'll meet you after work."

"Okay."

"Be safe, beautiful." His words and eyes were heavy with concern.

"Always."

CHAPTER 13

The bar was packed with Friday-night partygoers and business professionals with drunken ambitions. We decided on the Luxxe Martini bar downtown. I suggested the location due to the proximity to Rhett's office. He'd texted earlier he was going to be late, so I wanted to make sure it was close enough he could get here without getting stuck in L.A. traffic.

Riley had already landed and was in route. Joce and I parted ways when we walked into the bar. She set out in search of a table, while I headed to the wooden, oval-shaped bar to order our martinis. It sat in the middle of the space, with an island in the center holding a tower of glass shelves decorated with liquor bottles and colored lights.

I bellied up to the bar, looking around as I waited patiently for the bartender to make his way to me. The Luxxe was a trendy dive bar—stylish but mellow. The lighting was dim and intimate, making me yearn for Rhett to make his appearance, so I could cuddle up in his lap in a dark corner.

I watched the bartender work efficiently, mixing and shaking our martinis into delicious perfection. He handed me our drinks and I opened a tab, leaving to find Joce.

She'd snagged us a location with a perfect view of the entry. Joce and I chatted as we drank our martini cocktails. Mine went down a little too fast, and I was desperately wanting another. Joce still had half a drink, so I left her to hold the table, while I went for another round. Two wouldn't hurt. I'd stop after two, I decided.

I stepped up to the bar and ordered myself another round, idly standing, waiting for the bartender to return with my drink.

"Glad to see you're alive and well."

I flinched from the voice beside me, shame sinking my heart to my stomach. I turned to face an unhappy Owen leaning against the bar next to me.

"I guess that means you're just avoiding me."

"Owen. I'm sorry. I've been meaning to call you."

"Right. I get the hint."

"No, seriously. I've just been busy since I got back and—"

"Save your excuses, Ava. I'm not desperate. I'm not going to beg for a date." His words came out angry. "I just thought you'd at least give me the courtesy of not leading me on."

"Owen—"

"Have a nice life, Ava." He hesitated a moment, looking past me before turning his back on me, walking away.

I sank back against the bar, watching him disappear into the densely packed bodies. *Damn it.* That was not how I wanted that conversation to play out. I should've called him sooner. I turned back to the bar, picking up my martini that had unknowingly appeared, shaking off my humiliation.

I watched the entrance for Riley, anticipating his arrival. I listened as Joce talked, but was having a hard time focusing on her words, feeling lightheaded. The martini must've been stronger than I was used to. I knew I was a lightweight, but I hadn't even gotten halfway through my second drink.

When the dizziness wasn't subsiding, I decided to get some water. Getting up from the table, I told Joce I'd be right back. My body felt heavy as I attempted to walk to the bar.

I stumbled. The room spun. My mind was foggy. My body weakened. My vision blurred. I saw a hazy body coming toward me. I closed my eyes, trying to refocus them. I opened them—transfixed on a worried Riley running at me as I felt my body collapsing.

My body hit the ground hard. I couldn't move. I heard a yelling Riley and a terrified Joce. Then everything went black.

&

There was a steady beeping. It reminded me of the sound I heard before my father took his last breaths. My body felt weighted. There was nothing but blackness and deep, angry voices yelling in the distance. I felt a small warm hand clasped with mine. I wiggled my fingers.

"Ava?" A tiny grief-stricken voice spoke my name.

I tried opening my eyes, but I was blinded by a harsh bright light and closed them instantly.

"Ava, can you hear me?"

"Hmm," I moaned. I couldn't speak. My mouth was dry and throat sore.

"Rhett! She's waking up," the tiny voice called.

I now recognized it as Joce. The yelling in the distance ceased. The sound of Rhett's name had me forcing my eyes to open. I wanted to see him.

I squinted, letting my eyes adjust to the blinding light as his strong hand covered mine.

"Ava? Beautiful?" His voice was hoarse.

"Rhett," I tried to speak, but my own voice cracked.

"Yes, babe. I'm here. Joce, get her some water."

I opened my eyes fully as they adjusted, staring up at his strained face. Over his shoulder, Joce was pouring a glass of water and a distraught Riley stood in the doorway.

"I'll get the doctor," Riley offered.

Rhett ignored him, the tension between them tangible. Joce handed Rhett the cup of water.

"Here, beautiful. Drink this." He passed it to me then helped me sit up.

I drank as they both watched me intently, making me feel self-conscious. I finished the water as a gray-haired man, whom I assumed was the doctor, walked into the room, followed by a nurse and Riley.

"Ms. Conner, I'm Dr. Montgomery," he introduced himself. "We're just going to check your vitals really quick and then go over a few things. How are you feeling?"

"Okay, I guess."

The nurse moved, taking my blood pleasure and temperature. The doctor waved a light in my eyes and listened to my heart as Rhett sat on the other side of the bed holding my hand. Riley and Joce were wrapped in each other's arms, standing across the room.

The silence was making me uneasy. I racked my brain trying to figure out how I ended up in the hospital. "What happened?" I finally asked, not able to take the silence and solemn mood in the room.

Dr. Montgomery rolled a stool up beside the bed, taking a seat. "Ms. Conner, you arrived here in and out of consciousness. Your body was immobile, and you weren't responsive. We took a blood test and found traces of the drug Rohypnol."

"Rohypnol?"

"Yes, more commonly known as roofies or the date-rape drug."

"I don't understand. How?"

"Well, that's something we're hoping you can help answer. The police are waiting outside to ask you some questions."

"I don't know. I..." I glanced at Rhett for help.

"Ava, did you ever leave your drink unattended?"

I tried to recall the night's events. The last thing I remembered was returning from the bar after ordering my second drink. I don't remember ever leaving it, or the first one.

"No. I didn't. I had it the whole time."

"Did anybody ever approach you? Maybe distract you from your drink? Try to hit on you? Anybody you saw or talked to who could have wanted to do this?"

I shook my head as I searched my brain for answers. We had barely been there an hour. I was with Joce the whole time. Nobody had approached me except...no. No way. He'd never do that. Owen was a good guy. I looked away from Rhett and down at my hands.

"No," I lied.

Joce shift uncomfortably in Riley's arms. She looked at me as if she wanted to say something, but decided not to.

Rhett let out a frustrated sigh.

"I'm sorry," I apologized to Rhett.

"Don't apologize, beautiful." He took my face in the palm of his hand.

Two police officers knocked on the open door. "Are you up for a few questions, Ms. Conner?"

I nodded my head. They entered the room, going over questions similar to the ones Rhett had already asked me. I gave them the same answers, knowing I was no help at all. They thanked me for my time, and said they would let me know if they found out anything. They handed me a business card with a number to call if I remembered anything else.

After the police, doctor, and nurse left, the four of us sat quietly in my hospital room. Riley glanced over at Rhett, breaking the silence. "I'm going to take Joce home. I'll stop by the bar and question the bartender working that night. See if I can find out anything."

Rhett stood, turning on him, seething as he stared him down. "You've done enough, Riley. I don't need your help," he scowled. I was surprised by his reaction, having no idea why he was so angry with his friend.

"Rhett, I told you I'm sorry."

"Leave, Riley. Before I put you in your own hospital bed." Rhett's fists clenched at his sides, and Riley's body went rigid, his own temper starting to flare.

"Rhett. What the hell is going on?" I asked, sitting up

further in the bed in case I needed to leap out and stop him from pummeling his lifelong friend.

"You should've never been there, Ava. If it wasn't for him, you wouldn't have been."

"Rhett, this isn't Riley's fault."

"Don't bother, Ava," Riley interjected. "Let him be angry with me. It won't be the first time he refuses to take any of the blame."

Rhett stepped forward, ready to hit Riley.

"Stop it!" I yelled, slinging my upper body forward, halting him.

Riley shook his head, glaring at Rhett before grabbing Joce's hand to leave. Joce looked back at me with a sad expression. I hated her surprise visit had been ruined.

"I'll call you later," she mouthed as they left the room, leaving Rhett and me by ourselves.

I watched Rhett as he paced the room, trying to calm himself. He looked exhausted, like he hadn't slept in days.

How long have I been out?

"Come here." I patted the mattress beside me as I shifted over to make room for him.

He stopped his movement, turning toward me. His hardened face softened as he looked into my eyes. He climbed into my tiny hospital bed next to me. I rolled on my side, so we laid facing each other. He wrapped an arm around me, pulling me closer.

"How do you feel?"

"Like shit."

"Ava." His typical warning was weak.

"What? I don't get a pass?" I teased him, trying to lighten the mood.

He gave me a small smile and then kissed me, sweetly. I brought my hand to his face, dragging the backs of my fingers along the rough stubble on his jaw.

"It's not Riley's fault. Don't take this out on your friend."

He let out a heavy sigh, rolling to his back, shifting us, so I could rest my head on his chest. He kept one arm around me, while the other slipped under his head. "If anything would've happened to you...if someone had touched you, taken you."

"Nothing happened, because of Riley. He got to me before anyone else did."

"You would've never been in that position if he hadn't asked...if *I* hadn't asked...damn it! I know it's as much my fault. I allowed you to be at risk. *I* put you at risk."

"Rhett. Stop it. Please. It's not your fault and it's not Riley's. I'm not going to live in a bubble. It doesn't matter *why* I ended up at the bar. It could've been as simple as me wanting a girls' night out."

He didn't respond immediately. "Jim will be here in the morning. You won't be going anywhere without one of us with you."

There was no point in arguing. His worst fear had just come true. We'd compromise later. Instead, I changed the subject.

"When is the last time you slept?"

"Thursday night."

"What day is it?"

"Saturday night." I lifted my head to stare at his worn face.

"You need to sleep."

"I know, babe. I will, now you're okay and in my arms."

I dropped my head back to his chest, closing my eyes. I listened to his beating heart and let his breathing soothe me.

"I love you, Rhett Blackwood."

"I love you too, Ava Conner." He kissed the top of my head, before we both fell asleep.

~

Sunday, Rhett barely let me out of his sight. He even ignored work for the day, spending every minute with me. The only privacy he gave me was to call my mom. He'd called her on the way to the hospital and assured her he'd fly her out, if it was serious. She was in hysterics when she first answered the phone, but I was able to calm her. Knowing Rhett was with me helped her rest easier.

I knew he still felt guilty about asking me to go for drinks with Joce. It didn't seem to matter how many times I tried to convince him it wasn't his fault. He did finally give Riley a call Sunday night to apologize.

It was something, at least. I wouldn't be able to accept their friendship ending over something that neither of them could control.

Monday morning came quickly. Jim was waiting outside my apartment to take me to work. As ridiculous as it seemed, I didn't argue with Rhett. I'd go along with his crazy protectiveness for now, but at some point, we were going to have to set boundaries.

I begged and pleaded for Jim to drop me a few blocks away from my office. He didn't give into my charm, but he did finally agree to park a few yards away, where nobody—

Tom—could see me getting out of the fancy town car from inside my office.

I never had an opportunity to tell Tom on Friday about mine and Rhett's relationship. Okay...it wasn't so much there was *never an opportunity*, rather, I just didn't want to. I couldn't help it. Every time I ran conversation through my head, I imagined it either ending very awkwardly, or me being fired, or both.

I had already decided, if by chance Drew or Tom saw me getting out of the town car with Jim, I'd claim my car was in the shop, and he was an Uber driver. In his fancy town car, Jim looked nothing like an Uber driver, but I hoped they wouldn't notice.

I opened the door to my office and Joce's head popped up immediately, locking her eyes with mine. She gave me a forced smile as a greeting, remaining unusually quiet. I walked to my desk nervously. We hadn't talked since she'd left the hospital with Riley.

"Hey." I smiled softly once I made it to my desk.

"Hey." She glanced at me momentarily before refocusing on her work.

Things had never been awkward between us, and I hadn't been prepared for this.

"Do you want to go grab a coffee?" I asked, not being able to stand not knowing what the deal was. We needed to talk, and we couldn't do it here.

"Sure."

We both stood, not bothering to ask Drew. He had his headphones in his ears and a coffee cup already on his desk. We forced small talk as we crossed the street to the nearest

Starbucks. After ordering our drinks, we stood off to the side waiting for the barista.

"So..." I attempted to get her to say what was on her mind.

"So..." she said in response, pausing momentarily. "Look, Ava, I'm just going to come out and say it."

"Okay?"

"I think you should tell Rhett."

"Tell Rhett what?"

"About Owen."

"I don't know what you mean." I knew what she meant. I just hadn't realized she knew.

"Ava, Owen was at the bar that night. You guys talked. I saw you. And it didn't look like a pleasant conversation from where I was sitting...or do you not remember?"

I definitely remembered, but I was definitely not telling Rhett. There was no way it was Owen. I couldn't believe she would think for a minute it was.

"Joce, it wasn't Owen."

"How do you know that?"

"I just do. He's not the type of guy to do something like that."

"He looked pretty upset when you guys were talking."

"Of course he was. I'd blown him off without even an explanation. He had every right to be."

The barista called our names. We grabbed our drink orders, but didn't head straight back to the office and instead found a small table to sit at.

"Joce, honestly, I just want to forget about the whole thing."

"I don't like it, Ava."

Nervous fear spiked in me. "Did you say something to Riley?"

"No. I wanted to talk to you about it first."

"Please don't say anything. If Rhett finds out, he will kill him without a thought."

"That might not be a bad thing."

"It would be a terrible thing! I don't want to go around accusing an innocent man—someone I previously hurt Rhett with by dating."

"Fine, Ava. I won't say anything...but I think you should still consider it." I could see the concern in her eyes.

"Thank you."

"Sure. Just don't make me regret it." She raised her disapproving brow at me, signaling my weak smile lacked reassurance.

~

Once we were back at the office, things felt back to normal. I focused on my work, drawing up the house plans for Rhett's Malibu home. Tom wanted a set of drawings to review by the end of the week. I'd already completed the floor plan and was working on the exterior elevations when my phone vibrated on my desk.

R: I'll pick you up for lunch. x

Crap. As tempting as that sounded, it would be disastrous. I wouldn't be able to hide that I hadn't told Tom about us. I needed to keep Rhett away from Tom, until I could figure out a way to tell him.

A: I need to work through lunch. x

R: I'll bring food to you.

A: You'll just distract me. I'll get nothing done.

R: Are you avoiding me, beautiful?

A: Never. Just trying to get your house done.

R: It can wait. I'm in no hurry to move out of my current arrangement.

Shit. How am I going to argue with that? The man was impossibly determined.

A: Fine. I'll meet you somewhere.

R: Are you hiding me?

A: Nope. Only making sure Jim is earning the big salary I'm sure you're paying him ;) Text me time and place. x

When he didn't immediately respond, I set my phone down and went back to work. A few minutes later my phone vibrated again. I picked it back up, expecting it to be Rhett texting me where to meet.

O: Sorry about being an ass the other night. I hope you're okay. A little freaked out seeing you be rushed off in an ambulance.

O: If you never want to speak to me again, I get it. At least, let me know you're okay.

I reread his texts twice. Relief washed over me. There was no way it was Owen, and I was thankful I hadn't said anything. A small part of me had questioned whether I should tell Rhett after my conversation with Joce. But after getting his text, I was glad I hadn't.

A: I'm okay. Thank you for apologizing. I'd still like to explain why I didn't call, if you're willing...coffee sometime?

O: Sounds good. Let me know time and place.

Before I could reply, the front door to our office opened. My head popped up with Joce's and Drew's. Rhett strutted through the door like a cocky peacock.

Damn him! I jumped from my seat, hastily grabbing my purse and phone. I had to get him out of here fast. I glanced back toward Tom's office. He hadn't noticed we had a visitor, yet. *Thank God.* I moved quickly around my desk, telling Joce I was off to lunch. I grabbed Rhett's arm, pulling him with me hurriedly. The man was like a boulder.

"Joce." He greeted her with a smile as I yanked on his arm, ineffectively moving him toward the door. He was in no hurry to leave.

"Rhett, we should go," I tried persuading him while looking toward Tom's office. He was on the phone. For once, the gods were on my side.

"Excuse us Joce, apparently my girl is in a hurry."

Shit. I glanced at Drew. He already had his head back down with his earbuds in, blessedly oblivious to my struggles.

Joce grinned at him mischievously, waving her fingers. "Enjoy your lunch you two."

With that Rhett finally turned, allowing me to pull him out the door. We barely made it past the storefront when he turned, pinning me to the wall.

"You're still hiding me."

"No, I'm not. I just have a lot of work to do. I need to make this a quick lunch."

"Don't lie to me, beautiful." He smirked.

"Ugh…fine. I haven't told Tom."

He cocked his head at me.

"I will. Just give me a few days."

"Okay. You have until Friday." He released me from the wall, clasping my hand with his as we walked toward his car.

"Friday, huh? Why are you being so generous?"

He laughed his guttural laugh. "What makes you think I have ulterior motives?"

"Don't you always?" I raised my eyebrow at him.

A boyish grin overtook his face. He was definitely up to something. "Maybe. I need you to take some time off. At least a week."

"Rhett, no! I barely got back to work after vacationing for two weeks."

"Technically, that was work, not a vacation."

"No it—okay, yes. But we both know it wasn't much work. Why do you need me to take time off, anyway?" I asked as I slid inside his overpriced, fancy car.

"I have to go to New York for an extended period of time." He kissed my cheek, shutting the door with his response.

New York? I was not taking time off work just so he could work. That's ridiculous. He joined me in the car, starting the engine before buckling his seat belt.

"I'm not going." I looked at him pointedly.

"Of course you are. We won't be leaving for a couple weeks. That's plenty of time for you to put in your request."

"No, Rhett. I'm not taking off another week of work so you can keep tabs on me while *you* work."

"It won't be all work." He winked.

"Stop it. You're trying to use sex against me, again."

"Is it working?"

"No." It was…but I wasn't telling him that.

"What about using your friends?"

"What do you mean?" I looked at him curiously.

"Mike's restaurant is having its soft opening. I need to be

there. And I figured you'd want to be there, also, to support him and Lizzie."

Okay. That worked. "You're the investor."

"Yes. He has talent. It was an easy investment to make." He pulled away from the curb onto the road.

"I'm glad it's you." My defiance was only temporarily suppressed. "But that's only one night, why do we need to stay the whole week?"

"Will there ever come a day when you don't argue, beautiful?"

I couldn't help but laugh at his question. "Will there ever come a day you don't try to trick me into doing what you want?"

He glanced over at me, and his roguish grin and glinting blues told me it wasn't likely. *Same here.* He moved his hand to my lap, intertwining his fingers with mine as he drove us the rest of the way to the restaurant. Both of us dropped the debate, for now.

CHAPTER 14

"I can't believe that's why you refuse to eat a banana in public," Joce managed through fits of giggling.

"You're so ridiculous, Drew," I said through my own belly-aching laughter. Joce and Drew were providing their usual comedic relief during our lunch.

"You've been warned, ladies. If you ever look a man in the eye while eating a banana, only one thought will be going through his mind." He gestured, pumping his fist to his mouth while pressing his tongue to the inside of his cheek.

"It only took that one time for me. As soon as our eyes locked, I could see the filthy thoughts all over his face"—he shuddered—"and I prefer no man imagines me that way. He was big, too. All tatted up. I feared for my life." His face was serious as Joce and I tried not to fall out of our chairs.

"Poor Drew. Such a delicate flower," Joce sing-songed, taunting him.

"Stop! You may have ruined bananas for me." My laughter was uncontrollable.

"Not me. Next time Riley's in town, I'm getting a couple dozens of them." Joce smiled wickedly.

"You're the worst, Joce." I shook my head at her.

"Yeah we don't need to hear about what you do behind closed doors."

"Well, at least I'm getting some. It's obvious the only thing you do behind closed doors is eat bananas," she mocked Drew.

Our server approached, dropping our checks as our laughter subsided. "When will Riley be back?" I asked Joce.

"Not for another few weeks." She pouted as we paid our checks.

"Did you ever talk to him?"

"No. I feel like it's too early to talk about *our future*. I don't want to scare him away."

"You two are ruining my good mood," Drew interjected.

I nudged his shoulder for his lack of sensitivity.

"Shouldn't you be giving me advice from a male perspective? Otherwise what good is it having a guy friend?" Joce reprimanded.

"Hey, I didn't sign up for this shit when I took this job. When is Tom going to hire another dude? We need more testosterone."

"You have Tom," I pointed out.

"Tom doesn't count. He's just as emotional as the two of you lately."

I rolled my eyes at him, even though it was true. Marie was getting closer to delivering the twins and Tom was having some unusual mood swings. My guess was he wasn't sleeping much and was stressed about the twins' arrival. I used that as my excuse not to tell him about Rhett and me all week.

"Speaking of Tom, we should probably get back to work." I stood up from the table.

Joce and Drew followed suit, making verbal jabs at each other as we walked to the town car, where Jim was waiting.

I finally told Drew about Rhett and me. It was unavoidable. There was no other way to explain the burly, old man who followed me around every time we went for coffee or lunch. I swore him to secrecy until I could tell Tom. It's not like he had to keep quiet for long. It was already Friday, and my time was up if I didn't want Rhett to be the one to tell Tom.

~

By five o'clock, Joce and Drew were packing up to leave for happy hour. I was working on finalizing the drawings of Rhett's home before printing a set for Tom. I'd decided to talk to him when I dropped the set off in his office.

I stood at the plotter, waiting on them to print, going over how I'd start the conversation. No matter what I came up with, I still feared the whole thing would end with Tom canning me and calling me a lying whore. Okay, maybe it was a little extreme, and definitely a worst-case scenario, but it's still how I imagined it.

"Tom." I knocked quietly on the opened door to his office.

"Yes, Ava, come in. Come in." He waved me in without looking up from the sketch he was working on.

I walked into his office—palms clammy from nerves,

heart beating rapidly. My body broke into a sweat as I sat in the chair across from his desk.

"Ava, are you feeling okay? You look pale," he said, finally looking up at me.

"Yep," I lied. "I was just bringing you the Blackwood-residence plans." I handed the roll of prints to him.

"Great. I'll review them first thing Monday."

I forced a smile.

When I didn't move to leave, Tom looked at me curiously. "Was there anything else, Ava?"

I stared at my wringing hands in my lap. "Do you have a minute, Tom?"

I looked back up at him. His face sunk.

"Of course. Is everything okay?"

"Yes, well…I hope so," I paused.

"Go on, Ava," he encouraged, even though he was starting to look like a nervous wreck himself.

"I'm not sure how to tell you this, Tom. But—"

"Oh, dear God! You aren't quitting, are you?" he interrupted me, his eyes wide and fearful.

"What? No! I'm worried you're going to fire me."

"Why on Earth would I ever fire you?"

"Because I'm dating Mr. Blackwood!" I bit my lip with nervous anxiousness as soon as the words flew from my mouth.

Relief washed over his face and his body relaxed. "Oh, thank goodness." He wiped his forehead with the back of his hand.

Okay. Definitely not the reaction I expected.

"You're not mad?" I asked, shocked and confused.

He shook his head at me. "Ava, I'd already figured as much."

"You did?"

"I know I'm a bit older, but I'm not blind. I could see how he looked at you from the first day we met him. I knew it was only a matter of time. He's not the type of man to sit idle and not go after what he wants."

I didn't bother correcting Tom. It was easier to let him think it was all new. "I hope this doesn't mean you'll be taking me off the project."

Tom laughed at my assumption. "Ava, I think if I tried to remove you, Mr. Blackwood would not be pleased."

I smiled, knowing that to be true. "Thank you, Tom."

He returned my smile, dismissing my appreciation with a wave of his hand. We talked a little longer about the drawings before I left for the weekend. The conversation went so well, I even managed to get his approval for some vacation time. He was so relieved I wasn't turning in my notice, he was more than happy to give me the time off. It also helped I rarely took vacation in the three years I'd been there.

I texted Rhett as I stepped into the backseat of the town car.

A: Leaving the office. On my way home. x

R: Still working. Have Jim bring you to my office.

I started typing I'd just see him at home, not wanting to disturb him at work. Plus, I wanted to make him dinner. Before I could finish typing out my response, my phone chimed with another text.

R: Don't argue, Ava. I need to see you, beautiful. x

I smiled, giving Jim instructions to head to the Blackwood Industries headquarters.

~

I took the elevator of the office building that had already been emptied out, with only a few late-night overachievers remaining. The doors opened to the lobby of his office. I stepped out, recalling the last time I was here, and how desperate I'd been to escape Rhett. It was crazy to think how much things had changed in such a short period of time.

I walked past the empty reception desk where the sweet receptionist had sat. My heels clicked on the shiny wood floors as I walked toward the office where Rhett had previously held me captive.

His door was cracked opened, and I could hear his warm, deep voice as I drew closer. I pushed the door open, my steps stalling at the threshold when I realized he wasn't alone.

My heart pounded in my chest as a wave of possessiveness crashed through me. The pretty, skinny woman I recognized as Celeste was standing too close for comfort as they both looked over some papers on his desk. It was innocent enough, but her proximity to him made the hairs on my neck stand.

She was ridiculously pretty, with long, raven-colored hair that was straight as a board. All her features were petite, reminding me of a pixie fairy. Her arm brushed Rhett's shoulder as she moved to point at something on the paper. Her lyrical voice was like a siren, drawing you in until she had you in her tiny clutches.

I closed my eyes, chiding myself. They were doing nothing wrong.

I'd only been standing there a few seconds when I heard Rhett's voice directed at me. I opened my eyes to his sexy smile. He was already standing. Celeste had stepped aside, moving out of his way. I glanced past him to watch her as he walked toward me with his usual swagger. The expression on her face wasn't jealousy or distaste. She was actually smiling brightly at me.

I turned my eyes back to Rhett, who was opening his arms to pull me into him. He kissed me firmly on the lips as he hugged me, making all the dread I was feeling fade away.

He pulled back from our kiss, looking into my eyes. "Hi, beautiful."

I smiled in response; my insides liquefied as he disarmed me. *He's mine.*

"I want you to meet someone." He turned, putting his arm around me as he walked me to a smiling Celeste. "Ava, this is Celeste." He waved his hand toward her. "Celeste, this is Ava. The love of my life."

I looked at him, amazed by how forthcoming he was with an employee.

"Ava, it's so good to finally meet you." Celeste smiled genuinely as she put her hand out.

Damn it. She's nice. I don't like her. Okay, I like her, but I didn't want to. "Nice to meet you, too," I shook her tiny, delicate hand, smiling in return. It was time I moved on from my juvenile insecurity, I decided.

"Celeste is an old friend from Harvard," Rhett added. That explained his forwardness. "I recruited her to come work for me last year."

She gave him a friendly smile, "Yes, after hassling me for a year. I don't know how you tell this man no, Ava. He's relentless."

Preaching to the choir. I looked at Rhett, who was smiling proudly.

"Celeste is the best at what she does. I needed someone in place I could trust," he explained to me.

"I didn't realize you were in town, Celeste. If you guys still have work to do, I can leave you to it."

"Of course not, Ava. I actually have a flight to catch. I was only in town for a couple days. Rhett insisted I come here versus him flying to New York."

I looked over at Rhett, who looked at me with adoring eyes. "I wasn't leaving you again."

"Well, thank you for making the trip, Celeste. I appreciate you coming so he didn't have to leave." I gave her an appreciative smile.

"Don't thank me, Ava. It's my job," she replied, grinning between the two of us. "Besides, it gave me a chance to meet the woman who tamed the untamable Rhett Blackwood."

Rhett shifted with a slight clearing of his throat, his discomfort obvious with the mention of his dating history.

"Well...I'll give you two some privacy," she added quickly, realizing the sudden awkwardness she hadn't intended to cause. "Rhett, I'll finish going over the contracts on the plane and email you my comments." She moved, retrieving her things. "I'm glad I got to meet you, Ava. Hopefully, I'll see you soon."

"You too, Celeste."

She waved her goodbye as she left his office, closing the door behind her. Once she was gone, Rhett spun me to face him, taking my face in his hands. "I missed you. How was your day, beautiful?"

"Great, actually. Yours?

"Better, now you're here. I have something for you."

My brows pinched together. "What?"

"Come here." He took my hand, guiding me to the oversized leather couch in his office.

I took a seat on the couch, scooting backwards to rest against the backrest, my short legs no longer able to touch the floor. I felt like a small child, with a sudden urge to scissor my legs up and down as my feet dangled off the edge. I refrained, kicking off my heels before curling my legs under me.

Rhett walked over to his desk, picking up a medium black box wrapped in gold satin ribbon.

"What's this?" I asked as he handed it to me.

"A gift."

"It's not my birthday."

"I know. Just open it."

I narrowed my eyes at him before unraveling the ribbon. I wiggled the lid as I lifted, opening the box. Peeling the gold tissue paper away, I gasped. I lifted the black and white striped shoulder wrap I'd been eyeing at the expensive shop in Italy.

"Rhett," I said, wanting to reprimand and kiss him at the same time. "I can't believe you bought this. *When* did you buy this?"

"When we were in Italy. I had the tailor ship it with my suit. I saw you admiring it while we were there."

My head shook with astonishment. The sneaky man had gotten his way in the end. "You shouldn't have spent the money on it. I'll be scared to wear it."

"Get used to it, beautiful. I'll be spoiling you as often as I like." He sat next to me on the couch as I ran my hand along the silky, expensive fabric.

I looked at my frustrating, generous, stubborn, romantic man. "Thank you."

He moved the box from my lap, setting it aside. I climbed on top of him, straddling his hips, locking my hands around his neck.

"I have a present for you, too."

"It's not my birthday either." He grinned.

"No, it's not. But it's something I know you really wanted. It's not nearly as lavish or expensive as the one you got. It did cost me my dignity, though," I teased him.

His grin turned into a full-on toothy smile. "You told Tom."

"Yes, I did."

"And?"

"And...he was more than okay with it. It might've helped he thought I was quitting before I broke the news. I think he was worried about losing his help at work right before the twins came. He even approved my vacation time."

"That was a good tactic. Make him desperate to keep you before delivering the news. With those killer negotiation skills, maybe I should hire you to work for me."

"I don't think you need me working for you. It sounds like you already have your star pupil."

"Are you jealous?" He eyed me suspiciously.

"No!"

He cocked his head.

"Okay, maybe I was a little...but I like her. I'm curious about the stories she can tell me about the '*untamable Rhett*

Blackwood' in his glory days," I said, attempting to mimic her delicate voice.

"There will be no storytelling," he warned. "And I'm glad you like her. I didn't want to have to let her go."

"You wouldn't?!" My eyes widened as my mouth fell open.

"Depends. I'm not willing to let anything or *anyone* ever come between us again, Ava. I can always replace an employee. I can't replace you."

He was a magician, making my heart disappear from my body only to reappear in his hands, where he held it captive. It would never belong to anyone but him. Not even to me. It was his forever. I was his forever. I only wished I'd realized it years ago.

He cupped my face in his hands as he rubbed his thumbs across my cheeks. He placed a brief, tender kiss on my lips. It wasn't lustful or desperate. It was laced with his love. A love he gave to me only.

I slid my hands up his powerful chest, pushing his suit jacket from his shoulders. Loosening his tie, I removed it as he watched me wordlessly. I took my time with the buttons of his shirt, despite the urgent need for skin-to-skin contact.

His shirt opened, revealing the ripples I was aching for. I traced my finger over the ridges of his muscles, dragging it slowly south, watching its path as it went. He gripped my hips tight, restraining himself, desperate to be inside me. But he waited patiently, letting me admire him.

My finger landed on the button of his dress pants. I lifted up to my knees, making room to remove his slacks, but was hindered by the look of adoration in his stunning sapphires as I towered above him.

His hands slid steadily up my back, lifting my shirt. I raised my arms as he pulled it over my head, discarding it to the floor. His moves were slow and as deliberate as mine. He pulled my exposed belly to him, kissing my navel as he removed my bra at the same time.

I gripped his shoulders, needing my own form of restraint. He shifted below me, holding me to him as he guided my back onto the couch. He stood up, removing the rest of his clothes, his intense gaze on me as he did. I followed his every move closely as he stripped, heat settling between my legs.

He was naked in all his masculine glory, confident and unashamed—eyes hooded with passion. He was beautiful. Perfect. He kneeled back onto the couch, removing the last of my clothing, spreading my legs apart before finding his place between them.

He held himself above me, his eyes roaming over me before blue met blue. I brought my hand to his handsome, chiseled face, feeling the roughness of his stubble below my palm.

"I love you, Rhett Blackwood," I whispered softly.

He kissed me as he moved slowly inside me, causing my body to clench around every inch of him greedily. We fell into a slow rhythm, taking our time, savoring every minute, fusing our souls together.

∼

I freshened up in Rhett's office restroom, while he returned a few calls he'd ignored. Turning off the faucet, I heard his strained, raised voice. I cracked the door open, not sure if I should walk out or give him privacy.

My curious nature won over. I stepped out of the restroom cautiously. His back was to me, stiff and foreboding, as he listened to the person on the other end.

"Fine. Pay him whatever he wants. I don't care the price." He paused, listening again. "Get it done. I want them in my hands," he grated before abruptly hanging up the phone.

He looked out at the picturesque view of the bright lights of late-night L.A., not aware of my return, or at least not acknowledging it. I closed the distance between us, snaking my arms around his waist, tightening my hold as I pressed my cheek to his sturdy back. He was still shirtless with only his pants on, and the warmth of his skin on my cheek sent tingles cascading through me. His hands covered mine as his body started to relax with my embrace.

"Everything okay?"

"It will be, soon."

"What has you so upset?"

He twisted in my arms, so he was looking at me. His eyes were no longer filled with brightness from our earlier moment together. They'd been overtaken with darkness from his phone call.

"That was Eric, head of my security team. He's trying to obtain the security footage from the bar that night for me to review, so we can find out who drugged you."

My chest tightened. *Shit.* I knew what he'd see on the footage—Owen and me talking.

"Rhett, why don't you just leave this to the police? Let them handle it."

"I don't trust them to prioritize it, or do anything at all. Finding out who did this to you is my only priority."

"We don't even know if it was actually meant for me."

"That doesn't matter, Ava. The sick fuck who did this will do it again. Whether it was meant for you or not, the unlucky bastard will pay for it."

He was pissed. My attempts to comfort him failed. Instead, it had us both stressed. I dropped my arms from around him, breaking his hold on me also. I needed space to think. This wasn't going to end well if Rhett found out I'd lied about Owen.

"Ava," Rhett said, following closely behind me, grabbing my arm to stop my retreat. "I'm sorry. I didn't mean to let this ruin our evening."

"It's fine," I assured him, knowing that had nothing to do with my own distress. I needed to tell him. I couldn't let him find out the truth from watching the video footage.

I just had no idea how to tell him without him going after Owen. Now was not the time to tell him. He was already angry. I'd tell him later. I turned toward him, hugging him to me. "I'm ready to go home."

He kissed my forehead. "Sure, beautiful. Let me get dressed and we can go."

CHAPTER 15

I t was like I'd closed my eyes, chanted, "There's no place like home" while clicking my heels, and was transported to New York a week into the future. I had no idea where the time had gone. I was so busy with work—getting Rhett's Malibu home in for permit and out to bid—the week flew by.

I still hadn't found the right time to talk to Rhett about Owen. I'd barely seen him all week, with his demanding work schedule. The few moments we had with each other, I didn't want to spend discussing Owen or the "incident," as I was calling it.

Despite Rhett's busy schedule, he always made time to run with me every morning. In the beginning, I wasn't too thrilled with the idea. Running had always been a time I could clear my head, reflect, have some "me time." But after our first few runs together, I actually started to look forward to it, especially since it was the one time of the day I knew I could spend with him uninterrupted by his cell phone.

He had crazy endurance. I had a hard time keeping up with him as we ran. He pushed me past my limits, constantly encouraging me to go farther, longer, and faster. It also sparked some amazing, steamy, sweaty— *and did I mention amazing?* —sex afterwards as our bodies came down from their adrenaline highs.

I was now in the restroom of Rhett's New York penthouse getting ready. He'd be here in a few minutes to pick me up for a business dinner he requested I join him at. And by requested, I mean he told me I was joining him and not to argue. It wasn't exactly how I wanted to spend my evening, but if it was the only way I'd have time with him tonight, then I'd take it.

I stared into the floor-length mirror twisting, turning, and smoothing out the black cocktail dress I'd picked to wear for the night. It was a clingy, off-the-shoulder, strapless number showing off my collarbone and shoulders. The hemline stopped above my right knee, cutting up at an angle above my left knee. I'd gone shopping with Valerie earlier in the day to pick it out once Rhett had texted me about dinner.

I wore my hair down in large, loose curls, and my eyes were done up with golds and bronze colors. My lips shined with a rusty rose-colored lip gloss.

The penthouse door opened as I gave myself the final once-over. I picked up my clutch from the bed and walked into the hallway to greet Rhett.

Turning the corner, I stopped short at the sight of him. He hadn't seen me yet, so I took the moment to appreciate the stunning man before me. His posture was weary, as if he'd been carrying around the weight of the world. My heart sank. I hated how much he was having to work, and it had me wanting to demand we cancel dinner and crawl into bed where I could take care of him.

Despite looking tired, he was still strikingly handsome. He walked toward the bedroom, his head down as he rubbed the back of his neck. I moved again, distracting him from his approach with the clicking of my stilettos on the floor.

He looked up at me, his tired expression being replaced with brighter eyes and *that* smile—the one that is so contagious it can make me smile even on the worst of days. Everything bad in the world disappeared with that smile.

We both stood fixed in the moment, letting the vision of each other fade all our worries and stresses away.

"You look stunning." He started his progression toward me again.

I moved too, unable to resist the magnetic pull between us.

He rested a hand on my hip, as the other tangled in my hair. Our eyes met. "I'd say you look perfect, but something is missing."

The smirk on his face told me he was up to something. "And what's that?" I played along with his game.

"Something belonging here." His finger swept seductively across my collar bone.

I arched an eyebrow.

"And I think I have just the thing."

He reached into his suit jacket, revealing a small jewelry box he pulled from the inside pocket.

"Rhett—" I started to scold.

"Hush, beautiful. Open it." He handed it to me.

I took the box, glancing between it and him. He smiled encouragingly. I opened the lid, revealing a beautiful and very expensive necklace. The obvious expense of the ridiculous number of diamonds covering the necklace was not what had tears springing to my eyes. It was the shape of the pendant itself. The pendant was a smaller version of the antique key I'd given him years ago. But this one was made of white gold and was diamond encrusted, hanging from a delicate, white-gold chain.

I looked back up at him through my blurry eyes, speechless. My hands shook as he took the box from me. He removed the necklace, then reached around my neck to clasp it into place as I held my hair to the side.

"Perfect." His whisper brushed my ear as he fastened the clasp.

I turned my head into his face, caressing his lips with mine. "I love it. Thank you."

"I love *you*, Ava Conner." We smiled at each other for a moment, filled with silly happiness. "We should go. The car is waiting downstairs."

I reluctantly nodded my agreement, hooking my arm in his as he escorted me out the door.

~

Jim drove the limo down the busy New York street. Tucked into Rhett's side, I fingered the pendant around my neck, my other hand resting on his lap with our fingers intertwined.

"You seem stressed. Do you want to talk about it?"

Rhett exhaled, his head turning to me. "I need to warn you about who we're having dinner with."

"Okay?"

"We're meeting with Rex Archibald."

"Rex Archibald? As in Serena's father?"

"Yes. But Serena won't be there."

I fought to hold my temper in check. "I don't understand. Why are we meeting with him, and why would you insist I come?" I wanted nothing to do with Serena nor any of her family or friends.

"Trust me, beautiful. It's *not* something I wanted. He's been resistant about selling his shares of our company in London. Part of me feels like Serena has been in his ear. I didn't expect him to be this difficult to negotiate with"—he rubbed a hand roughly down his face—"Celeste has been trying to handle most of the negotiations for me, so I could keep my distance. But he's been impossible. Only wanting to deal with me. And now, you."

"Me? I don't understand."

"We've finally come to an agreement on the contract, but he put a contingency on signing it. He wanted to have dinner with you."

"Why?"

"Honestly, I have no idea. I'm just hoping this isn't some kind of manipulation of Serena's."

"I see," I replied nervously.

"Babe, I don't want you to worry. I'll be with you. I've told you nothing and nobody will ever come between us."

I smiled weakly at him. "I know. I trust you."

He pushed my hair behind my shoulder, kissing me as the limo rolled to a stop. He pulled back. "Are you ready?"

"As ready as I'll ever be."

He squeezed my hand, comforting me as Jim opened the door for us. "Let's go, beautiful."

~

Rex Archibald was already waiting for us at the table when we arrived. I'd only seen the man a few times before tonight—both times I'd been serving him, not joining him for dinner. To say I was apprehensive was an understatement. I'd never officially been introduced to the man, and I had no idea what to expect.

Will he be kind and genuine like his best friend, Charles— Rhett's father—or will he be spiteful and manipulative like his daughter, Serena?

The atmosphere of the restaurant didn't help with my anxiety and self-consciousness. It was filled with pretentious, wealthy diners. Only New York's most elite could afford to dine here, with the plates costing up to a thousand dollars apiece.

My body was rigid with anxiety as we approached the table. Rhett held my hand tight, placing a gentle kiss on my temple to help calm me. His previous stress had seemed to disappear into thin air. His present demeanor was calm and confident. It made me wonder if he was in business mode, masking his true emotions.

Rex stood upon our approach. His smile was genuine enough, which helped me relax—but only a little. He was still an intimidating man. Rex was handsome for his age, which wasn't surprising after seeing his evil, but unfortunately beautiful, spawn.

He was distinguished looking, with gray hair—one of the

few things aging him. He was lean and fit, with a few wrinkles around his eyes and brow.

"Rex," Rhett greeted him with a shake of his hand.

"Rhett. Good to see you, son." Rex gave Rhett a manly pat on the back as they shook hands. His greeting had more endearment than I expected after our conversation in the car.

"And this must be the beautiful Ms. Ava Conner I've heard so much about." Rex smiled at me.

"Ava, meet Rex Archibald," Rhett introduced us. I shook hands with Rex.

"It's a pleasure to meet you, Mr. Archibald."

"Call me Rex, please." I nodded, smiling shyly. "Let's sit"— he waved us toward the table where he'd previously been waiting—"I hope you don't mind. I ordered a bottle of wine for the table."

I'd barely settled into my seat before the server was at our table, pouring us each a glass. Rhett and Rex made small talk, inquiring about each other's families. After ordering our food—I relied on Rhett to order for me— Rex began inquiring about me, my family, my life.

The entire dinner was pleasant, and I concluded Rex was definitely more of a Charles than a Serena. There was no discussion of business at all during dinner. Our plates were cleared by the server and more wine was poured in our glasses, but Rex declined a top off of his nearly empty glass.

I glanced over at Rhett, wondering if this was the end of the meal. Rex glanced between us, seeing the questioning look I gave Rhett.

"I suppose you're both wondering why I asked you to have dinner with me."

Rhett shifted slightly in his seat as he held my hand in his, preparing us both for what was to come. He nodded at Rex in response.

"I wanted to be able to apologize to the both of you in person."

My brows furrowed together in confusion, while Rhett remained impassive.

"On behalf of my daughter and my family," he continued. "Rhett, I know Serena has caused a lot of unnecessary pain and grief for you. And honestly, I have no excuse for her behavior. Sometimes, I wonder if it was her way of lashing out or crying for attention. I know I was an absentee father for most of her childhood—always busy with work. I regret it every day, and I hope I can make it up to her somehow.

"If I may offer you one piece of advice, Rhett, remember to make time for the ones you love." He quieted, lost in his own regrets. Shaking his head, he cleared his throat. "Anyway, I've taken enough of your evening. I do hope you both can forgive her someday."

"I hope you can understand I don't see it happening any time soon," Rhett replied apologetically.

Rex gave him a slight nod. "I completely understand. But as her father and someone who sees you as the son I never had, I hope you don't blame me for trying. I'm sure you'll understand someday, when you have kids of your own." He smiled between us.

As Rex stood to leave, we both stood with him. "Ava, it was a pleasure finally meeting you. I can see why Rhett is so enamored by you. I wish you all the best. Rhett's a good man, and I believe you're both lucky to have each other."

"Thank you, Rex. It was a pleasure meeting you, too."

"Enjoy the rest of your evening. The check has been taken care of. Rhett, give your parents my regards."

"Will do," Rhett confirmed with a handshake. Once Rex had disappeared, we both sat back down to finish the last of our wine.

"Well...that was unexpected." I turned to Rhett for his reaction.

He smiled. "Not really. Rex is an honorable man, who cares very much about his family and friends."

"As much as I hate to admit it...I like him, despite him being Serena's father."

Rhett chuckled, pulling me to him as he kissed my head. "Are you ready? I plan to start taking Rex's advice right now." He leaned in closer, placing his lips next to my ear, "I've been picturing stripping you out of that dress all night. I want you in my arms—naked and panting my name."

My breath hitched as the familiar tingles trickled through my body. I'm not sure we would be making it all the way home. *Thank goodness for the limo.*

"He's a very smart man. And I'm a big supporter of your plan," I said, grinning.

⁓

Making it back to the penthouse still clothed was a feat. We'd barely crossed the threshold before Rhett had me naked, wearing nothing but my necklace.

I was now cuddled in Rhett's side after multiple orgasms —*yes, multiple*—feeling, understandably, weak and gratified. It was my happy place.

I admired the brilliant view of twinkling city lights

through the large floor-to-ceiling window across from Rhett's bed. In these moments, I struggled between wanting to live in L.A. or New York. I was enchanted by the bustling city of New York, but I longed for the peaceful, soothing ocean.

I let my thoughts continue to wander as the city lights hypnotized me, like watching the flames of a fire. Rhett stroked my arm, "What are you thinking about, beautiful?"

"You."

"What about me?"

I rolled in his arms to face him. "You work too much...I worry about you. You aren't sleeping enough. And I can't watch you do this to yourself."

"I'm fine, babe," he assured me, running his fingers through my hair. "It won't always be like this. Once I get things transitioned and up and running in L.A, it'll be better."

"Do you promise?"

"Yes. Do you believe me?"

"Always. Besides, if you don't, I'll destroy your phone, so at least you can't work when you're in my presence."

"My phone?"

"Yes. It's the devil. I've plotted its destruction on more than one occasion."

He released his deep, powerful laugh, the vibration of his chest making me want to meld into him. "Should I get my phone its own security detail?"

"Possibly," I deadpanned. I really despised that thing lately.

"Noted." He gave me a chaste kiss. I laid my head back down, pulling him into me, wanting to ask him something else weighing on me after our conversation with Rex.

"Rhett..."

"Yes, babe?"

"Do you think you'll ever forgive Serena?"

His body tensed slightly with my question. He didn't speak for a few moments, contemplating his answer. I wasn't sure what I wanted him to say. Part of me wanted him to never forgive her, but at the same time, I almost needed to know he *could* forgive her. Despite her deceit, she'd been a very close friend his whole life. The man I knew wasn't someone who could throw away a relationship like that so easily. At least, I hoped not.

I found myself sympathizing with Serena. There was no way I agreed with what she did...but I understood her desperation—the desperation to keep him. After knowing the pain of losing him, I'd do anything to keep us together. I'd never trick him into anything, but I'd never give up on us again.

"I already have a little, just not fully. I'm sure I will some-day, but even when I'm able to...I'll still never let her back into my life. She lied and put me and both of our families through hell. I'll never trust her again."

My own body tensed with guilt. I was lying to him, also, and I knew once I told him about Owen he'd be hurt by my deceit. The longer I waited, the worse it would be. I needed to tell him. Now.

"Rhett—"

"No more pillow talk, beautiful," he interrupted me. "We should both get some rest. We have a long day tomorrow."

I agreed, allowing him to silence me. Because no matter how much I knew I should tell him, it was hard, and I'd rather him never find out. But I also knew my lie was like a ticking time bomb that could explode any minute, destroying my world. Destroying us.

I rolled over and tried to force myself to sleep. I grasped the pendant around my neck as I closed my eyes.

~

I awoke to the murmurs of Rhett's deep voice in the distance. The moon and city light shining through the window revealed I was alone in bed. Rhett slipped back into the bedroom as I lifted to my elbows. He stopped in the dark, seeing my movement.

"Did I wake you?"

I nodded my groggy head.

"I'm sorry." He climbed onto the bed, sidling up to me with my back to him, holding me close, his arm snaked around my stomach.

"Who were you talking to?"

"Nobody."

"It must be important if it has you getting out of bed in the middle of the night," I yawned.

"Don't worry about it, babe."

"You're not going to tell me?"

"We can talk about it tomorrow. Close your eyes. Sleep," he commanded as he kissed my temple.

I debated for a minute whether to keep pressing. But as I felt his breathing slow, I knew he'd already fallen back to sleep. I didn't want to be the one to keep him awake. He needed his rest. I closed my own eyes, drifting back to sleep.

CHAPTER 16

We arrived to a squealing Lizzie greeting us as we walked through the door of the restaurant.

"Oh my goodness, Lizzie! Look at your tiny bump!" I squealed back as she charged me. We threw our arms around each other. I laughed as she squeezed me like a boa constrictor.

"Because I love you, and I'm so glad you're here, I'm going to ignore the fact that you just pointed out I'm fat." She smiled after releasing me.

"I wasn't calling you fat." I rolled my eyes at her.

"Lizzie. How are you feeling?" Rhett asked, giving her a small hug and kiss on her cheek.

"Good, now the morning sickness is over."

"I'm definitely glad we're past that part," Mike said, walking up behind her in his chef's apparel. He hugged me and shook Rhett's hand. "She was starting to give me a complex. Every time I'd have her try a new recipe

240

I was testing she'd run to the bathroom gagging." He smiled at Lizzie as she playfully elbowed him in the side.

"Can I feel?" I asked hopefully, glancing toward her stomach. It was so surreal seeing Lizzie, of all people, pregnant. We both always thought I'd be the first to marry and start a family.

"Sure. Grope away. It may be all the action I get for a while."

I grinned ear to ear as I placed my hand on her tiny baby bump. "Have you felt her move, yet?"

"Not yet. I think it's still too early."

"I can't believe she's letting you touch. She hasn't let anyone touch her belly, with the exception of me, of course," Mike interjected with a smirk.

"Ava isn't just *anyone*," Lizzie responded.

"That's right! I'm Auntie Ava. And I plan to spoil my little niece from the day she arrives."

"She?" Mike crinkled his nose.

"Yes, *she*," I replied sternly.

"What makes you so sure it's a she?" he asked, still looking perturbed by the thought.

"Call it a hunch."

"No way. I want a boy."

"Whatever. You'll love our baby no matter what it is." Lizzie looked at him, annoyed by his dismissal of having a girl.

"True. But I'll love it even more if it's a boy." His playful grin spread across his face.

"Why don't you want a girl?" I asked curiously.

"Girls scare me. I wouldn't know what to do with a girl.

241

Plus, with a boy, I only have to worry about one dick. With a girl, I'll have to worry about a lot more."

That earned him an eye roll from me and a slap on the back of the head from Lizzie. Rhett chuckled and from the look on his face, I knew he agreed with Mike.

Men. As if they are any easier to deal with.

"Enough baby talk. I want to see the place! Give me the grand tour."

We'd arrived early to Nouveau, Mike's restaurant, so I had a chance to see the space and visit before the crowd descended on the place. The soft opening was by invitation only. Friends and family were invited, along with a few high-profile bloggers and food critics to help spread the word.

Lizzie led the way to show us around the restaurant, while Mike returned to the kitchen to continue with food prep and helping his staff set up for the evening.

The space was long and narrow. As you entered the restaurant, there was a small hostess stand and waiting area. To the left was the main dining area, and straight back led to the kitchen and a small bar fully stocked with glass liquor bottles accented by concealed, softly glowing lights behind them.

The walls were adorned with white subway tile contrasting well with the dark, walnut booths, forming a galley-style seating arrangement. The booths had high backs, giving diners a sense of privacy. The tile, wooden booths, and layout, along with the globe pendant lighting suspended above from an open structure, set the tone for the food to be served.

The restaurant had a trendy, hip café vibe. It was where fine dining met local diner. The plates served were upscale versions of favorite comfort foods, with medium-to-high-range pricing.

We ended our tour in the kitchen, where we stood out of the way, watching Mike and his team of chefs work. They diced and sliced efficiently and effortlessly, preparing for tonight's opening.

Mike was a natural leader in the kitchen. I glanced over at Lizzie as she looked dreamily at her man, watching him work confidently. As if sensing her gaze, he glanced up, winking at her, giving her his cute smile. I looked up at Rhett, who was holding my hand in his, feeling content in this moment, with the man I loved and the friends I loved.

Rhett excused himself to make a few calls in Mike's office off the kitchen, while Lizzie and I headed back toward the front of house. Guests were starting to arrive, and I wanted a drink from the bar.

I sipped my frilly cocktail at the bar as Lizzie sat glaring at my drink. "Maybe they can make you a virgin," I offered.

She shook her head, "Nah. I'll be fine with water. I'll just squeeze a lime in it and pretend it's a gin and tonic."

"Suit yourself," I said, polishing off my drink and ordering another.

The place was filling up fast. Most of the guests I didn't recognize. A few I'd met at social events I'd attended with Rhett. Lizzie and I remained at the bar chatting, while everyone milled about. Her face contorted with concern when someone at the door caught her eye. I turned to look over my shoulder in search of the subject of her troubled expression, finding Stephen and Amber standing just inside the door.

I don't know why I was surprised to see them. He is, after

all, Mike's brother, and they've always been close. Of course he'd be here on one of the biggest nights of Mike's career.

Lizzie was watching me carefully when I turned back to face her. "I'm sorry. I forgot to warn you they'd be here."

I dismissed her apology. "Lizzie, I'm fine."

She tilted her head at me.

"Honestly. I'm actually kind of glad they're here." I smiled reassuringly.

To show her I was indeed fine, I decided to make the first move. I stood from my stool, heading to greet them. Lizzie waddled slowly behind me. Stephen smiled halfheartedly, his eyes full of unease as they connected with mine. Amber flashed her pretty, friendly smile at me as she stepped forward, releasing Stephen's hand to hug me.

"Ava!"

"Hi, Amber," I said, wrapping my arms around her shoulders. "How have you been?"

"Great! It's so good to see you."

"You look beautiful *and* happy." I smiled genuinely at her.

She glanced back, grinning at Stephen, who was still standing like a scared puppy by the door. "I am happy."

"I'm glad to hear that." I gave her arm a light squeeze.

I was honestly happy for her and Stephen. I always thought they'd be good for each other. Stephen stepped cautiously forward after hugging Lizzie hello. "Ava, it's good to see you."

"You too, Stephen."

We stared uncomfortably at each other.

"Amber, how about I take you to the bar to get a drink?" Lizzie interrupted our awkward silence.

"Sure, lead the way," Amber agreed, smiling back at

Stephen before they left us. We both watched them walk away before turning back to face each other.

"So—"

"Look—"

We started to talk simultaneously, then stopped. "Go ahead," he said with a small smile.

"No. You go first."

He nodded.

"Ava, I'm sorry—really, really sorry. For everything. For the night at the hospital. For the kiss and ruining our friendship..." He hesitated, looking up at the ceiling for a moment before looking back down at me, a hand rubbing the back of his neck raw. "I wish I could take it all back. I didn't mean to hurt you. I thought...I thought I was doing the right thing that night. Sending him away. But now...now I just think I was being a jealous prick."

I snorted a laugh.

He gave me a crooked smile. "I'm sorry, Ava. Will you ever forgive me?"

"I already have." I smiled back at him.

He hugged me to him, lifting me off my feet as I squealed. He placed me back down, holding us arm's length apart with his hands on my shoulders.

"I missed you, pumpkin."

"I missed you, too. And thank you. For apologizing. I know you thought you were doing the right thing at the time."

"I wish I could go back in time." He dropped his hands from my shoulders, looking defeated.

"It doesn't matter, now," I told him, because it didn't matter. He wasn't the only one to blame. And Rhett and I were together now. It was all that mattered. "So...you and Amber, huh?" I grinned knowingly at him.

His sexy smile spread across his face as he looked past me in search of her. "Yeah. She's the best thing that's ever happened to me."

"I'm excited for you. For both of you." His smile faded as he continued looking past me, his body stiffening. I started to turn to see what had made his happy mood instantly vanish, but stopped when I felt Rhett's hands grip my hips from behind.

"Stephen."

"Rhett." Stephen responded.

Their terse greetings put us all slightly on edge. I covered Rhett's hand on me, trying to ease his tension. I wasn't going to push them to be friends again. I'd given up on that a long time ago. Before Rhett even had a real reason to dislike him. But I hoped they could at least be cordial.

"The place looks great," Stephen said, looking around the restaurant.

"All compliments should be aimed at your brother. It's his doing," Rhett responded.

"Right. Well...I appreciate you backing him on it."

"It wasn't out of charity. He more than earned it. He's a hard worker. I'm glad to have him as a partner."

Stephen nodded.

"You should head to the bar. Lizzie and Amber are there. Drinks are on the house tonight," Rhett said firmly, dismissing Stephen from our presence.

Stephen smiled tightly, moving past us. He stopped, looking over his shoulder. "Rhett...for what it's worth, I'm sorry. I apologized to Ava already, but I felt I should apologize to you, also."

Rhett turned, looking Stephen in the eyes. "I appreciate that."

Stephen nodded his head once before turning to walk away, leaving us to ourselves. Rhett looked back at me as I spun in his arms to look at him.

"Are you okay?"

"I'm more than okay." I smiled up at him as I squeezed him tighter.

"Good. Let's get a drink and grab our table. There's one reserved for us with your friends and my family. They should be here soon."

"Lead the way," I said, hooking my arm in his.

~

The food was fabulous. I overindulged in everything brought to our table. I'm pretty sure Mike had prepared everything on the menu for us to try. We passed plates around, sharing them as we all ate.

The bartender kept our drinks coming, and except for Lizzie and maybe Rhett, we all had a pretty good buzz going on. It was so good to laugh with my friends, Rhett, and his family. I even saw Rhett crack a small smile at some of Stephen's jokes. *Progress.* But I wasn't getting my hopes up.

I leaned into Rhett, feeling a little frisky from all the lighthearted amusement and alcohol. My hand moved under the table around his thigh, brushing against him. His body came to attention. I grinned, biting my lip, loving what my touch did to him. He shifted, clenching my hand with his, restricting my movement. He looked down at me with a raised eyebrow. I smiled up at him unashamed. I wanted him, and I wanted him now.

"I think someone's had a little too much to drink." Mischief danced in his eyes, telling me he wasn't really upset.

"What can I say? I'm drinking for two," I teased, putting my martini glass to my lips.

"Yep, it's her responsibility as my best friend," Lizzie, who was sitting next to me, interrupted our conversation as the rest of the table continued visiting.

He leaned in, "Not here, beautiful," his husky whisper floated near my ear. "Meet me in the office."

I sucked in a puff of air, butterflies fluttering in my stomach with excitement. I nodded. He kissed my head, excusing himself from the table to make a call. The next few minutes were the most excruciating minutes of my life.

After what felt like enough time, I excused myself from the table in search of Rhett. I started to make up what sounded like a legitimate excuse—I needed the restroom. Lizzie wasn't buying it.

"Just make sure you sanitize the area thoroughly when you're done." She winked, giggling.

I blushed, automatically glancing over at Rhett's family. Thankfully, they were all too deep in conversation with Amber and Stephen to hear Lizzie alluding to my promiscuous endeavor. I flipped her the bird, blocking my crude gesture from the others before walking away. I heard her loud laughter roaring behind me.

I pushed through the swinging door of the kitchen. Mike glanced over at me. He smiled knowingly, nodding his head toward the office to point me in the direction of

Rhett before returning his focus to the dish he was preparing.

Do I have "I'm horny" written on my forehead? I subconsciously rubbed my hand above my brow.

I maneuvered through the busy kitchen, making sure to stay out of the way of the staff rushing around. The office door was cracked open, and I could hear Rhett on the phone.

I pushed the door open, closing it gently behind me. He was sitting at the desk, his elbow resting on his thigh, holding up his head, while the other hand held the phone to his ear. His previous flirty playfulness was gone. His body was now rigid with stress.

"I know. I'll talk to her," he said, releasing a weary sigh. "Let me know, if you hear anything else. Thanks for the call, Jackson."

He hung up the phone, staring momentarily at the ground before he looked up at me with a troubled expression.

"Jackson?"

He nodded.

"What did he want?"

He leaned back into the chair. "Come here, babe. There's something I need to tell you."

My heart pounded hard against my chest. Panic obliterating my emotions from earlier. The last time Jackson called Rhett late at night, my father was being rushed to the hospital. "What's wrong? Is everything okay? Is it Nana?"

"Nana's fine. Your family is fine. Come here." He reached his hand out to me.

I walked hesitantly to him. Something was wrong. Something Jackson told him had him upset. He clasped my hand, pulling me onto his lap, brushing my hair away from my face.

"Has Chris contacted you? Have you seen or heard from him?"

Chris? My forehead wrinkled. "No," I replied warily. "Why?"

"Ava, I've been keeping something from you…and I need you to promise to hear me out."

"I promise." And I meant it. I'd learned the hard way I needed to trust him and listen to what he had to say. Had I done that in the past, all the misunderstandings between us would've been resolved a long time ago.

"Chris's wife left him earlier this year. He'd started drinking and becoming verbally abusive with her."

"That's terrible. That doesn't even sound like Chris."

"I know, babe. But he's not the same man you might've known back then. He's had a streak of bad luck, from what Jackson has told me. He turned to alcohol and has been arrested a few times for bar fights."

I shook my head, confused. "I'm not sure how this concerns me. I don't even talk to him. The last time I saw him was in the store."

"When his wife left him, he started asking around about you. At first, it was innocent conversation with mutual acquaintances, but he eventually approached Emily. When she wouldn't tell him where you were living, he got a little aggressive with her. Luckily, Jackson was there to intervene."

"When was this?"

"Earlier this year." He studied my eyes as I connected the dots.

"That's why. Why you moved to L.A. Why you came for me."

He nodded.

I stared at him, processing it all. *Am I mad? Am I relieved?* This was the other piece of the puzzle. The reason he stopped waiting for me. The reason for his protectiveness. *Is Chris the one who's been causing my paranoia?*

"What are you thinking, beautiful?"

"Why are you telling me this *now*?"

"Chris showed up to his ex-wife's house drunk and angry a few weeks ago. He was yelling at her. Blaming her for ruining his life. He hit her—"

"Oh my gosh!" I gasped, horrified, covering my mouth as I shook my head. "Is she okay?"

He nodded. "Their little girl walked in on it. As soon as he saw her, he took off. Nobody has seen him in a few weeks. He hasn't been home. They don't think he's even in town anymore."

"You think Chris is the one who drugged me?"

"I don't know, Ava. He's my main suspect, but I can't be sure, yet."

I nodded my head as I looked down at my trembling hands. He moved his hands to cup my face, lifting my eyes to his.

"I won't let anything happen to you, beautiful. My security team is looking into his disappearance, trying to track him down."

I nodded weakly.

"Ava, if he ever contacts you, approaches you, if you see him, you need to keep your distance. And you need to tell me."

"Okay," I promised, nodding my agreement. I couldn't stop thinking about his poor little girl. To see him hit her mother...the thought of it made my heart ache.

"Is anyone keeping an eye on his ex-wife and their daughter? What if he comes back after her?"

He slid his hands down my shoulders, resting them on my arms, rubbing them slowly. "The local police are aware of the situation and are keeping an eye on their house. But everyone is pretty sure he's long gone."

"Thank you. For telling me."

"I'm sorry I didn't tell you before. I didn't want you to worry, but with the potential of him now being in L.A., or here—"

"Rhett—" I touched his face with one hand, intertwining our fingers with my other. "It's okay. I'm not mad. I understand why you didn't tell me before."

He leaned in, pressing his lips to mine. I slid my hand through his hair, deepening our kiss. His tongue swept against the seam of my mouth. I opened while shifting in his lap to straddle him.

His hand moved to the zipper of my dress, sliding it down as I worked at the buttons of his shirt. I grinded my hips on his lap, already desperate to take things further. There was a knock at the door. We ignored it. The door slowly opened.

Shit. I forgot to lock it.

We both froze. Rhett wrapped his arms around me protectively, even though I was still fully clothed, other than the back of my dress being unzipped.

"Cover your baby makers! I'm coming in," Lizzie teased as

she opened the door more, pretending to cover her eyes, but peeking through the cracks between her fingers.

"Lizzie, what the hell?" I laughed.

"Sorry to bust up your little love fest, but Rhett's family is leaving. It was either this or I tell his family you two were playing hide the salami in the office." A grin glided across her face. "I figured since I'd already seen the goods before, this was the preferred option."

"Out!" I laugh-yelled, wanting to throw something at her. Lucky for her, she was pregnant.

"I'm going," she said with her hands up in surrender. She laughed, closing the door behind her.

"Well, I guess we should go tell your family goodbye."

"I guess we should." His grin grew wide.

"What are you grinning about?"

"I'm just thinking about the things I'll be doing to you in the limo on the drive home."

I shook my head teasingly. "You and your fetish."

CHAPTER 17

M arie was scheduled for her C-section the week after our return from New York, which meant Tom would be at home with her for at least four weeks, if not longer. He'd left Joce and me in charge of all the projects, managing to come into the office on occasion to give us feedback on things we were working on. But for the most part, his communication with us was limited to phone or email. Between Tom being away and construction starting on the Malibu home, things were hectic for me, to say the least.

I hadn't heard anything about Chris since our conversation that night at Nouveau, other than that Rhett's security team had a lead they were following up on. Knowing Chris was the prime suspect, I didn't rush to tell Rhett about talking to Owen at the bar.

I was out of time, though. Eric had negotiated to pay the owner of the bar a ridiculous amount of money to release the security footage and would be giving it to Rhett soon. I planned to tell him after Valerie's visit this weekend, not wanting to ruin her time in L.A. We planned to help Valerie find a place to live when she moved here at the end of the month.

After work, I had Jim take me to the store to pick up a few items I needed to make dinner. Rhett was actually going to be home at a time I considered "early." It was a special occasion, so I made him promise to be home no later than seven. They both tried to convince me to go out to dinner. I refused. I wanted to make a meal for them. I'd decided to cook my mom's chicken parmesan recipe, one of my favorite dishes to make. It also happened to be one of Rhett's favorites I cooked.

The evening weather was beautiful, so Jim helped me rearrange the balcony, so I could set up a table and chairs outside. I set the table with some candles and a nice white tablecloth. It wasn't as refined-looking as what the Black-woods were used to, but I was still proud of my arrangement.

I pulled the boiling spaghetti off the burner, draining it, tossing the spaghetti with some butter. There was a knock at the front door.

"One minute!" I yelled as I rushed to make sure all the burners were off.

I scurried to the door, stopping to look through the peep-hole before opening it. I'd promised Rhett I'd be more cautious opening the door, with Chris's whereabouts still unknown.

"Ava! *Hurry.* I have to pee!" Valerie yelled through the door.

I laughed as I opened it.

"Hi!" she said hurriedly, brushing past me, bee-lining it to my bathroom.

I shook my head at her greeting, or lack thereof, closing and locking the door behind me. Returning to the kitchen, I pulled the French bread from the oven. A few minutes later, she graced me with her presence, giving me a proper hug.

"Sorry. I'd been holding it since we left the airport. The traffic here is ridiculous."

"Tell me about it," I snorted. "You'll never get used to it either. How was your flight?"

"Ugh…flying first class sucks," she pouted, leaning her hip on the counter, arms crossed.

I rolled my eyes at her.

"You know, Val, most people would love to be able to fly first class."

Rhett's parents had been enjoying their retirement by globe-trotting around the world the last few weeks, forcing poor Valerie to fly commercial like a normal person. At least, a wealthier normal person.

"Whatever. I guess I should get used to it. I plan to make some changes in my life when I move here."

"Oh?" I asked, curious.

"Yes." She looked down at her hands, lacking her usually fun-spirited mood. "I need a fresh start when I move to California. Like you did."

"What do you mean?" My eyebrows furrowed in concern.

"Just that I want to make a name for myself."

Before I could inquire any further, the front door opened. Rhett walked through the door with wine and a bouquet of white roses.

"Rhett!" Valerie squealed, charging at her older brother, her mood instantly lifted.

She leaped into his arms, clinging to him like a spider monkey. He laughed his deep, masculine laugh, making my insides swoon. She jumped down from his body, and he kissed her forehead.

"Hey, Val. I see you managed to survive first class," he goaded her.

"Barely," she huffed. "Nice flowers."

"*These* are for Ava." The corner of his mouth lifted into a half-smile as his eyes searched for me.

I moved from the opening of the kitchen to greet him.

"Does that mean the wine is for *me?*" she asked hopefully, smiling as she exaggerated batting her eyelashes.

"Nice try." He narrowed his eyes at her, unaffected by her charm.

Her face straightened with frustration. "I don't see what the big deal is. It's not like you weren't drinking at my age."

He glared at her, giving her a warning look. "Whatever." She rolled her eyes, walking away. "Ava, where's your water?"

"There are some bottles in the fridge," I tossed over my shoulder, turning my focus back on Rhett.

He set the flowers and wine aside. "Hey, beautiful."

I wrapped my arms around his waist. "I missed you today."

His blue eyes heated. For a moment, I wished we were alone.

"I missed you, too. Smells amazing." He nuzzled his nose into the crook of my neck. I tilted my head to the side, allowing him better access.

"Chicken Parmesan."

257

"I meant you," he whispered, kissing my neck, "tastes good, too." He pulled back, grinning his naughty smile, eyebrows bouncing.

"*Hello.* Little sister. Still here," Valerie called from behind me.

"Don't remind me," he groaned under his breath. "Yes, Val. How could we ever forget?" he flung at her sarcastically.

I laughed, taking the flowers and wine from Rhett. "Let me get these in some water and then we can eat."

We spent the rest of the evening on the balcony, enjoying each other's company, eating and drinking wine. I even convinced Rhett to let Val have a few sips of my wine. She was under supervision, after all.

"We'll have to swing by the Malibu property, after we house hunt tomorrow," I told Valerie. "They broke ground the other day!"

"Broke ground? What does that mean?"

"You know, they started clearing the land, moving the dirt around to get it pad ready."

She stared at me blankly.

"They're getting it ready so they can start building the actual house," I tried explaining further.

"I prefer to see it when there's an *actual house.*"

I sighed, "This is the fun part, though. Watching it be built and come to fruition."

She looked at Rhett. "Does she always get this excited about dirt?"

He shrugged. "I think it's cute. Sexy actually." He winked at me with a grin.

"Eww. Gross." She covered her ears and closed her eyes. "Can you two keep your clothes on at least until I leave?"

I rolled my eyes at both of them, standing to clear the plates. "You two are impossible."

Rhett and Valerie remained on the balcony at my insistence, laughing and catching up while I cleaned up the kitchen. I'd barely finished loading the dishwasher when I heard them walk back inside. I dried the counter and hung the towel before stepping into the living room.

"Are you leaving?" I asked Valerie.

"Yes, I should get to the hotel."

"Are you sure you don't want to stay here? I can make up the couch. It turns into a bed."

Her nose wrinkled. "I think I'll take my chances at the Wilshire."

"Jim is waiting downstairs. He'll take you to the hotel," Rhett directed Valerie. "We'll pick you up in the morning."

"See you guys tomorrow." She gave us both a hug.

~

"I still don't understand why you insist on living in an apartment," Rhett said to his sister as we drove down the road, "when you can have a private residence in Beverly Hills."

"Because, Rhett, I want to fit in with my classmates," she muttered, frustrated by his insistence on her living in a big fancy house. "What's so wrong with an apartment? *You're* living in an apartment."

"Yeah," I agreed with Valerie, "What's so wrong with an apartment?"

"That's temporary," he replied pointedly. "Ava and I will both be moving to the Malibu home as soon as it's ready."

Wait, what? "We are?" We hadn't exactly discussed this. I loved my apartment.

He ignored my question, turning his unreasonable demands back onto his sister. "Apartments make it more difficult for security. Too many people are able to come and go."

"Can't you hold your judgement until we see the places first? You haven't even given it a chance."

Rhett contemplated her request. "Okay. But if I don't like it, we're going to look at houses."

When we pulled up to the first stop, Rhett barely slowed the car after seeing the neighborhood and the homeless people milling about.

"Absolutely not," he said as he drove off toward the next apartment option.

"It wasn't that bad," Valerie mumbled, barely able to convince herself, much less Rhett. I shook my head at the two of them.

The whole morning went about as expected. The two of them were both hard headed and determined individuals. It was quite entertaining for me to watch, seeing Valerie challenge her unreasonable brother. He couldn't charm his sister or seduce her to get his way like he always did me.

The few apartments we did make it inside to tour were dismissed almost immediately by Rhett as unsuitable for his little sister. After the fifth one, he told her we were done looking at apartments. She begged and pleaded with him to look at one more.

Hearing the defeat in her voice and seeing the sadness in her eyes had me intervening and negotiating a compromise between them. We would look at one more apartment of Rhett's choosing. Of course, the apartment of his choosing was a high-end, modern complex with a concierge and security staff in place.

The place was like a luxury resort, with its clubhouse, fitness center, and Olympic-sized pool surrounded by comfy outdoor seating and fireplaces. It'd be like being on vacation year-round. It was impressive and fitting for the Blackwood family. For some reason, though, as much as I could tell Valerie loved the place, she was wavering on committing to living there.

"Fine," she finally conceded as we finished walking through a floor plan, "but I'll need at least two bedrooms, so I can have a roommate."

"Roommate? You don't need a roommate, Val," Rhett stated firmly, biceps bulging as he crossed his arms.

"I know I don't need one. I want one."

He studied her carefully, "Why?"

"Because, I want one!" she said, exasperated with her overbearing brother, not explaining her reasoning any further.

I could tell by his furrowed brow he wasn't too keen on his little sister having a roommate, but he let up on his demands. "They'll have to undergo a background check."

"You're absurd, Rhett. I'm not forcing people to do background checks."

"Background checks or no roommate."

She looked at me for help. I shrugged, not wanting to jump on this grenade for her.

"Fine, but it won't determine whether the person is allowed to live with me. That decision is mine to make."

"We'll see," he said with a confident smirk.

～

We drove to Malibu after finalizing the lease for Valerie's two-bedroom, two-bath apartment and grabbing some lunch. I hadn't been out to the site since the contractor broke ground, and I was anxious to see the progress.

As we walked the site inside the stakes placed to outline the exterior edges of the foundation, I tried giving Valerie a tour of the floor plan. "And here is where the kitchen will be!"

"All I see is dirt." She crossed her arms, unimpressed.

"Use your imagination, Val." I rolled my eyes.

She closed her eyes, pretending to imagine, then flicked them back open. "Yep, still just dirt." She grinned.

"I give up." I sighed, frustrated.

She laughed. "I'm sure it's going to be awesome when it's all done, Ava. I mean, this view alone is incredible, and the beach cove will be the perfect spot for some college parties when I house sit." She winked.

"There'll be no college parties in our home," Rhett warned as he draped his body around me from behind.

"You're seriously no fun, Rhett," she whined, walking off to check out the secluded beach cove. We watched her as she disappeared out of view.

"So...I'm moving, huh?"

"Of course."

"You didn't think this would need to be a conversation we should have? A decision we should make together?"

"No," he said, unwavering.

"Rhett—"

"Ava," he challenged, smiling at me. "You can't pretend you didn't know. I've been upfront from the beginning. This is *our* home. For it to be our home, you have to be living in it with me."

I tried to hold back the cheesy smile slicing through my face, but I couldn't. "Is this your way of asking me to move in with you, Mr. Blackwood?"

He laughed. "I think it's clear, I'm not asking. It's not even a question. I love you, Ava Conner. And I don't plan on sleeping in separate beds ever again." He skated the back of his fingers across my jaw, bringing his lips to mine.

~

Sunday, Rhett left Valerie and me to our own devices to have a girls' day. We were on a shopping spree to purchase furniture and necessities for her apartment. Halfway through the day, we had most of the main furniture items purchased and decided to grab some lunch.

Near the end of our lunch, Valerie's phone blew up with a slew of texts and alerts. She retrieved her phone from her purse as I paid for our meal. I watched her as she scrolled through her phone, her earlier lighthearted mood slowly draining as she read. Her face sagged, and she slammed her phone harshly to the table. She didn't look at me, but I could see the hurt.

"Val," I soothed, "is everything okay?"

I rarely saw anything get Valerie this upset. I was suddenly feeling very protective.

She shook her head, not answering me immediately. "I'm fine." She forced a smile, pretending to be unaffected by whatever was on her phone.

"Are you sure? Do you want to—"

"I'm fine, Ava," she said forcefully.

I sat quiet for a moment. "Okay," I surrendered.

She let out a sigh. "I'm sorry, Ava...I didn't mean—"

"It's okay," I said, reaching for her hand. "You don't have to say anything...but if you need someone to talk to, I'm here."

"Thank you, Ava." She smiled weakly.

It pained me to see her hurting, and I wondered if this had anything to do with why she wanted a fresh start in California. The ride back to my apartment was silent, making more worried about what was upsetting her. I didn't push her for answers, though. It was obviously something she didn't want to talk about.

By dinner time, Valerie was back to her old self—at odds with her brother.

"You don't need a car, Val. You don't even have a license," Rhett sighed. Valerie was in the middle of begging him to take her car shopping.

"I'm getting my license. And I *do* need a car," she demanded. "Especially now you made me live in an apartment so far from campus," she huffed as she sat back crossing her arms.

"You'll have a driver. The same as you do in New York."

"What part of 'I want to fit in' are you not grasping? I want to be like every other person on campus," she complained.

"Val, you aren't like every other person. You're a Blackwood."

"Yes, I don't need the reminder," she sighed. "Ava gets it. Don't you, Ava?"

"Nope. You two aren't dragging me into this one." I grinned, taking a sip of my wine, enjoying that Rhett's infuriating demands were for once not directed at me.

"So much for sisterhood." She glared.

I shrugged sympathetically.

"Are Dad and Mom aware of all this?"

"Do you tell them about every move you make in your life?"

Rhett rubbed a hand over his face in frustration. "Fine."

"Really?"

"Get your license, Val. Then we can talk."

"Thank you! Thank you! Thank you!" she squealed, jumping to hug him.

I washed my face and brushed my teeth, getting ready for bed. Valerie had left my apartment after dinner. She was on the way back to the hotel in better spirits, but I still couldn't get the thoughts of our earlier conversations out of my head.

Rhett snaked his arms around me, his chin on my shoulder as I applied nightly moisturizer to my face.

"Rhett…" I looked at him through the mirror.

"Yes, babe?" He dropped kisses down my neck to my shoulder, leaving tingling sensations in his wake.

"Did Valerie seem…. I don't know…different to you this weekend?"

"Besides being more aggravating than normal?"

I let out a small laugh. "Yes."

"She had an odd desire for independence all of a sudden, but I figure it's a typical teenage-girl thing. Why?"

"Never mind. It's nothing."

"Ava." He gripped my shoulders, turning me to look at him, his eyes demanding me to start talking.

"Promise me you won't tell her I said anything."

"Tell me," he commanded.

"Promise me."

"Fine. I promise."

"I'm probably reading too much into it. It's just, she said a few things this weekend and her mood at times seemed like something was bothering her. She got some texts at lunch that seemed to upset her pretty badly. I wasn't sure if maybe she talked to you about it?"

"No. I'll look into it though."

"By 'look into it'…I hope you mean you'll talk to her, not get your security team to invade her privacy."

"Okay, I'll talk to her."

"Good."

"Though you just made my task harder by denying me the use of my security team and making me promise not to tell her it came from you."

"I have faith in you. You're a smart, determined man when you put your mind to it." I grinned.

He tickled my side, causing me to squirm with a fit of laughter. I wiggled away, running to the bedroom for protection. I jumped on the bed, grabbing a pillow as a poor choice of weapon as he chased after me.

"Stop!" I laughed, warning him with the pillow.

He skidded to a stop at the edge of the bed, still ready to pounce. "And what are you going to do with that?" He nodded toward the pillow.

"Come any closer and you'll find out," I threatened.

His eyes glistened with intrigue, not backing down from the challenge. He stalked around the edge of the bed with his devilish grin on his face. I stepped across the bed, the mattress providing an unstable foundation below me.

He pretended to lunge for me, and I fell for it, swinging the pillow at him, missing him as he ducked. He lunged again while I was off balance from my swing, tackling me into the bed. I screamed with laughter, trying to crawl out of his arms. He tickled me relentlessly as I squirmed in his arms, his own laughter harmonizing with mine.

"Okay!" I choked out through my giggles. "You win!"

He ended his torturous tickling with my surrender. "You should know by now, I'll always win, beautiful." His smiling face hovered over me as he pressed his body over mine.

"We'll see," I said, unperturbed.

"Yes. We will," he said with a smirk.

He skirted his hand up my thigh, looping his thumbs in the waist band of my pajama shorts and panties, pulling them down my body simultaneously as he lifted onto his knees. He discarded them to the floor, staring down at me with a gleam in his eye.

My body tensed with the suspense of waiting for him to make his move. He lowered himself, leisurely trailing kisses up my leg, starting at my inner knee and moving toward the apex of my heat. My breath hitched.

"Is this you winning or me?" I breathed.

His head lifted with a juvenile grin. "Both," he stated simply before dropping his head again, working his magic with his lips and tongue. My magician.

I'm definitely the winner.

CHAPTER 18

M ondays. I hated Mondays. They always came too fast and they were always hectic at work. This particular Monday I was dreading its beginning as much as its end.

After work, I texted Rhett from the back of the town car, letting him know I was on my way home. My phone vibrated with his response.

R: Will be late.

I responded, disappointed.

A: Okay. x

Although lacking his usual sentiments, his response wasn't a surprise. I was becoming accustomed to his late nights. I still hated it, though. Especially tonight. Tonight, I'd planned to tell him about my conversation with Owen when he got home.

The car slowed in front of my apartment building. I looked up from my phone as Jim opened the car door.

"Thank you, Jim." I stepped out of the car, searching through my purse for my keys as I walked to my building. I was halted by Jim's strong hand on my arm.

"Ms. Conner," his voice was firm.

I glanced at him, a stern expression on his face. He signaled toward the door of my building. I followed his eyes to Owen, who was leaning against the wall.

"Ava." Owen smiled, pushing off the wall, coming toward me.

"Hi, Owen," I said, my brow wrinkling.

"Sorry to drop in on you unexpectedly. I hadn't heard from you, and I was in the area. Figured I'd check up on you. See if you had some time to talk."

"Oh," I responded, caught off guard.

"You still want to talk, right?"

"Yes…sorry. I do. Do you want to come up?" I offered. I did still need to close this chapter with Owen. I guess now was as good a time as any. I could knock both Owen issues out all in one night.

"Works for me." He smiled.

I stepped forward but was halted once again by Jim. "Ms. Conner, I don't think that's a good idea," he said in a low voice, only audible to me.

"It's fine, Jim. It'll only be a minute." I smiled reassuringly at him. "He's a friend."

Jim nodded, reluctantly releasing my arm. I walked past Owen, letting him in the building to follow me to my apartment. We walked in an uncomfortable silence. As I nervously unlocked the door, I started to feel like maybe this *was* a bad idea.

We probably should've gone to a coffee shop or something, somewhere public. If Rhett were to come home and see him here, this wouldn't look good. I closed my eyes, taking a deep breath through my nose as I opened the door. It'd be fine. I'd explain things to Owen quickly, and he'd leave. Rhett was working late anyway.

I walked into my apartment, stepping aside to let Owen in, and closed the door behind him. I watched him, letting the door hold me up for support as he stood in the middle of my living room, looking around.

After taking it all in, he turned to face me. We stared at each other awkwardly. At least, awkward for me. He was smiling brightly, not knowing I was about to tell him nothing would ever happen between us.

"So."

"So…how are things, Ava?"

"Good." I moved away from the door. We stood in another awkward silence.

"Can I get you something to drink?" I finally asked. I didn't know why I offered. I didn't want him to stay long enough to have a drink, but I couldn't think of another way to break the ice. This whole situation was putting me on edge.

"I'd love a drink."

I could hear the salaciousness in his voice; he was getting the wrong impression. It was too late now. I'd already offered.

"What would you like?"

"Do you have a beer?"

"Sure," I responded hesitantly. I moved toward the kitchen, needing the space. I opened the fridge in search of a beer.

"How are you feeling?" he called from behind me. "Did they ever figure out who drugged your drink?"

I halted, startled by his question. My hand trembled around the bottle of beer. The pounding in my chest drowned out the sounds around me. I never told him what happened in the bar that night. *How does he know about the roofy?* Realization dawning on me. I remained frozen in the opened fridge door, trying to figure out how I could get to my phone to text Jim without Owen knowing.

"Ava?"

I jumped, his voice too close. My entire body went rigid. I slowly closed the fridge door, turning toward him. He was inches from me, his eyes blackening. Panic fired through every nerve in my body as the fight-or-flight instinct kicked in.

"Is that for me?" He looked at the beer in my hand.

I nodded, shakily handing it to him, unable to find my voice. He took it, setting it on the counter, stepping closer as a coldness spread through me. I stepped back, hoping he'd get the hint. He stepped forward, closing in on me until my back was against the wall.

I was trapped. There was only one way out of the kitchen and it was through him. His hand moved to my hip. I flinched, my chest constricting, breathing becoming difficult.

"God, Ava…you're so fucking sexy." His hot breath hit my face as he stroked his hand down my long hair, cupping my breast. He pressed his body against me, and I could feel the erection in his slacks. I closed my eyes, trying to black out what was happening.

"Owen," my voice shook, "please—"

"Shhh"—he pressed his finger to my lips—"you don't have to beg, Ava. I'm going to give you exactly...What. You. Want."

I shook my head no, leaving my eyes closed tightly. He pressed his lips aggressively to mine. My hands flew to his chest, pushing hard against him. I flicked my eyes open when I no longer felt his lips.

His eyes narrowed. He was seething as his jaw tightened. "I know your game, Ava," he gritted out. "You fucking want this. I've watched you...you like a man who takes what he wants."

"No." I shook my head at him, anger surging through me now.

He pushed back against me. I tried forcing him away again, but his hands tightened around my wrists, pinning them above my head. "Stop fighting it, Ava," he hissed in my ear.

He used one hand to keep my wrists pinned to the wall—his grasp painful—while the other worked hastily to rip the buttons open on my shirt. I twisted and squirmed, fighting my way out of his grip. I bent my knee, slamming it upwards into him. He grunted with pain.

"Fuck!" The back of his hand connected with my face.

The pain stung as I hunched over, feeling with my hand where it radiated from my cheek. I looked back up at him as he charged me. My scream pierced the air as he pushed me back up against the wall. I closed my eyes, continuing to kick and scream, thrashing out at him. A single tear escaped from the corner of my eye when I felt myself losing the fight.

The weight of his body was suddenly gone. I heard the repeated pounding of fists hitting and bones cracking. I flung my eyes open. Rhett was wailing on a crumpled and bleeding Owen. Jim flew into the room, pulling Rhett from him. Rhett charged again, but his effort was impeded by Jim.

"Rhett!" he yelled in warning, breaking Rhett out of his uncontrollable rage. "I've got the fucker," Jim assured him.

Rhett's body remained hardened as it heaved up and down with enraged breathing. Rhett nodded. "The police?" His voice was strangled.

"They'll be here any minute," Jim stated.

Jim hauled a lifeless Owen to his feet, dragging him out of my apartment. Rhett's eyes shifted to me. The color drained from his face as he took me in. My legs lost their strength as I collapsed onto the tile floor, sobbing. His arms were around me instantly, pulling me into his powerful body.

They had the power to protect me and comfort me all at once. I clung to his shirt with my fists, letting the tears cleanse the fear and guilt from my body. "I'm s-sorry," I cried. "I'm s-so sorry."

"Shhh, babe. You're okay. Everything's okay."

I shook my head as he reassured me, knowing this was all my fault. Once again, I'd ignored his requests and my better judgement.

The hard floor disappeared below me as he scooped me up in his strong arms, carrying me to the living room. He sat us both on the couch, keeping me in his arms, clinging to him.

"Are you okay?" he asked softly. "Did he—"

"No." I shook my head, responding through my tears. "You got here before anything…"

He let out a breath of air and kissed my head as he pulled me even tighter into him. I could barely breathe, but I didn't care. His tight embrace made me feel safe. I heard his heart pounding rapidly in his chest. I squeezed him back. He saved me. *If he hadn't shown up when he did...* I shuddered. I didn't want to think about what would've happened.

"How? I mean...you're here," I finally managed to say, looking up at him. He was here. I needed him, and he was here. I searched his eyes for answers, unsure how he was home so early.

"Eric sent me the footage."

Oh. I dropped my eyes.

"I saw the little prick talking to you, and the look on his face..." He grinded his teeth, his breathing becoming forced. "I'm sorry, Ava...I should've been here sooner. But when I saw you two...I was pissed. I didn't want to come home angry and out of control— damn it!" he yelled, throwing his head back on the couch, taking a deep breath.

"I missed it the first time I watched. I was too distracted by seeing you two talking. I had to replay it a few times. It was hard to see, but I saw him flick the drug into your drink. As soon as I saw, I left the office to come home. I was already driving when I got a text from Jim saying you had company, so I didn't waste time getting here."

"I'm sorry, Rhett. I'm sorry I didn't tell you Owen was at the bar that night. I—"

"It's okay, beautiful"—he tucked my hair behind my ear —"we don't need to talk about this now. I know you had your reasons."

"They were stupid reasons. Stupid. I was going to tell you. I'm such an idiot. I can't even trust my own instincts."

"Stop," he demanded, his voice leaving no room for argument. "Listen. *This* is not your fault. None of this."

I nodded.

There was a knock on my door. I jumped, Rhett's hold tightening on me. "That's probably the police."

He shifted me reluctantly from his lap to answer the door. He stepped aside, allowing two officers to walk in. Rhett spoke first, filling them in on what he saw in the videos and what he found when he arrived. I worried he would be in trouble for beating the crap out of Owen, but they assured me it was in defense and not to worry. Either way, I knew Rhett had the best attorneys and nothing would happen to him.

After they spoke to Rhett, they started questioning me, getting my statement. When they were done, they thanked me for my time and suggested I see a doctor as soon as possible. And then they were gone.

Rhett locked the door behind them, turning back to me. I was still sitting on the couch, bundled in a ball of remorse and fear. Rhett walked back to me, crouching on his heels in front of me.

"They're right. We should get you to the hospital tonight."

I shook my head. "I don't want to go."

He watched me, contemplating whether to give in or demand I go.

"I'm fine," I assured him.

His thumb brushed the spot on my face where Owen had hit me. I flinched at the pain of his light touch. His eyes darkened. "I think we should go. Get you checked out."

"Please, Rhett," I pleaded, not wanting to go.

He was quiet for a moment, finally relenting with a sigh. "Okay, beautiful."

I gave him a weak smile of gratitude. "I want to shower." He nodded his understanding, shifting to help me up. Once he got me settled in the bathroom, he left to make a few calls and get some ice for my face.

I stepped into the warm spray, letting it purge my body of Owen's touch and smell. I scrubbed harshly, ignoring the pain in my wrists and face. I thought about all my conversations with Owen and whether there were any warning signs I missed. When I couldn't find any, it only heightened my self-doubt. I sat on the tile floor huddled in a ball, crying as the water pelted my back.

The water ceased. I stared up at Rhett standing over me with the saddest eyes. I knew I had to look like a broken mess. It was how I felt. He grabbed a towel, wrapping it around me, and lifted me in his arms.

Placing me on the toilet, he delicately dried my body. I sat motionless, letting him do all the work. He disappeared from the room, returning moments later with an oversized T-shirt.

"Raise your arms." His voice was soft but firm.

I complied. He pulled the T-shirt over my head. I breathed it in, his scent immediately making me feel safe, like nothing could hurt me as long as I was wearing it. It was a ridiculous notion, but I felt secure nonetheless.

His arms hooked under my knees and behind my back as he picked me up, carrying me to the bed. Setting me down, he picked up the ice pack waiting on the nightstand.

"This might hurt a little." He sat on the edge of the bed as he moved the ice pack to my bruised face.

I flinched, a small hiss releasing through my teeth.

He held it in place as he observed me. "I spoke to Eric… They found Chris."

"Where?"

"In a rehab."

Relief fell over me. "That's good…right?"

"Yes. It turns out he checked himself in. Apparently, when his little girl interrupted his attack on her mother, it triggered a wakeup call for him."

"I'm glad he's getting the help he needs."

I was. It told me there was still a chance the old Chris was in there somewhere.

"Ava…even if he does get better, I still want you to keep your distance from him."

"I will."

And I would. I'd learned too many times I needed to trust Rhett's judgement. He obviously read people better than me. I gripped his free hand to reassure him. He flinched slightly at my touch. My eyes dropped to his hand, seeing it bruised and slightly swollen.

"Rhett, your hand."

"It's fine. I'll ice it after you're taken care of."

I opened my mouth. "Don't argue, Ava. I need to take care of you first."

"Okay," I replied, fully understanding his need.

He leaned in, kissing my forehead in appreciation. The rest of the time he was quiet and so was I. I closed my eyes, feeling drained from everything.

After a few more minutes, I felt the cold ice pack lift from my face, and the bed shift below me. I opened my eyes, finding Rhett standing. He stripped out of his clothes as I watched his muscles ripple. He crawled into bed next to me, pulling me into my spot at his side.

"You need to ice your hand," I tried again.

"Go to sleep, beautiful."

I lifted my head to his mouth, connecting my lips with his, needing his mouth to be the last thing my lips touched. Not Owen's. I laid my head on his chest to listen to his heart. It was back to its normal rhythm. I let the steady beat soothe me as I fell asleep.

～

The morning after the attack, I had a pretty good shiner on my cheek. I took the day off, calling in sick, not ready to face my co-workers. As embarrassed as I was to be in public, I insisted on going into work the following day. It was probably one of the most heated arguments Rhett and I had ever had, besides the time at his place in Boston.

Rhett wanted me to take the rest of the week off, even trying to bribe me with him doing the same, but I refused. With Tom already out, I wasn't going to leave Joce and Drew stuck with handling everything on their own. Besides, I needed to work, so I could have something to get my mind off what had happened. I also found it hard to be in my apartment.

We finally compromised: he would take me to and from work, and we would have lunch together. This went on every day for the next few weeks.

Going back to work was the easy part. Explaining to Joce and Drew what happened was the hard part, especially Joce. She had her own guilt for allowing me to refuse to tell Rhett about Owen, and for not saying anything to Riley.

I kept telling her it was all on me, but it didn't seem to matter. I could see it in her eyes, she still felt responsible. Having to look at my bruised face was a constant reminder of her guilt, and mine. When the weekends rolled around, I was more than relieved.

As the weeks went on, the bruise faded. But my guilt and regrets didn't, so I did what I did best: threw myself into my work.

I kept busy, working late at night, not wanting to be in my apartment alone. I would stay until Rhett was finished with his work, only leaving when I knew he was already on his way home, or when he came to pick me up himself.

He worried about me, wanting me to talk to someone, if not him. I dismissed his concerns, convinced I only needed some time. Time and distraction was how I healed. And running.

I would run, sometimes twice a day. If Rhett couldn't run with me, Jim would. Unlike Rhett, though, Jim would purposefully lag behind me, giving me my space. I appreciated it.

After a few months, I started feeling better. The Malibu house was nearly complete, and Valerie had officially moved to L.A. She was a great distraction, keeping me company when Rhett was working.

Things with Joce were also getting better. I'd avoided hanging out with her after the attack. It was hard to look at her and be around her remorseful face beyond work hours. It was awkward for both of us. Plus, Riley was making more frequent visits on the weekends to be with her.

What helped the most was Owen's sentencing. It was the closure I needed. I hadn't realized it until it was done. I was finally able to breathe easier. Rhett took me to place a restraining order on Owen for once he was released. I didn't think Owen would ever try to approach me again, but having that in place helped me feel a little safer.

~

I lay back against the lounger on my apartment balcony one last time, bundled in the beautiful wrap Rhett had given me. It was our last night in my apartment. We were leaving for Litchfield in the morning to visit my family and celebrate Lizzie's baby shower. The movers would be coming while we were gone to pack and move all my things into the Malibu home.

Rhett had left to pick us up some food for dinner. I declined going with him, wanting a little time to myself in my apartment.

I watched as the ocean waves crested, turning over into a sheet of water rolling onto the sandy beach. The consistent movement and sounds they made put me in a tranquil state as I reminisced. Despite the recent horrible memory, this apartment had been a place I could heal and grow. I'd miss this balcony, this view, this beach. I'd miss living here.

The breeze hit my face, and I closed my eyes as the sun began to set. I heard the front door open. A few minutes later, Rhett's strong, warm hands were on my shoulders. His lips pressed against the crown of my head.

He didn't speak. I didn't open my eyes. We both sat quiet, letting the ocean do all the talking. He moved to the side of the lounger. I opened my eyes, sitting forward as he climbed behind me. His legs and arms cocooned my body as I lay back on his muscular chest. My head rested against him, and

I tilted it to the side, letting his kisses sprinkle my neck and shoulder.

I wrapped my hands on his forearms, squeezing him tighter to me.

"Everything okay?"

"Perfect." I smiled. "I love you, Rhett Blackwood."

"Not as much as I love you, Ava Conner."

I grinned inwardly.

We remained on the balcony until the stars cluttered the night sky and the moon reflected over the blackened ocean. We ignored our dinner, letting the food get cold. Instead, Rhett carried me inside, where we fed our hunger with each other, making love one last time in the bed of my apartment until we fell asleep blanketed with each other.

CHAPTER 19

I took a couple weeks off work to go home to Litchfield. I didn't have a ton of time to work on all the little details of Lizzie's baby shower, so I hoped with the help of my mom and sister, I would be able to pull it all together last minute.

The two of them were skilled organizers and helped me throw a beautiful baby shower for Lizzie in a short period of time. We held it at Nana's home, since she had the most space and a large screened-in porch to set up the shower. September, with its beautiful weather, was the perfect time of year to hold the party outdoors.

"Lizzie!" my sister said excitedly, greeting Lizzie and her mom as they walked in the door. "Holy shit! Look at your baby bump! It's so—"

"If you say big, I swear to God I'll clock you, Emily," Lizzie threatened.

"Round. Perfectly round," Emily amended her statement.

She opened her arms wide and mouthed the word 'big' to me once Lizzie's back was to her. I shook my head, laughing. Mom came into the foyer, hugging and greeting Lizzie and her mom, dragging Mrs. Taylor away after we all gave her a proper greeting.

"Thank goodness for your mother," Lizzie said to Emily and me. "I swear mine is going to cause me to go into early labor from stress. The woman is driving me crazy, hovering over me constantly and criticizing everything I put in my mouth. It's not my fault this baby has a sweet tooth."

"Well, Mom should keep her distracted for at least the afternoon," I assured her.

Our mothers had always gotten along well, and it had been awhile since they caught up, so I had no doubt Mrs. Taylor would be occupied.

"Come on. Let's head to the porch. There's a whole table of sweets just for you and my sweet niece," I said.

Yep. She was having a girl. Despite Mike's insistence on having a boy, his eyes watered with tears of joy when they finally found out the sex of the baby. I knew he would be smitten as soon as she arrived.

The shower was a success. We had a full house, with pretty much everyone invited making an appearance. We had to ditch a few of the games due to Lizzie's sensitivity to the size of her belly, but other than that everything ran smoothly. There were lots of laughs and tears, most of which were Lizzie's tears.

After all the guests had left, the men—Rhett, Jackson, Mike, and Stephen—arrived with dinner and drinks so we could all hang out at Nana's for the evening. They had been hiding out at Mom's during the shower doing "men stuff," they explained when we asked. Whatever the hell that meant. All I could envision was them all sitting around, watching sports, drinking beer, and burping. Strangely, the only one I couldn't picture behaving that way was Rhett.

We all ate, drank, and played games while Mom and Nana observed our shenanigans. Nana remained glued to Rhett like a bug on flypaper. It was all my favorite people in the world in one room, laughing and having a good time with each other, even Rhett and Stephen.

It seemed they'd actually turned a new leaf. They weren't best friends or anything, but now they were able to hang out in each other's presence without glaring threats at one another.

As the night went on, Mom and Nana were the first to excuse themselves and head off to bed, stating they couldn't keep up with us young kids. Lizzie, Mike, Stephen, and Amber left shortly after that—Lizzie unable to keep her eyes open any longer.

Emily, Jackson, Rhett, and I moved into the den to have a nightcap and visit some more after saying our goodbyes to everyone.

"Has Mom mentioned any more about selling the house?" I asked Emily.

Mom hadn't mentioned it to me since the first time she brought it up. I was curious if she had abandoned the idea. Emily turned, looking up at Jackson, who quieted his own side conversation with Rhett. He looked at her as they had a silent conversation with each other the way married couples can. After a few seconds, they both turned their eyes to Rhett and me, their faces impassive, making me suddenly nervous.

"What?" I asked, unable to take the silence.

"Well…" Emily started, a smile slowly creeping across her face as she linked her fingers with Jackson's, "Jackson and I have decided to buy it from Mom."

"But you already have a home," I pointed out.

"Yes, but it's kind of small…and well, we're going to need some more space now." She grinned ear to ear as Jackson gazed adoringly at her.

"Congratulations." Rhett smiled, immediately standing to give Jackson a manly hug and pat on the back. "I wish I had some cigars on me."

"I have some for us to smoke out back," Jackson grinned proudly.

Huh? I stared at them all, confused.

"Do we need to spell it out for you, Ava?" Emily teased.

I slowly pieced their comments together. "You're pregnant." I stared in a state of shock, suddenly realizing my sister hadn't touched a drink all night.

"Yes, Ava," she said, laughing at me. I screamed with excitement, jumping up to hug her.

"This is so awesome! Congratulations you two!" They all laughed, whether it was with me, or *at* me for being slow on the uptake, I wasn't sure. But I didn't care. This was the best news.

After our excitement settled, Rhett and Jackson went out back to smoke a celebratory cigar and drink a glass of whiskey while Emily and I discussed the details of her pregnancy and purchasing Mom's home.

I crawled into bed next to Rhett, curling into my place in his side. I couldn't stop smiling. This had been one of the best days in a long time.

"What has you so happy?" he asked a glint in his eye.

"You. Everything. It was a good day."

"I'm glad," he said, and kissed my forehead. "Since you're in such a good mood...I have something to ask you."

"What?" My eyebrow raised with curiosity.

"Would you be willing to spend the last few days of your vacation in the Hamptons with me?"

I smiled. He was actually asking for once. I hadn't been back to the Hamptons since the night I worked his father's birthday party.

"I hate to ask you to cut your time short with your family—"

"Rhett," I interrupted him, "I would love to. I've had plenty of time with my family this week. I want to spend the rest of my time off alone with you...but...only on one condition."

"What's that?"

"No phone," I said, determined to see this demand through.

He smirked. "No phone?"

"Yes. I want you all to myself. No interruptions."

"I think I can manage that," he agreed without hesitation, a smile on his face.

"Really?" I asked, a little surprised he'd so easily bend to my demand.

"Yes, beautiful. Really."

Well...that was easy. "When do we leave?" I smiled, pleased.

"Thursday, unless you want to leave sooner?"

"Thursday works."

"Good."

I sat quiet for a moment. "Did I ever really have a choice?"

"No," he said, unrepentant.

I shook my head at him in disbelief. This man. I couldn't help but love him. And I planned to show him exactly how much I loved him tonight. I pushed him to his back, straddling his hips.

"You're so arrogant."

"I prefer confident." He smiled.

I leaned forward placing a light kiss on his lips before having my way with his delicious body.

The remainder of the week we went through my childhood room, sorting through all my belongings. With Jackson and Emily purchasing the home soon, I needed to clear out my room, so they could move in. We packed up the things I wanted to take with me to L.A., and Rhett handled making sure they arrived to our Malibu home. Other items I threw out, donated, or packed up for storage at Nana's house.

We also helped Mom with some of the packing and sorting of her and Dad's things. She had planned to go ahead and move out before the sale was finalized. Jackson and Emily wanted to remodel the place a bit before they officially moved in.

They planned to do new floors and paint—along with

remodeling the kitchen, opening it up like Mom had always talked about doing. It was kind of sad to think they would be changing our home, but I understood. They needed to make the home their own. I was just glad it was staying in the family.

Rhett and Jackson carried various boxes for my mom to the Pod she had rented, while all of us ladies continued to pack. We spent more time laughing and reminiscing, as we found various items evoking memories, than we did packing. A few times we even teared up when we found photos or things that had belonged to my father. The days were an emotional rollercoaster for all of us, yet felt very cleansing, giving us all a little more closure.

Our last evening in Litchfield, we went for burgers and beers at our favorite spot. We played a few games of darts, with Rhett and I on one team and Emily and Jackson on another as my mom cheered us on equally. We eventually switched teams to girls against guys. Watching the comradery between Jackson and Rhett was endearing. The two of them had become very close over the years, both taking on the responsibilities involved with being protectors and providers for the women in my family in my dad's absence.

∼

Thursday morning, I walked through my very empty child-hood bedroom, looking around one last time before it would be transformed into a nursery. The walls were now bare, other than the outlines of old posters and frames that had hung there for so many years. The closet doors were open, exposing the empty shelves and racks. The only thing left in the room was the furniture, which would be either sold in a garage sale or donated.

"Are you ready?" Rhett's deep voice came from behind me.

I spun to look at him. He stood in the doorway of my bedroom with a T-shirt and faded jeans on, his forearms resting on either side of the doorframe. His blue eyes shimmered as they observed me.

Simply looking at him had me licking my lips, wanting to devour him. Those damn jeans. They did it to me every time. A grin broke through his impassive face.

"Should I call for a limo?" he said with a smug smile.

I rolled my eyes, walking toward him. I bit my lip, rubbing up against him as I sauntered past. He groaned as my hands took the liberty of feeling him up.

"No need. The plane will do just fine," I threw over my shoulder as I left him in my doorway as needy as he'd made me. I heard his deep chuckle from behind me as I continued my path outside the house.

We gave my family repeated hugs and kisses as we told them goodbye. I made Emily promise to keep me up to date on the progress of the house and pregnancy. I wanted regular growing-belly pictures and before/after pictures of the remodel.

When we finally made it inside the car, Rhett linked our hands together on my lap as we drove to the airport. I glanced over at him, smiling and looking forward to our mini vacation in the Hamptons.

"Don't forget...no phone," I reminded him.

"Already off, beautiful. Just you and me for the next four days." He winked as he glanced over at me.

∼

Turning down the long drive to his family's Hamptons estate, I sat up to admire it once again. I'd almost forgotten how impressive it all was. He pulled the car to a stop at the front entrance, where a man dressed in formal butler attire greeted us, opening my door for me.

Rhett handed another man keys to the car as the butler removed our bags from the trunk. I stood there awkwardly, feeling like I should help with my bags. Rhett took my hand in his as he guided me into the house.

When we entered the house, the woman I recognized as the head housekeeper was standing there to greet us. She looked at me curiously, and I wondered if she recognized me from the night I worked the party. If she did, she didn't say.

"Mr. Blackwood, we are glad to see you made it safely."

"Mrs. Williams," Rhett greeted her. "This is Ms. Conner," he introduced her to me.

She bowed her head slightly, "Ms. Conner."

I waved my hand awkwardly at her. She gave me a curt smile before turning back to Rhett. "Your lunch has been set up on the patio as requested. Let me know if you require anything else."

"Thank you," Rhett dismissed her.

Once she was out of earshot, I turned to him. "I don't think she likes me."

"Don't take it personal, beautiful. She's never been the

friendliest person, but she keeps this place immaculate and the staff on the top of their game."

"Probably because they fear her deathly glare."

"Yes," he laughed. "Probably. Come on, babe. Let's eat."

We dined on the patio, looking over the pristine gardens of the estate. Our conversation was light as we mostly made desperate eyes at each other.

"So, what are the plans for the next few days?" I asked, taking a drink of my water.

"What would you like to do?"

"I don't know," I shrugged. "What would you like to do?"

He grinned his devilish smile as his eyebrows danced up and down.

"Other than *that*," I laughed.

"I want to do whatever you want to."

"You aren't helping me out here, are you?"

"Nope."

"Okay…fine. I want you to show me your favorite things to do in the Hamptons."

He contemplated this. "I hope you brought your sailing clothes then."

"You sail?"

"I do."

"Impressive."

He laughed. "Wait until you see my boat."

"Is it big?"

"Huge," he winked, smiling naughtily at me.

I shook my head, laughing at his innuendo. He wasn't lying. I knew that for a fact.

We spent the whole day Friday on his sail boat. It *was* impressive, but I'd had no doubt it would be. Watching Rhett sail through the waters of the Hamptons back bays had me even more in awe of him. When I thought he couldn't be any sexier, he proved me wrong.

The whole experience was exhilarating. Especially when he taught me how to steer the boat. As much fun as it was cutting through the waters, when we stopped and anchored, I was glad. I was having a hard time controlling my urge to jump him the whole time he navigated the waters like a pro. Once anchored, we spent a good portion of our day below deck, tangled in the sheets.

As the sun set, he sailed us back to the marina. I squeezed between him and the helm, letting his arms trap me in place as he steered us home. He leaned into me, planting a small kiss on my neck, dropping one hand from the wheel to wrap around my waist.

"Can we have dinner on the deck, once we dock?" I asked, not ready for our time on the boat to end.

"Anything you want, beautiful," he said smiling.

When we got back to the marina, Rhett left to grab us some food to eat on the deck. I showered in the cabin of the boat, wanting to freshen up and fix my windblown hair. I put on a flowy, white dress and brown sandals, leaving my hair down and makeup light.

I gave myself the once-over then headed up the stairs to sit on the deck and wait for Rhett's return. I stepped back outside to find Rhett already waiting for me. He had a table set up, with small votive candles lit and our dinner already set out.

"Wow"—I smiled at the romantic man standing in front of me—"you work fast."

"Only on some things." He sauntered toward me. "But there are *some things* I like to take my time on."

His fingers skirted down my bare shoulder, sending chills down my body. His head dipped as he brought his yummy lips to mine. I tasted him, his mouth only intensifying my body's craving. My fingers weaved through his hair as I pressed my body to his. Suddenly I was only hungry for one thing, and it wasn't food.

He pulled back barely, trying to break our kiss but with little determination. I could feel his grin through our kiss. "Babe," he tried ineffectively. "We should eat," he said, brushing his lips against my neck.

"Not hungry," I panted.

He chuckled. "You need food."

"I need you," I countered through our fevered kissing.

My hands found their way to the button of his pants.

His hands instantly stopped mine as he broke us apart.

"Food," he said firmly, his own breathing heavy. "Then I promise to take care of you."

I could tell he was fighting to control himself. If I pushed him, he'd give in, letting me have my way. Unfortunately, my stomach betrayed me with a growl.

"Damn it," I complained.

"Mouth, beautiful," he warned with a smile.

"Fine. Food first," I pouted.

He took my hand, leading me toward the table, where he had the food laid out and a bottle of champagne iced.

"This is some fancy takeout," I goaded him, looking at the spread before me.

He had raw oysters, lobster, and steamed veggies waiting for us. He released my hand, giving me a smack on the butt. "Sit. Eat."

I did as I was told.

Initially, I had planned to scarf the food down, but it was so good, it had me savoring it instead. We ate and drank under the stars—the champagne giving me a light buzz by the end of the meal. I lay back in Rhett's arms as we stared up at the dark sky after dinner, the boat's steady rocking lulling me into a relaxed state.

"I wish every day could be like today," I said dreamily.

He kissed my temple. "We can have as many days like this as you want, beautiful."

"If only that were true. There's this obligation I have…it's called a job."

"You don't have to work."

"Yes, I do." Technically I didn't, now that I was moving in with Rhett. With my car and student loans paid off, I didn't really need the money. I also had an inheritance my dad left for me. I'd never touched it, though. For the longest time I resented the thought of the money…as if it could really replace the loss of my father.

"I can provide for you, Ava. You can have anything you want." That was an understatement.

"I know. But that's not what I want." His body tensed. I looked back at him. "Don't take that the wrong way. I just mean my job is important to me. It's not only about money."

He smiled down at me. "I understand. But know, if that ever changes, and you decide you want something else, you have that option."

I lifted, giving him a peck on the lips. "Thank you."

His eyes locked with mine, telling me everything he was feeling. Our heads moved slowly together, our lips brushing lightly, each kiss becoming more intense.

He moved our bodies forward, standing to lift me in his arms. I locked my arms around his neck as he carried us to the bed below the deck. He made good on his promise for the rest of the night.

CHAPTER 20

We had a leisurely morning on the boat when we awoke Saturday. Neither one of us was in a rush to get out of bed. By mid-morning, Rhett finally deemed it important we eat, so we cooked breakfast together in the tiny kitchen on the boat.

"What are the plans today?" I asked him as we sat down to eat.

"Do you want to sail again? Or we could visit some of the shops or vineyards in the area?"

I contemplated the options as I ate. "I wouldn't mind seeing the shops. The last time I was here, it was off-season and most of them were closed."

"Shopping it is, then."

"Window shopping," I clarified.

"Whatever you say, babe," he chuckled as he shook his head.

After breakfast, we disembarked from the boat and set

out on our window-shopping excursion. We strolled around some different boutiques until we both got hungry for lunch. Rhett took me to one of his favorite restaurants, where we ate on their patio, taking advantage of the last of the warm-weather months on the East Coast.

We headed back to the estate after we ate, wanting to spend the rest of the day splashing around and soaking up the sun on the beach. When night fell, we traded in our swimsuits for warmer clothes, while Rhett's staff set up a bonfire for us on the beach.

"Something on your mind?" I asked as we cuddled in front of the fire, listening to the waves. Rhett had been unusually somber and quiet since we came back down to the beach.

"Only you," he spoke softly.

"Care to elaborate?"

"I keep thinking about how long I've waited to have you in my arms, here on this beach. Just like this."

"How long?"

"Since the night I saw another man's arms holding you."

My breath caught.

"That night..." he continued, "it was one of the first times I felt myself losing complete control. Seeing you and him. I'd never felt so jealous in my life. It took everything I had in me not to go after you anyway...of course, I had no idea at the time you weren't with him."

"I wish you had...come after me anyway."

"Knowing what I know now, I wish I had too."

"Why didn't you? What held you back?"

"You. You looked so comfortable and content. No matter how much I wanted you, I didn't want to be the one to make things difficult for you. All that mattered to me in that moment was knowing you were happy.

"I spent weeks trying to purge you from my mind. Nothing worked. And as if things couldn't get worse for me, you showed up in my club looking sexy as hell and determined to drive me insane," he smirked.

"Your club?" I asked, confused. I had no idea.

"Yes. It was one of the reasons I'd been staying in Boston."

"You never told me that. When you took me to that room, I just thought it was an extra-special VIP room."

He laughed. "No."

"Stephen was with me that night, though. You still came to get me, anyway."

"I did." He smiled. "I tried to stay away, but I couldn't. I had to have you. It was the first time I believed in fate. After the number of times our paths crossed, I wasn't going to walk away again without at least trying to talk to you.

"Plus, you were making it impossible to stay away. I can still see you in that dress, dancing around. I didn't want another man laying his hands on you."

"It seems so crazy—how many times simple misunderstandings have stood in our way or deterred us from each other. Yet, somehow, we always find our way back to each other. Why do think that is?"

"Simple. Because we belong together, Ava. You're the only one for me. You always have been, and you always will be."

I faced him, needing to see his eyes. I loved his eyes. They told me everything between us was pure and true. He could disguise his face to hide his feelings, but his eyes always gave him away to me.

"I love you, Rhett Blackwood. More than anything in this world."

He kissed me. It was a simple kiss. But as simple as it was, it held so much meaning. It was more powerful than any kiss he'd ever given me.

"Come with me."

"Where are we going?" I asked, not quite ready to leave our moment on the beach.

He stood, offering his hand to me. "Don't argue, Ava. Come with me."

There was so much hope and love in his eyes, there was no way I could deny his request. I would follow this man anywhere. I gave him my hand, and he pulled me up from my sitting position on the ground. He linked our hands together, and we walked back toward the house.

Neither of us said anything. Our silence was always comfortable. Once we made it inside, he took us to the room where we were staying. The door was closed. He cracked it open then stepped aside, letting me go in first. I looked at him curiously as he nodded toward the cracked door with an encouraging smile.

I pushed it open, suddenly forgetting how to breathe. The room was filled with candles and white roses. Even the bed had white rose petals sprinkled across the top. I stepped slowly into the room, taking it all in.

When I spun slowly to look at him, Rhett was no longer standing, but down on one knee. I gasped, my hands flying to my mouth, my heart skipping a beat as tears welled in my eyes.

"Ava Conner, from the moment you crashed into me—"

I snorted a laugh as I shook my head in shock, tears already streaming down my cheeks.

"I knew you were the only one for me. I'd never been so sure of anything in my life. You saved me that day, beautiful. Saved me from myself and the dark path I was on. Saved me from a guilt I had lived with for so long. You made everything dark in my world bright again. I love you, Ava Conner. Marry me."

"Are you asking me or commanding me?" I smirked through my tears.

He grinned. "Both."

I laughed.

"Well, for the record…my answer is yes." I grinned ear to ear. No matter how infuriating and arrogant he could be, I loved him. He was mine. Forever.

"You know what this means, don't you?" He stood, his own sexy grin stretching across his face.

"What?" I arched an eyebrow. *What was he up to now?*

"I get to buy you whatever the hell I want. And you have to accept it without argument…including this." He pulled a ring out of his pocket as he took my left hand in his.

He slipped a beautiful, vintage-style white gold band over the tip of my finger. The diamond was a massive European-cut stone sparkling in a compass-point setting. The center diamond was flanked by two blue sapphires.

My hand trembled as he slid the expensive piece of jewelry in place on my left ring finger. I looked at him, filled with more love than I knew I was capable of. I linked my hands around his neck, pressing my body into his.

"I love you, Rhett Blackwood."

"I love you, future Mrs. Blackwood."

I smiled. "I like the sound of that."

"You better," he smirked, lifting me in his arms.

I squealed with giddiness.

He carried me to the bed, setting me down on my feet beside it. The palm of his hand moved to my cheek, as he caressed it with his thumb. "Ava, you're the most beautiful woman I've ever known. Inside and out. I don't think I'll ever fully believe you're mine. It all seems too good to be true."

"I'm yours. Always. It has never even been a question." I raised my own hands to cup his face. "I knew it from the moment we touched. Sparks flew through every nerve ending in my body, and I knew I would never feel that with anyone else. Ever."

His lips pressed against mine as his hands lifted my shirt. Breaking our kiss, he pulled it over my head. I reached behind my back, unclasping my bra as he removed his own shirt. I sat back on the bed as he slowly stripped me of the rest of my clothes before removing his own.

I slid back, laying my head on the pillow as he moved over me, keeping his eyes locked with mine the whole time. He pushed my hair aside before placing a delicate kiss on my lips, then traced a trail from behind my ear down my body.

With every inch his lips touched, my body ignited with more need. He took his time though, no matter how impatient and needy I became. He made his way down one side of my body, resting at my core, manipulating me into a frenzied state, and then moved back up the other side. I was milliseconds away from pushing him onto his back and taking control, my body and mind tortured to the edge of madness.

"Eyes, beautiful," he quietly demanded. I hadn't even realized I'd closed them. I fluttered them open, looking into his beautiful sapphires that now reminded me of the ring residing on my finger. I caressed his face as he moved inside me.

The satisfaction of finally having him had me instinctively closing my eyes as my back arched with pleasure. "I need to see you, beautiful," he whispered his reminder.

I opened them, staring back at my frustrating man I loved so much. I held onto his shoulders as he expertly controlled our bodies.

He controlled every part of me: my body, my heart, my soul.

∾

To say our families and friends were excited about our engagement was the understatement of the century. I am pretty sure I temporarily lost my hearing when I told Lizzie and my sister. The screaming wasn't any less subdued when we told Valerie. My mom was overjoyed. Nana was a blubbering mess. I just hoped they were tears of happiness for me, and not because she felt like she no longer had even a sliver of a chance with Rhett. Maybe it was a little of both. By the time we finished announcing our engagement to everyone, I was exhausted.

I relaxed in a lounger on the patio beside the pool of our new Malibu home. It was our first night in the house, but amazingly, it looked like we had lived here for months. The house had already been furnished with the belongings we had purchased and moved from my apartment. The only boxes remaining unpacked and needing put away were the ones we had shipped from Litchfield.

I looked back toward the house, watching Rhett pace inside as he talked on the phone. Being out of touch for four days meant he had a lot to follow up on after we finished all the engagement announcement calls.

Seeing him in this house and knowing both belonged to me, seemed unreal. The day I collided with Rhett my whole world changed. No matter how much I fought against it, I was never going to win. Rhett was right. I had never been a big believer in fate or destiny, but there was no other way to explain it.

Of course, I know Rhett's determination had something to do with it. But he had that determination for a reason. He never gave up on us, and that alone meant more to me than anything. I knew the road ahead of us would not always be smooth, but knowing I had him as a partner to navigate with, someone so dedicated to me—*to us*—I no longer feared those challenges.

I smiled, feeling stronger and having more faith in us than ever.

"What has you smiling so big, beautiful?" Rhett walked out on the patio to join me.

"You."

He kissed my head, sliding in behind me.

"Are you done making all your calls for the night?" I asked.

"Yes. How about you? Have you let everyone know?"

"Yes. Well…everyone but one…" I trailed off, thinking of my father.

"Who's that? Do you want to call them really quick?"

"It's not someone I can call."

He looked at me quizzically.

"I was referring to my father…it's moments like these I miss him the most. Not being able to share this with him is hard."

"I see…" He paused. "Ava. He knows."

"I know, I know…he's watching from above. I get that, but it's not the same thing."

"That's not what I meant. I meant he knew."

I turned to look at him. "What do you mean?"

"I asked him for your hand in marriage."

"What? When?"

"The day of your graduation."

My heart stopped momentarily as the tears brimmed in my eyes. I shook my head in disbelief. "You?"

"Yes. I told you. I knew from the day I laid eyes on you for the first time. I had no doubt in my mind, so I wanted to make sure your father knew. Knew my intentions. Knew I would be protecting and looking after you for the rest of my life."

"Rhett," I said, shaking my head. I couldn't believe what I was hearing. "He said yes?"

His deep, baritone laugh reverberated from his chest. "Seriously, babe? Do you have any doubt?"

I laughed. *No.* I knew my dad respected Rhett and would have been happy to see him as my husband. "Thank you," I said sincerely when our laughter died down. It was the best gift he could ever give me.

I kissed him sweetly and turned back around, leaning into his chest as he held me tight to him. It was where I belonged. I was the only one for him and he was the only one for me. There would never be anyone else.

EPILOGUE

RHETT BLACKWOOD... FOUR YEARS AGO...

I pulled to the curb, parking my car outside of Brewed. Turning off the ignition, I leaned my head against the seat, taking a deep breath. I was not looking forward to this meeting. I would've much rather stayed in bed, having my way with...*Ashley? Or was her name April?* I couldn't remember. Didn't really care. The point was I would rather be doing her than doing *this*— meeting my father.

I knew it was only going to be another lecture about taking on more responsibility. I rubbed my hand down my face in frustration before getting out of the car. Time to get this over with. There was no way around it. He'd made the trip all the way down here.

He pretended it was to see me, but I knew it was actually because he wanted to try out the restaurant of the chef my mother hired to cater his birthday party. I opened the door to enter the coffee bar. I walked past the hostess, nodding my greeting. I knew my father was already here. I was ten minutes late, and my father was a punctual bastard.

Feeling my phone vibrate in my pocket, I pulled it out to look at it. *Serena.* I groaned internally. She had the worst timing.

S: *I'm in town. Can you come by tonight? I need to talk.*

I wanted to tell her no. I hated going to talk to her. All she ever did was rehash the past and make me feel worse than I already did. But the guilt I always felt made me do things I didn't want to. It was part of the reason I drank and fucked my life away. I sent a quick response.

R: *I have plans. Will stop by later.*

I looked back up from my phone, glancing around the coffee bar for my father. My steps came to a standstill. I stood, blatantly staring at a sexy figure as she drew nearer. She was headed right toward me with her head down. I should've moved out of her way, but I couldn't. She was the most beautiful woman I'd ever seen—and I'd seen and been with a lot of beautiful women.

She was different though, something about her felt like a rope was pulling taut between us. I instantly wanted her. More than I wanted anything. *What the hell am I saying? Why can't I move?*

The next thing I knew, she was colliding with me. Her petite, sexy, curvy body hit mine, sending her bag and books everywhere.

Now I felt like an asshole. She scrambled on the floor, trying to gather her papers and books as I stood there like a jerk. She was obviously in a hurry, and this hadn't helped. I still couldn't move, though. I was mesmerized by her.

The filthy thoughts running through my head with her crouched below me were rendering me incapable of doing anything.

Shit. Snap out of it.

She stopped, finding the phone I'd dropped. Her eyes slowly moved up my body until they locked with mine. *Damn.* Those eyes. If I thought she was beautiful before, those big, beautiful, blue eyes made her a freaking angel.

Her eyes were such a pure, crystal blue they made me hopeful, made me feel like there was a light at the end of this dark tunnel I'd been living in. They made me want to be a better man, for her. Those eyes gave me everything I didn't know I was looking for. She was making me feel things, things I'd never felt before, things I didn't know how to control.

Everything about her was beautiful—from her breath-taking eyes to her luscious, long brown hair, her petite little frame, and those fucking lips. I wanted to taste those perfectly pert lips. My heart pounded in my chest, reminding me I was still alive and not dreaming.

Losing her balance in her squatting position, she fell back on her ass, knocking me out of my trance. I squatted down, offering her my hand, worried she might've hurt herself. "Are you all right?"

"I'm...I'm fine," she stuttered, before ignoring my hand and helping herself up. "I guess this belongs to you," she continued, handing me the phone as she stood over me.

Aggravated by her rejection of my offer to help, I gathered her remaining papers, needing a minute to get these unfamiliar emotions under control. I didn't like being out of control, especially when it came to women.

As I stood, I handed her the papers while taking my phone. When our fingers brushed, an electric current shot through me. It was like nothing I'd ever felt, and I immediately wanted to feel it again. She flinched, quickly withdrawing her hand. I fought the urge to grab it back into mine. By her reaction, I knew she must have felt it, too.

"Thank you... and sorry... for bumping into you," she stammered out while shoving her books back into her bag as she moved past me.

"I'm not—sorry that is." I grinned mischievously.

I wanted her, and I was glad my body had been frozen in her path. She didn't respond. Instead, she gave me a cute, nervous smile before running out the door.

Where the hell is she going? I didn't even get her name or number.

I started to run after her, but my father called my name.

Damn it.

I turned, finding him seated at a table near the bar. He stood as I approached, shaking my hand and giving me a pat on the back. "Son. Glad you finally made it."

"Dad," I greeted him. "Sorry. I got held up."

"I saw," he said disapprovingly, which immediately had me on defense. "Rhett, you need to get your head in the game."

Here we go...

"I'm not saying you have to settle down and get married. I'm only saying you need to be a little more focused on work and less on the women you bed."

"Dad. Seriously?" I sighed, roughly rubbing a hand on my neck, agitated by his concern for my personal life.

"Yes. It doesn't look good for the company image. You

know your mother wants me to retire soon. I need to know you're ready for this."

"I'm ready."

"Then prove it. I'm not saying you have to stop dating all together, but at least pick one and try something steadier."

In the past, when he would give me these pep talks, the last thing I wanted to do was think about marriage, or even a relationship for that matter. But when he brought it up this time, my thoughts suddenly went to the brown-haired, blue-eyed beauty I'd just collided with. She was different than the other girls—not just because of her looks, or because she didn't throw herself at me like every other woman. In fact, she did the exact opposite. She ran out of here, like she couldn't get away from me fast enough.

"What about Serena?" My father's voice interrupted my thoughts.

"What about her?" I asked, my brow furrowing.

"Well, you guys have always gotten along. I mean, I know you guys have a little bit of a rough history, but maybe..."

"No. Absolutely not," I stated pointedly.

"Okay"—he threw his hands up in surrender—"I don't care who it is or if it's nobody. Just stop showing up in the tabloids, parading different women."

"Fine."

The rest of our breakfast, he kept the conversation focused more on business with the club and less on my personal life, thankfully.

"In a couple weeks, we're going to have dinner with the Archibalds at Christopher's. I would like you to join us," he said as he paid our tab.

"Aren't you eating there tonight?"

"Yes, but Rex and Charlotte have been wanting to eat there, so we'll all be having dinner. Serena will be joining us."

"Dad—"

"I know. You already told me. Humor your mother for at least this dinner," he said as we stood to leave.

"Fine. Send me the time. I'll meet you all there."

"Thank you, son." He gave me a pat on the back.

"Give Mom and Val my love."

"Will do. Talk to you soon."

I texted my buddy, Riley, as I headed into the Hamilton Pub, telling him to order me a beer. I was meeting him and Adam for drinks tonight, and I was looking forward to it. I had been so busy with the club and well...other *things*, I hadn't spent much time with them lately.

I moved through the crowd of bodies, locating them at a table near the bar.

"Hey, man. How's it been?" Riley greeted me with a handshake.

"Good," I responded before turning to Adam. "Adam." I shook his hand, taking my seat.

"Beer is on its way. This place is packed tonight," Adam said.

"How was the meeting with your dad?" Riley asked.

"Same shit as normal," I answered as the cute little waitress brought me my beer. She smiled at me desperately. I ignored it. She pouted and sulked away.

"What the hell, Rhett? I figured you'd be all over that," Riley laughed.

"Yeah, well my dad gave me his normal 'you need to settle down for the company image' speech today," I explained. It wasn't the real reason why, though. Annoyingly, I was only interested in one blue-eyed beauty at the moment. I couldn't get her out of my head and suddenly, no other woman was even appealing to me. Unfortunately, I had no idea who she was or where to find her.

I knew she must be a student, based on her books and notes this morning, which is one of the reasons I agreed to hang out at the Hamilton Pub tonight versus meeting the guys at a bar in Boston.

"That never seemed to stop you before," Adam interjected, throwing my explanation out the window. *Asshole.*

"Well, maybe things are different this time," I scowled.

"Does that mean you're giving in to the idea of Serena?" Riley smirked.

Adam tensed at the mention of Serena. I knew he had a thing for her. But for some reason, he was too much of a pussy to do anything about it. I don't know if it was out of loyalty to me or what. He could have her for all I cared.

"Hell, no," I clipped.

I started to change the subject, when I was distracted by some girls yelling and cheering on their friend at darts. I glanced past Adam to see what they were so excited about, almost choking on my beer.

She was here. She was actually here. I'd hoped she would be, but I wasn't really counting on it. She was lining up to take her throw at the dart board. I couldn't take my eyes off her.

"Rhett, man, what are you staring at?" Adam asked as he and Riley tried to follow my eyes. "Oh yeah, saw her earlier tonight. She has a nice little body. Her friends are pretty hot, too. Maybe we should all head over there."

"No," I said forcefully, and louder than I meant to, looking over at my friends. I could see the confusion and curiosity all over their faces.

I didn't want them anywhere near her. It already pissed me off, knowing Adam had been checking her out. I felt strangely possessive of her. I needed to protect her from other guys. I respected my buddies, but they were as bad as me when it came to women. I turned back to look at her. She was standing frozen in the same spot. I missed her throw, but from the look on her face, it wasn't a good one.

Her friend approached her with concern, making me irrationally worried about her. She looked over the friend's shoulder straight at me, her eyes locking with mine, once again. I instantly felt the need to be next to her—to touch her again.

"I'll be back," I excused myself from the table to head toward her.

She was on the move, grabbing her things hurriedly. *Why was she always in a hurry?* She was headed for the door, pushing her way through the crowd.

I maneuvered through the thick mass of bodies, being halted by a desperate blonde trying to get my attention.

"Hi," she purred, licking her lips as her eyes greedily roamed over me. "Want to buy me a drink?"

"No," I sneered bluntly. *Shit. Where did she go?* I scanned the bar, looking for her, finding her already breaking through the exit.

"Okay, we can skip the drink then." She rubbed her hand up my chest, not getting the hint. I removed her hand from me, brushing past her, heading toward the exit. I was not letting her get away this time. I busted open the door in a rush.

I was too late. She disappeared into the darkness. *Damn it!* I scanned the streets, hoping she would suddenly reappear. I ran a hand through my hair, groaning in frustration.

As if this day and night could get any worse, Serena texted me again, giving me her hotel information, letting me know that the shit luck I'd been having tonight hadn't run out yet. I went back inside the pub, aggravated. I'd need to finish my beer if I was going to deal with Serena tonight. I might even need to have a few more.

"What the hell was that about?" Riley asked when I returned.

"Nothing."

"Didn't look like nothing."

"Yeah, I'm pretty sure that's the first time I've seen you chase after a girl. Come to think of it...I think it's the first time I've seen a girl run from you," Adam said with a smirk, as if pleased with the thought.

"Shut the hell up, Adam," I warned. It was the truth, which only pissed me off more.

They both laughed under their breaths, Riley shaking his head at me.

I spent the rest of the time at the pub drinking beer with my buddies while watching the group the beautiful girl had been with. I was half-tempted to walk up to them and ask them for her name, but there was one guy eyeing me suspiciously. I'm sure I looked like a creeper, so despite my urge, I didn't. The last thing I wanted was for her to be freaked out by me. I chugged my beer before leaving for the night.

No matter how hard I tried over the next few weeks, I couldn't get those blue eyes out of my head. Every time I closed my eyes, I saw visions of her. A few times, I even tried using other women to wipe her from my mind. But every time I attempted to take them home, I immediately felt guilty for some ridiculous reason. I ended up dropping them off at their houses instead, leaving them alone and desperate.

I almost backed out, last minute, the night I was to meet my parents and the Archibalds for dinner at Christopher's. I was not in the mood for socializing or dealing with Serena. But, I hadn't seen my mother in a while and the dinner was at her request. I would do anything for my mother, so I put on my suit and left to meet them all at the restaurant.

They had barely sat down at the table when I arrived. The hostess led me to the private room, where they were all waiting. I kissed the women on the cheek in greeting and shook my father's and Rex's hands before taking the one open seat next to Serena.

We all visited while we waited for the server to arrive. After a few minutes, the one girl I could not get off my mind walked through the door. My eyes focused on her instinctively. She stood frozen in place without saying a word. It was like the whole world faded around us. All I could see was her and the only voice I wanted to hear was hers, but she wasn't speaking.

In fact, she looked as shell shocked as I felt. I suddenly realized the room had fallen silent. I stood instinctively, wanting to go to her and hold her. *Why is she not speaking?*

"Rhett, dear, what are you—" Serena grabbed my arm to stop me. I ignored her.

Feeling as if I should introduce her to my parents for some insane reason, I offered some help. "This is…uh…" But I didn't even know her name. I was acting like a fucking lunatic and I knew it. I couldn't seem to help myself whenever she was near.

"Ava," she said, tearing her eyes from mine. "I'll be your server this evening."

I slowly sat back down in my seat as she continued to speak. *Ava.* I finally had her name, and there was no way she could run from me if she worked here. This time, I was determined to end the night with at least her number.

I watched her closely as she spoke. Her voice captivated me like a lost sailor drawn to a siren. I couldn't take my eyes off her, and I felt a weird sense of pain at the loss of her eyes on me. She was refusing to look at me. The refusal was like keeping the last drop of water from a man dying of thirst. And I was that thirsty man.

I was so busy staring at Ava, numb to the world around me, I didn't even realize Serena had linked her arm in mine until Ava had disappeared from the room. I moved my arm, forcing her hold on me to release. I glared at Serena, warning her to keep her hands to herself.

I was pissed, but I kept my control. The last thing I wanted was Ava thinking Serena and I were together. I am sure it had appeared that way with our parents sitting here, and Serena being more touchy than normal.

When Ava returned to the room with the wine my father had ordered, I immediately trained my eyes on her, willing her to look at me. She didn't. And it drove me crazy. *Why is she being so resistant? Can she not feel the pull between us?* No. I knew she could. She was fighting it. I could see that. *But why?*

She moved around the table, filling our glasses. I tried to stay involved in the conversation around me, but it was impossible. All I wanted to do was watch her every move. Every sway of her hips had my cock coming to attention. I was thankful I was shielded by the table.

As she stepped close to me, filling my glass, I could smell her delicious, floral scent. She was inches from me. I was tempted to reach out and touch her, desperate to feel her and that surge of electricity that made me feel alive. For the first time in my life, I wanted something more than meaningless sex. I wanted everything, as long as it was with her.

The rest of the dinner, I studied her. I knew she felt my eyes on her, but somehow, she resisted looking at me. I could tell she was the strong, independent type. It only drew me to her more.

There were a few times a guy came in to fill our glasses. I immediately recognized him from the bar. He seemed to recognize me, too. The way he was glaring at me made me wonder if they were dating. Simply the thought had me feeling jealous and possessive of her.

I planned to pull her aside at the end of our dinner, but she never returned after our food was served. Christopher arrived in her place, letting us know the meal was on the house. He spoke with my parents for a bit. Before he departed, I stood, stopping him.

"Christopher, do you have a moment?" I asked, guiding him out of the room into the hall as my family and the Archibalds finished off their glasses of wine.

"Of course, what can I do for you, Mr. Blackwood?"

"The young woman who waited on us..."

"Ah, yes. Ms. Conner."

"Yes. Ms. Ava Conner," I said, trying her name on my lips. "Could you please give this to her in appreciation for her service? She did an excellent job." I handed him a wad of cash. I didn't even know how much was in it. It didn't matter. I would give her the world if I could.

"I'm glad to hear that," he said, taking the money from me. "She's a hard worker. She's one of the servers who will be coming to help with your father's party in the Hamptons."

"Good to hear," I replied, more than pleased to hear that. It meant I would be seeing her again and soon. "Well, I won't take any more of your time. Thanks again. The food was excellent."

She would be at the party. Suddenly, I was looking forward to the weekend—to seeing Ava Conner again. There was something about her and the way our bodies seemed to respond to each other. I needed and planned to delve into that further. I was determined to find out more about her and what made her tick.

Leave it to Serena to ruin the first night in a long time I'd actually been looking forward to. We were running late for my father's party. I was moments away from leaving her to find another way there. I hadn't wanted to show up to the party with her anyway, knowing Ava would be there. But she begged me to escort her.

She was one of those girls who was always concerned with her appearance and social standing. She wouldn't dare show up at a social event alone. It was annoying. Despite her being hot, her pretentious attitude had always made her unattractive to me.

When we finally walked into the foyer of my family's Hamptons home, my parents greeted us. "Serena, dear," my mother said, air kissing Serena, "You look stunning."

"Thank you, Vivie. You look gorgeous yourself."

"Son," my dad greeted me with a handshake as Serena annoyingly remained attached to my other arm.

"Happy birthday, Dad."

"Glad you guys made it."

"Of course," I said, suddenly distracted from our conversation. I could feel her presence before I even saw her. I turned my head, searching for her, for those eyes. I found them immediately. Our gazes connected. I started to excuse myself, but just as quickly as I found her she was gone. Again. Running from me. *Shit.*

I guess I would just have to wait for the right moment. She was serving champagne, so I could easily talk to her, pretending to only be interested in a drink. I would have to be discreet about my approach. I knew Mrs. Williams ran a tight ship and would be watching the staff.

I waited for her to make her way over to me, but she never did. She frustratingly kept her distance. I watched her from the corner of my eye, not wanting to draw attention to myself. I also couldn't seem to shake Serena from me, which only irritated me further. To an outsider we would appear to be a couple, but that couldn't be further from the truth. When I did finally get the chance to speak to Ava, I needed to make that clear.

I saw her disappear back into the kitchen, I assumed to

refill her tray, but when she didn't return for a while, I excused myself in search of her. I went into the kitchen, finding Mrs. Williams's disapproving stare, but no sign of Ava. I ignored Mrs. Williams. She worked for me, after all. She would keep her mouth shut and get over it.

I continued my search in the servers' quarters, concern growing that something had happened to her. I had no idea where she would be until I heard some commotion in one of the rooms. I stood in front of the door. I was about to knock when it opened. Ava stepped through it, nearly running into me, once again.

I thought she might scream from my mysterious appearance. She didn't. Instead, her beautiful eyes swept down my body. I could see the craving in her eyes, which fueled my own. *God. She was gorgeous.* I had to have her, and not just once, like all the other women. I wanted her to be mine for as long as I breathed. It was a ridiculous thought. One I chose to ignore.

When her eyes dropped to where I couldn't see them, I instinctively raised her chin with my hand. Her body was already responding to me, telling me everything I was feeling was mutual.

"I'm not with her," I told her, needing her to know the truth immediately.

"What?" she asked, confused, her brows furrowing together.

"The girl. We aren't together. She's only a family friend," I said, attempting to elaborate on exactly what sort of relationship Serena and I had.

"Why are you telling me this? It's none of my business and you don't owe me an explanation."

Her voice was shaky when she spoke. The way her body was begging for me made me question what she was scared of. It made me want to wrap my arms protectively around her.

"I know I don't owe you an explanation," I said firmly. "I wanted you to know."

"Why?"

She asked the question, but I knew she knew the answer. The chemistry between us was undeniable. My face stretched into a smile. I stepped forward, gently pressing my body into her, pushing her up against the closed door as I stared down into those eyes that reminded me of the bright, blue sky. I could get lost in them.

"I think you know why," I said, letting our bodies do the explaining as hers melded into mine.

Her body felt so right, fitting perfectly to me like the puzzle piece I had been looking for. As much as I wanted to savor our first time together, I was about to lose it and take her right here in the hallway. Before we could continue our conversation, someone interrupted us.

"Ava? Is everything okay here?"

I turned, seeing the same guy who'd been with her the last few times, standing in the hall with an angry, protective look that told me he was ready to fight. She hadn't said she was taken, so as far as I knew she was fair game. I clenched my fists, ready to make that clear.

She pushed her body forward from the door, forcing me to step back slightly. She looked between the two of us, concern growing on her face. "Yes, I'm fine. I was just headed back," she explained, turning away from me to walk away.

Not wanting her to leave, I latched onto her elbow to

stop her. I felt the sparks shoot through me like a bottle rocket. I knew now was not the time. She was working, and Mrs. Williams likely sent this guy to find her.

"I'll find you," I promised in a voice low enough only she could hear.

She didn't respond, but I didn't expect her to. She turned, walking away from me, leaving me alone in the hall, desperate for her. I took a minute to gain my composure before rejoining the party.

I kept my distance from Serena the best I could, and I continued to watch Ava. I knew my parents would have paid the hotel expenses for Christopher and his staff, so I could find out where they were staying. I impassively asked my mother and she looked at me knowingly, glancing across the room. I didn't follow her gaze. I knew Ava was there, and I knew it was who my mother was looking at.

"Rhett," she warned. "Your father—"

"Mom, it's not what you think. It's different."

She studied me carefully and then nodded with a small smile, telling me where they were staying. Her hand caressed my cheek. "I really hope this is different, Rhett. I want to see you happy again." She kissed my cheek before walking away to bid farewell to the departing guests.

I waited around awhile until all the guests had gone, and I knew the staff had departed. I told Serena to find another ride. She looked disappointed, but I didn't care at the moment. I had plans, and I wasn't letting anyone or anything deter them, not even my own guilt.

I knocked on the door to the room where she was supposed to be staying. When there was no answer, I tried again. I waited for a moment. Still nothing. I threw my head back in frustration, a hand running through my hair. A group of rowdy people walking down the hallway, headed toward the beach grabbed my attention. I recognized one of them from the party.

I followed behind them, keeping my distance, hoping they would lead me to Ava. They walked out onto the beach toward a bonfire with a group of people surrounding it. I halted my strides, spotting her. My heart dropped, my body tensing.

She was sitting by the fire with the same prick's arms around her. Seeing him touch her had a rage boiling inside me I'd never felt before. *What the hell?* She never mentioned she wasn't available. She could have said something in the hallway.

I felt myself losing control. I started to walk toward them to demand an explanation and fight for what I wanted, but I was halted by her smiling face. She looked up at him so sweetly, it was endearing. I felt an ache shoot through my chest. I wanted her in my arms, looking at me that way. She seemed so happy, sitting there with him. Content. *Fuck.*

I couldn't be the man to bring her pain. I wanted to protect her, not hurt her. I watched her for a few more minutes, knowing I should walk away, but having a hard time moving. Her laugh carried across the cold, dark sky, knocking me from my internal debate. I glanced at her one more time before reluctantly walking away.

I felt more loss and pain in that moment than I had ever felt in my life.

~

Over the next weeks, I felt like I was in a darker place than I had been before Ava crashed into my life. Knowing she existed and I couldn't have her was like living in my own personal hell. I spent most nights at the Biltmore, sitting in my private office. It was more like a party room than an office. I had spent more late nights drinking with my friends and screwing random women there than I had actually doing work.

It had a perfect view of the club. And tonight, I sat alone, watching people mill about, dance and get wasted. It was a typical, boring night. Nothing exciting happening—no fights to break up or pricks to throw out. Everything at the bar was running smoothly.

I was tempted to call it a night and go home. Our manager was here, so there was no need for me to stay. Most nights, I only stayed here to drink after going over paper-work and signing off on various things. I didn't bother drinking tonight. All I was doing tonight was sulking.

I stood to leave, but was halted by the vision below on the dance floor. I couldn't see her face, but I knew that body and those soft locks of brown hair. I watched as she swayed her hips with the music, her damn body taunting me. She was sexy as hell.

I started to go to her, but stopped, the appearance of her boyfriend impeding me. *Shit.* I gripped the back of my neck. He hadn't been dancing with her initially, but now he was.

I sat back down, watching them. I had no idea why. It was torture watching him touch her when I wanted to be the only one to have my hands on her. She was so beautiful. I don't think I would ever want anyone else the way I wanted her. If I couldn't have her, then I would likely be alone forever.

He left her side again, leaving her on the dance floor alone. *Idiot.* I watched her dance near a couple of friends, but they were too focused on each other to notice Ava. *Fuck it.* I didn't like her exposed and vulnerable down there by herself. I threw my resolve to keep my distance out the window.

She was the only one I could see, the only one I've ever wanted like this. And she was here. In my club. That had to mean something. I had to at least try to make her mine. The number of times we had crossed paths—that had to be fate bringing us together. I couldn't give up on the idea of us without even trying.

I stood, determined, striding out of my office to the dance floor. Nothing was going to stop me from making her mine...

THANK YOU FOR READING!

I sincerely hope you enjoyed reading this book as much as I enjoyed writing it. If you did, I would greatly appreciate a short review on Amazon, Goodreads or your favorite book website. Thanks again!

THE BLACKWOOD SERIES CONTINUES IN

A REASON TO LEAVE

REDEEMING

Lottie

Now Available

Click Here!

Subscribe for updates on my blog!

Website:

www.melissaellenwrites.com

ACKNOWLEDGMENTS

First, I want to thank all my readers. Hearing all the excitement, feedback and support, makes writing so much more enjoyable and worthwhile. It has been a fun adventure writing this series so far. I can't wait to share all that is to come in the Blackwood Series.

As always, I would also to like to thank my personal support team – my sister, Christy, my friend, Ryan, and my mother, Mary. Thank you for always being willing to be my beta readers and give me feedback. This book wouldn't be what it is without having you guys to bounce ideas off of.